Also by Jean Chapman

Both Sides of the Fence
A Watery Grave
Deadly Serious

DEADLY ZEAL

JEAN CHAPMAN

W⦿RLDWIDE®

TORONTO • NEW YORK • LONDON
AMSTERDAM • PARIS • SYDNEY • HAMBURG
STOCKHOLM • ATHENS • TOKYO • MILAN
MADRID • WARSAW • BUDAPEST • AUCKLAND

Recycling programs
for this product may
not exist in your area.

ISBN-13: 978-0-373-28236-4

Deadly Zeal

Copyright © 2015 by Jean Chapman

A Worldwide Library Suspense/March 2017

First published by Robert Hale, an imprint of The Crowood Press

www.Harlequin.com

Printed in U.S.A.

DEADLY ZEAL

ONE

'Do YOU REALIZE,' Liz Makepeace whispered from the business-side of the bar, 'that we have a poacher, a publican, a painter and a professor on our team?'

Helen Jefferson, off duty, in a multi-green dress like a Hockney tree print, turned to look around the packed but silent public bar of The Trap. 'Well,' she whispered back, 'your John's the publican, my Paul's the painter, old Alan Hoskins is, or hopefully was, the poacher, so does that mean—' she nodded to the other member of their team, Michael Bliss, a relative newcomer in the area '—is a professor?'

Liz nodded. 'So I understand. Had a bad car accident, retired here and turned what was just a bric-a-brac shop in the village into a good antique shop, and he trades on the internet.'

'What was he a professor of?' she asked, only to be shushed by those nearest the bar.

'Can you repeat the question?' A call from the far table of contestants.

'Don't know,' Liz mouthed to Helen, 'something to do with the arts, I think.'

'Can everyone please keep quiet?' John Cannon turned and, catching his partner's lips moving, scowled disapprovingly at her.

'What was the *full* name of the American president who resigned *and* the name of the scandal that caused him to resign?' The question master repeated the question, adding that this was the last one of the political section.

There were ten teams in this opening round of the Fenland Interpub Quiz, four members in each team. There was much whispering, shaking of heads and finger pointing with varying degrees of certainty before this answer was written down. John Cannon nodded as the professor wrote down 'Watergate' but shrugged when he added 'Richard Milhous Nixon'.

'The next category is sport.'

There were quite a few cries of relief at this announcement.

'Again there are five questions.'

'How…many…more…questions?' The sentence sounded as if the speaker had a mouthful of food and there was a full stop after each word.

'Five questions, and there is just one more category after sport, so ten questions in all, Timmy,' the retired primary school headmaster and question master obliged.

'You're not answering them so why worry?'

The gibe was cheap and unnecessary. There was always one insensitive joker in the pack who liked the sound of his own voice, John Cannon thought, as he glanced over to where Timmy sat next to Niall Riley, his father. A local baker who must be retiring age, Niall Riley had jerked himself upright and now sat tense as a coiled spring.

Cannon tutted as this joker who had arrived with the team from The Stump's Shadow in Boston added, 'He wouldn't get too many right by the look of 'im.'

'Can we have best of order and some quiet, please,'

Cannon called loudly in his most officious landlord manner.

'Come on, boy, we're going.' Niall Riley rose, pushing a half-drunk pint away, and waited while his middle-aged son, looking bemused but as amiable as ever, linked arms with him and informed all and sundry that he was 'going home to my mother'.

'She'll tuck you up in your little wooden bed,' the same man scoffed.

Timmy turned and beamed at him. 'Yes,' he said. 'My mother loves me.'

'We all love you, Timmy,' another local called.

The joker's loud sneering laughter now made Paul Jefferson spin round in his seat. 'Don't say another word, sunshine,' he advised, but Riley had already disengaged himself from his son and asked a friend to take Timmy to wait outside. 'I'll just get you some crisps, son,' he told Timmy, and seeing him out swept round and back towards his tormentor.

'Now there'll be trouble,' Liz muttered. 'Riley's so protective of his boy, he won't stand for this.'

'You have a problem?' Riley demanded, stumbling over chairs and feet in his haste to reach and confront their tormentor.

'No, mate, seems it's you 'as got the problem, big time, I'd say,' and as the irate father reached him, he rose from his seat. He looked enormous under the low-beamed ceiling.

'I've taken on people like you all my son's life,' Riley said, looking like an enraged little terrier who doesn't know its own size, snapping at a great black bear. 'I'd sooner have one loving son like mine to a thousand such as *you. You great oaf!!*'

Cannon was on his feet and on his way to Riley's side, Paul with him.

'My son'll be loved and care for, while you—' Riley was leaning forward fairly spitting the words up into the face of the man who towered about him '—you'll be an unloved bully. I pity *you*, you know that! I pity *you*.'

'Save your pity for yourself, you need it,' the joker sneered.

There were cries of outrage from all around the bar now.

Cannon had his hand on Riley's shoulder, as he seemed about to launch himself at the huge man. Riley tried to push him away as the joker waved a clenched fist under his nose, inviting him to, 'Just give me an excuse.'

'Take your son home,' Cannon advised, and from the corner of his eye he saw Liz hand two packets of crisps over to Paul, who in turn scrunched them into Riley's hands and took his stance alongside Cannon. The two tall men were completely shielding Riley from his opponent.

'Reckon I could take you two, no problem,' the joker declared.

'I presume you're drunk; no one could be so objectionable if he were sober,' Paul said.

'You *presume*...' The joker assumed a prissy tone, turned to the company, repeating, 'He presumes.'

'Aye,' Alan Hoskins shouted, nodding towards Helen, 'and his missus is a police chief inspector so think on.'

'Thanks, Alan,' Helen muttered, but thrust into the spotlight she said calmly and briefly, 'I'd advise you to sit down and be quiet,' adding as the aggressor's lips curled and he looked her up and down, 'And my powers are the same off duty as on.'

Her comments emboldened others to urge the man, in a variety of different ways, to sit down and shut up.

'See Mr Riley out to his boy,' Cannon prompted Paul. There was some argument, for it was Riley now who definitely did not want to back down.

'No one pokes fun at my boy and gets away with it,' he protested, but by simply not allowing him to pass he was eventually edged towards the door and persuaded to join his son. All the time Cannon kept a weather-eye on the aggressor, remembering so many moments in his former Met days when such men either went berserk regardless of consequences, or stepped back to smoulder and wait for another chance for revenge—usually on someone more vulnerable.

It seemed Liz, Cannon's working partner in the Met and here in their Lincolnshire pub, had recognized the moment too as she reached over to collect and clink together a few empty glasses from the counter. The sound was loud in the still-tense atmosphere and, he thought, could either signal a return to normality, or the bell for round one. Then someone else, whether by design or accident, clinked a glass in another part of the room. The man swept around like an aggressive animal distracted from its prey, grunted, made a swinging threatening gesture towards all and sundry with his fist, then turned and went back to his seat, muttering that he'd been in better pubs. No one had the stupidity to contradict him.

Cannon signalled to the question master, who cleared his throat and continued.

The rest of the quiz was quickly over, for the spirit and enjoyment had gone out of it. Prompted by Cannon, the question master announced that there would be a fifteen-minute interval before teams swapped papers and marked each other's answers.

'By which time,' Cannon announced, 'as we are running a little late, it will be after closing time, so if we could make it last orders now, ladies and gentlemen, please.'

A good section of the assembly rose as one and made for the bar, and Paul, as he had often done in the past, came behind the counter to help as some ordered more than one drink and a few ordered brandy chasers to calm their nerves and keep them going until the end of the evening.

Papers exchanged and marked, The Trap won by two points. No one else had got the full name of Richard Nixon.

The Stump's Shadow's team and their supporters, including the joker, were among the first to leave.

'Bloody good riddance,' someone from another team called. 'Let's hope that particular "gentleman" is not around for the next round.'

'So say all of us,' Paul called back.

'Aye, up The Trap and good night, Chief Inspector,' Hoskins said, on his way out to pick up his bike and cycle away to his lonely cottage on The Fens.

'Good night, *Mr* Hoskins,' Helen said, 'you old…'

'Bugger,' he suggested as the doors swung to after him.

'Going to stay and have a cup of tea with us?' Cannon said when only Paul, feeding the last of the glasses into the sterilizer, and Helen, remained.

'Better not,' Paul said. 'Know we've got Helen's mum babysitting but mustn't take advantage. She takes it all so seriously—hovers over the child like a guardian angel.'

'We'll be over during the week,' Helen promised.

John saw them out, walking with them to the side car park, waving as they gave him a brief parting salute on the hooter.

Normally he would have stood and enjoyed the peace, the solitude, the brilliance of the stars, the smell of the sea, the contrast to the busy evening, but tonight it had been soured. The quiz was an annual event organized after the height of the holiday season was over, when it was more peaceful on The Fens. He gave a humph of ironic laughter and walked slowly to the back porch and into the pub's kitchen where Liz had everything ready for their nightly brew of tea.

She had loosened her long blonde hair so it fell free over her shoulders; this and what he called the nightly tea ceremony she put on were usually like signals that passed him through to their private world. He watched her use the strainer to pour tea from the teapot into the china cups and saucers; any other time of the day it was mugs and teabags but this was a soothing kind of wind-down, the sounds and smells, the excellence of loose tea—and Liz's loose hair. It was special for him.

'That could have been nasty tonight,' she said, still holding on to his cup and saucer. He reached for it. 'Timmy always reminds me of a family I knew as a child. They had two sons, one special needs like Timmy, loving, affectionate, always smiling, the other a really bright boy—but he never smiled.'

'Two extremes,' Cannon concluded, but Liz was not done with the memory as they sat sipping their tea.

'I remember Dad took me to a swimming gala, and

the older boy, he'd be about ten then, was in it. He won his race and helped win the relay race. I remember feeling proud just because I lived near him. His parents were there but all their time and attention was for the son who sat between them. I remember they were running a little toy car up and down his legs and arms to amuse him. He was about four. The older boy—wish I could remember his name—was presented with two little cups…' Liz looked up, her eyes still full of regret for the long-ago injustice as she shook her head and added. 'I saw him leave his two prizes behind a door as he followed his parents and brother out. We exchanged looks, and I knew he did not want me to say anything. Strange how vividly one remembers some things.'

'I'm not surprised you remembered that!' Cannon exclaimed. 'Wrong, very wrong, to exclude the other boy to that extent. What happened to the family?'

Liz shook her head again. 'We moved just after that, so I never knew.'

'Well, Timmy is an only child so it's all different,' Cannon said.

'I suppose it was just Niall Riley's reaction, the single-minded devotion to the boy, that reminded me of those parents.'

'I heard someone say the big chap's been banned from more than one pub in the area and he's not long taken to going in The Stump,' Cannon said. 'I might have a word with the landlord in the morning, see what he knows about him. Sod's law that our next round is at The Stump!'

'Hmm,' Liz mused, 'I wonder if he goes home and

takes it out on his wife and children, if he has any. He's the type.'

'There's usually some spin-off from such incidents—some casualty,' Cannon said.

TWO

CASUALTIES SEEMED EVERYWHERE the next morning. On the television news a gas explosion and a collapsed block of flats in the north, a bad pile-up on the M25—and a flattened rabbit on the road where Cannon climbed over to head for the beach and his habitual early-morning run. He had set off in long-sleeved sweatshirt and joggers, but shorts and sunglasses would have been more appropriate as the autumn sun rose with what seemed like abnormal heat.

Perhaps because of the unpleasantness the night before, and his intention to ring the landlord of The Stump as soon as he got back, he had run faster and further than usual, deciding how he would phrase his questions about the big man. He was now well beyond Paul and Helen Jefferson's beachside home. He thought of calling. He and Paul still needed to agree on an advertising programme for the New Year, when they intended to begin a new venture. Together they would run painting holidays, with Paul, well-known watercolourist, providing the tuition and John and Liz providing accommodation in their recently converted stable block.

He smiled as he looked towards the roof of the bungalow where Paul had returned some years ago to care for his ageing mother, and where Cannon had later thought Paul would end his days as a bachelor. Then Police Inspector Helen Moore had come along, now

Chief Inspector Helen Jefferson, back on duty after maternity leave.

Cannon had found himself to be inordinately proud when Paul named his son for Cannon. John Paul Jefferson was now eighteen months old.

He turned to run back along the sea's edge, still wondering if he had time to call on Paul. Then he was diverted by the sight of three dogs in the distance, racing at top speed towards him with no one else in sight.

They headed so directly for him, he began to wonder if the dogs, a collie and two Alsatians, were going to attack him. They came on, the collie just ahead, and as it got nearer he could see its mouth gaped and its sides heaved with the effort of running. Its eyes looked glazed with terror. The Alsatians were chasing the collie with intention.

Cannon was not going to let this happen; no one and nothing was going to be a victim if he could help it. As the Alsatians reached him, he yelled at the top of his voice: 'Leave! Leave! Leave it!'

The result was that the chasing dogs split and ran either side of him, but as they came together on the far side they brushed shoulders and one fell. Immediately the other turned back and, for a moment, Cannon thought it was attacking its fellow, but then he realized that the two were merely playing, rough and growling tumble, but playing. Meanwhile the collie was nearly out of sight, and still running as if the hounds of hell were at its shoulder.

'Come on, where do you two belong?' His voice and approach distracted their attention. They shook themselves and stood, tongues lolling, panting, as he consulted their collars. 'Blackburn,' he said. 'You're a long way from home, and neither of you are very old, I'd say. I guess you two are on holiday, so back the way you came, I think. Come on!' he ordered and after seeming to consider the options, they fell in with him, jogging alongside as if they did it every day of their lives.

After fifteen minutes or so he came in sight of the usual spot where he turned from the beach, went up through the dunes and fields to the back of The Trap. He was speculating what might be the best course of action with regard to these dogs when he saw someone, a man, running towards him. He wondered if he had come from the caravan park a mile or so away, though Cannon thought it had already closed for the winter. The man waved urgently, and as they all neared each other the dogs picked up his scent and tore to him, wagging their tails, jumping up.

The man stood and waited for Cannon, calming the dogs, not fussing them, a tenseness in his manner alerting Cannon to something more that was troubling him.

'The collie ran on,' Cannon told him.

The man frowned, shook his head, staggered a little as he stooped to clip a double lead on to the dogs.

Cannon judged he was young, in his twenties, half his own age. 'Is the collie yours as well?' he asked.

The man shook his head again. 'No, I...' He turned aside, retched several times, staggered and would have fallen had Cannon not caught his arm. 'Sorry,' he said when the spasm was over.

'What's happened?' Cannon asked, and as the man's knees threatened to give way, he supported him to where the sand was dry and sat him down, crouching next to him. The dogs flopped companionably down beside both of them. Cannon quickly realized it was not rest the man need for his agitation increased and his colour worsened as he sat. This man was in shock.

'Now, what's happened, Mr Sutton?' Cannon asked and was startled by the alarm in the other's eyes.

'How did you know my name?' he asked.

Cannon indicated the dogs. 'On their collars,' he said.

Sutton stared at his dogs, wiped his mouth on the back of his hand and said, 'It's not just them as was running away,' he said.

'You'd better tell me,' Cannon said.

Sutton turned to look at him more carefully. 'Are you police?' he asked.

'Years ago,' Cannon said. 'Does it show?'

'A bit.' Sutton made an effort to smile but then dropped his gaze again. 'So perhaps you are the right man—not just for the dogs—thanks for stopping them.'

'Why would I be the right man?' Cannon prompted quietly.

'They, the dogs, then I…found a body…my God… A man, I think.' Sutton covered his face with his hands. 'I never… I mean, real life's not like…'

He guessed what Sutton meant was that real death was not like that on any sized screen, large or small. 'You are sure the man was dead? Have you phoned for help?' Cannon asked, his hand going to his pocket for his phone.

Sutton shook his head, swallowed hard. 'He was on his face but—' And Sutton retched again '—he's dead. He must have had the collie's lead still in his hand and when my two ran up to it, it went mad and pulled out of its collar and my two chased it, and…then I ran. He's not alive.'

'I'll phone the police and ambulance and you can show me where you were.'

Sutton looked horrified.

'You can point from the beach,' Cannon told him, 'then wait there with the dogs.'

'All right.' Sutton seemed more controlled now Cannon had taken over.

Cannon phoned the emergency services as they jogged back, gave their location and then the details as far as he knew them.

'I have deployed an ambulance and will inform the police now,' the operator told him. 'Please give us more details as soon as you can.'

They went past the point where Cannon usually left the beach and on to where the end of Sea Lane meandered in a well-used footpath from village to beach. It was a regular route for dog walkers and often horse riders.

'I've rented a cottage in Sea Lane for a fortnight,' Sutton told him. 'This is my first morning. I came for a walk, let the dogs off when I reached the beach, thought they'd run down to the sea but they went up into the sand dunes, and I followed.' He stopped walking and pointed. 'That way over to the left. There are some bigger dunes, it was somewhere there.'

'Will you come a little further with the dogs?' Cannon asked. 'They'll find the way better than either of us, and it is possible the man may be alive. You obviously didn't get very near.'

Sutton shook his head, and reluctantly took a few steps off the main path. The dogs immediately got the idea and pulled hard on the lead. Cannon tried to remember the statistics about dogs being able to smell onc drop of blood in so many million gallons of water.

Sutton pulled the Alsatians to a standstill as thcy reach the brow of a large sand dune. 'It's over the other side of this,' he said.

'Wait here until I make sure,' Cannon said, hoping Sutton had seen a little blood and was exaggerating the injury, even that the 'body' might even have managed to get up and stagger home—it happened—but not this time.

Even from the top of the dune Cannon recognized violent death when he saw it. His phone in his hand again, he turned and shouted back to Sutton. 'Go back to Sea Lane and direct the emergency services when they arrive, and then stay there, wait for me. All right?'

He waited for the man to shout back, then turned to glissade down, making sure he did so well away from where he might destroy any evidence. But it was evident the dogs had not been so careful.

Reaching the bottom he could see a fair amount of sand had been dislodged and fallen over the legs and torso, making the exposed mass of battered skull, bone and blood more stark. Cannon thought it was like a picture in three separate parts, a triptych: one part delicately covered in sand, the mutilated head, and the third part, the man's right hand and arm pulled out from under his body, arm full stretch and from his hand, also pulled to its complete length, a dog leash and collar.

He found the shaft of a broken child's spade and, standing in the mass of already disturbed sand, he leaned over and carefully lifted the dog collar until he could read the engraving on the small brass plate: 'Patch' in scrolled large gothic and a telephone number, a local number, but this was smaller and the plate was well worn.

In the distance he could hear the sound of sirens. There's no hurry, he silently told the racing emergency services, not for this chap, though if he too had been on an early-morning walk with Patch his killer might not be far away.

While he waited, he looked around, reflecting that if this was a hate crime he could not imagine what evil the victim had inflicted on his murderer to deserve such a beating—and what weapon had he used? Nothing he had found casually lying around, that was for sure.

He phoned Liz as the sirens got nearer. Her silence as she took in the main facts felt like a black hole they might well fall willy-nilly into. 'Liz?' he queried.

'You'll come straight back when the police arrive?'

'Of course,' he said.

'You won't get involved?'

The head and shoulders of the first policeman appeared above the dune even as he said, 'The dog's collar has a local telephone number on it.'

THREE

CANNON, AS HE saw it, was never in a position to go straight home and leave Sutton. The man was becoming more and more distressed and his lively young dogs increasingly restive and vocal. When the uniformed Helen Jefferson arrived and heard Sutton's holiday cottage was nearby, she agreed John might usefully take him there and stay with him until she could join them.

As they walked, Cannon asked Sutton if there was anyone on holiday with him. He was to regret the question for Sutton immediately stopped walking, hung his head and gave way to tears.

'No,' he sobbed, 'my partner decided we'd have some time apart to find out if we could resolve some…difficulties. How can I think clearly now?'

'That's not going to be too easy,' Cannon agreed, feeling it was a pretty inadequate reply. 'Let's get you inside,' he said, taking the dogs as they reached the cottage gate, and thinking tea and sympathy would be the best he could do. Sutton did not console easily and when Cannon glimpsed Helen coming towards the front door he hurried outside to meet her, and out of earshot explained the situation.

'I think he must have been on the edge of a breakdown when he came here. Finding…has not helped.'

'I really just need his statement,' Helen said. 'Sergeant Maddern's coming to take it. He's a fatherly soul.'

'No idea who the victim is yet?' Cannon asked.

'No answer from the number on the dog collar.' She shook her head. 'As soon we have the address I shall go there myself.'

He gave her a sympathetic glance. It was one of the worst tasks any police officer faced, telling someone their loved one had died; an accident or sudden death was bad enough but murder was in a different league. Murder in this part of the country was like a large boulder dropped into the middle of a still lake, the ripples going on and on, sometimes turning back on themselves and making things doubly complicated.

'There might be something on the body to help identify him,' Helen went on, 'but if we're not careful forensics will be having to dig him out. The whole blessed sand dune begins to slide down if we get near.'

'It could be someone who lived alone, of course,' Cannon mused as they both turned to the sound of footsteps behind them.

'Ah! Here's Maddern, good,' Helen said.

'Hi, Jim,' Cannon greeted him.

'Bit near home this one, ma'am,' Maddern said.

'Yes, give him your special old-fashioned treatment, Sergeant, the man's in a state. John, I'm sure, will go in with you. I must get back to the scene.'

The two of them watched her go. 'What you'd call a smart bit of stuff,' Maddern said. 'Not to her face, of course.'

'Well, not while she's in uniform,' Cannon agreed.

'Just introduce me,' Maddern said as Cannon gave him a quick résumé of what he knew of the man, 'and tell him I live in the same lane. He may find that some comfort.'

Cannon did just that, and was struck, as so many times in the past, by Maddern's gift for stillness, observing, listening, waiting for the right moment to take charge. Cannon made more tea as Maddern took the statement, then left to get back to his public house and Liz. When he arrived he found only Alamat, their live-in help there, and remembered Tuesday, one of the slacker days at the pub, was Liz's day for shopping. Business, of course, had to go on.

Alamat had just two customers, a couple, finishing two of the pub's renowned all-day breakfasts. They were all smiles and well satisfied with the service they had received from the dapper little Croat in his pristine white apron.

Cannon thought of ringing the landlord of The Stump in Boston but felt no wish now to talk over last night's events, which seemed trivial compared to those of the morning.

The customers left, Alamat went to spend the afternoon in his quarters in the stable block, and Liz arrived back. They unpacked the car, the bulk of food items not so geared to sausages, chips and breaded chicken shapes school-children seemed to prefer. The end of October would see their winter opening hours come into force, and they should really make the effort to go away for a complete change. Liz could do with a holiday, preferably somewhere scenic so she could do some sketching and painting. Cannon, on the other hand, rather enjoyed the winter at home; he always had the feeling that the whole of the Fenland stretched out, wider, expansive in its emptiness, resting, recouping, and he loved it all— the rougher seas, the empty beaches, the cosy nights with the regulars in the pub.

Liz was bringing old stock to the front of the deep freeze and stacking the new at the back when the police arrived.

Helen led the way in, followed by a tall, gangling figure they knew well, Regional Detective Inspector Derek Betterson. Both looked grim, Helen's greeting a tight-lipped nod and Betterson's little more.

'It is not good news,' she told them, 'and there's a chance it could be linked to the trouble here last night.'

'What!' Cannon exclaimed. 'So the victim…'

'Was here last night.'

Cannon's thoughts immediately went to the huge man who had antagonized the whole bar but he was certainly not the victim: the body was nowhere near his size.

'So what's happened so far?' Cannon heard himself ask, and knew immediately it sounded too officious—he'd no right to know police business these days, and added, 'I mean, has the body been officially identified?'

'Not officially, but the papers in his wallet, and my own knowledge of the man's build, et cetera…'

Cannon felt a chill of goose-bumps creep up his spine. He glanced at Liz and saw her expression change to horror as Helen went on.

'I am afraid there is little doubt that the dead man is Niall Riley,' Helen said.

'Timmy's father? His father!' Liz exclaimed incredulously. 'Oh no, how awful, and why? Why! His poor wife! How will she cope?'

'We have checked that Riley is not at the bakery working, and with Mrs Riley's consent Sergeant Maddern's gone over to alert her sister in Reed St Thomas. Apparently she's a widow. Maddern knows the family details,' Helen went on, 'and has just let me know the sister is coming back with him. She'll stay with her nephew while we take Mrs Riley to view the body. That is, once the pathologist has done his investigations and has the deceased reasonable enough for a relation to see.'

'That won't be easy,' Betterson said, 'someone's given him a right walloping about the head. Shouldn't be any problem with the cause of death though.'

There was a short silence after these remarks.

'I wonder how Timmy is taking it?' Liz wondered. 'Mr Riley once told me he has the intelligence of a bright six-year-old.'

'Mrs Riley was helping him wash and dress when the phone was ringing,' Helen told them, 'and when I was there he obviously thought his father was at work, but was really upset that the dog was not at home. He was asking all the time after Patch.'

'It was going down the beach like it was heading for John O'Groats,' Cannon said, 'but that was hours ago.'

'I've alerted all the motor patrols to keep a lookout for it, a rough-haired collie, yes?' Betterson queried.

'Yes,' Cannon confirmed, 'white patch like a saddle on its back.'

'I'd like you both to give statements, your versions of what happened here last night,' Helen said, 'as I and Paul will do, of course, and I'd like a list of all the people you know by name that were here, or failing that a list of the teams who took part in the quiz.'

At that moment the telephone rang, Cannon answered and was told, 'The name's Ladkin, landlord of The Stump's Shadow in Boston. I understand there was trouble at the quiz last night involving someone who travelled with our supporters. What's it all about?'

'The police are with me now,' Cannon told him.

'Are they?' Ladkin did not sound impressed. 'Didn't sound like the kind of trouble the police bother about.'

'Just a minute,' Cannon said, and put his hand over the receiver and told Helen and Betterson who it was.

'Let me speak to him,' Betterson said.

'Mr Ladkin, Detective Inspector Betterson, I shall be coming to see you. We want to talk to Mr Maurice Spier but he did not return home last night according to his wife.' He paused and held the receiver away from his ear as the landlord made loud protests that Spier was a man he hardly knew. Betterson let him continue until the voice dropped in volume then putting the receiver back to his ear added that the situation had become much more serious. When he rang off he said, 'Any landlord would be better off without Spier. He's been known to the police since he was a great lad, broody individual. Anything said he doesn't like he can be nasty, very nasty, and…' He shrugged, then went on, 'He's also on a suspended sentence from his last outburst; any further trouble and he goes down for two years.'

'It still leaves us with a lot of enquiries to make of a lot of people,' Helen said. 'I wondered if there was anything in particular either of you remember about last night, any reaction to the trouble that caught your eye?'

Cannon remembered Paul sitting very tense, then swinging round to tell Spier to be quiet. Hoskins had clenched his fists and put them out of sight under the table. The professor had knocked over his walking stick, Cannon had retrieved it when he stood up. There had been other reactions all around the bar but certainly not against Riley.

'This man, Spier, was the only one to show aggression towards Riley,' Liz said, adding, 'Though to tell the truth it was Riley who became the more aggressive. John and Paul had to intervene.'

'Could, of course, be nothing to do with what happened here,' Betterson commented with a shrug.

Cannon frowned; his time in the Met had left him with little belief in coincidences.

When they were once more on their own, neither Liz nor Cannon could settle to rest.

'We've got until six,' he began, then in spite of how anxious Liz always was to keep out of police affairs these days, he drew in a great breath to make a suggestion. Her eyes were on him immediately.

'Why don't we go for a walk along the beach?' he suggested. 'Look for the dog. I can't think it would head off and go wandering about the streets; my guess is it will eventually turn and come back towards home.'

'Just look for Timmy's best friend,' she said, looking at him sternly, 'no involvement, just find the dog. I wouldn't mind doing that.'

'Shouldn't think anything has ever had a closer view of a murder than it did,' Cannon mused. 'If that dog could talk it would be a star witness.'

'There's always the possibility of forensics,' she muttered as she rummaged around in the cupboard, brought out a packet of arrowroot biscuits, opened it and put some in her pocket. 'Should we take a piece of string as well, something to tie round its neck if we find him?' she suggested.

'As practical as ever,' Cannon said.

'Maybe, but not involved,' she asserted.

'No, no,' he said and retreated to the porch for their outdoor coats.

It occurred to Cannon as they went across the meadows at the back of the pub that they did not often walk together. He ran in the mornings but Liz said she found enough exercise in the pub, although she loved to be out on the marshland or seashore, painting landscapes. Sometimes, and a little diffidently, she would ask for Paul's opinion and advice, which he gave very willingly.

They reached the beach well out of sight or sound of police activity and turned the opposite way, the way Cannon had seen the dog running. The sun had gone and the wind was stronger now, blowing straight into their faces. Cannon drew her attention to sand being whipped up from nearby dunes and flying like a pennant from each top. Obliterating evidence, he thought, but not murder, which would always surface. He felt a sudden certainty that this was going to be a much more complex case than might at first appear, and wondered if Spier, who he had thought of as just a blustering, bullying joker, might be something more sinister?

They were both leaning forward now to walk against the wind and it was difficult to keep one's eyes open as they searched for any sign of Timmy Riley's dog.

Cannon turned to walk backwards a few steps to point at his watch and say they would walk for an hour one way, then he thought they should make their way back. She nodded agreement.

By the time the hour was nearly up they had reached a point where the beach was divided by waters draining from the land, making a gully several feet deep. That will be it then, Cannon thought. We'll turn back at that point. We've seen nothing; no point getting wet through as well as wind blasted.

At that precise moment Liz raised her arm and pointed to the sea end of the miniature ravine where darting black shapes appeared and disappeared in and out of the gully.

'Children,' he said, 'playing in the water.'

As they got nearer they could see that there was a small group of nine- or ten-year-old boys, who were throwing objects at something in the water. As they got nearer he could hear them shouting and screaming, egging each other on, running to find more pieces of driftwood, and Cannon had a terrible premonition that he knew what they were aiming at.

He ran, shouting, towards them. They were so intent on their occupation that they neither heard nor saw him until he was nearly on top of them. Then they saw his anger and ran, one shouting back, 'It tried to bite me!' as if it justified the torment.

'I'll bite you if you don't clear off!' Cannon bellowed after them.

The dog lay on a small island in the middle of the gully, wet through, shivering, trembling, bits of driftwood all around it and floating away on the current to the sea.

Cannon was immediately in the water, wading towards the dog, talking to it, calling it by its name.

Only its eyes moved as he neared it. 'I'm not going to hurt you,' he told it, 'I'll take you back to Timmy. Timmy,' he repeated louder as the dog's ears lifted a fraction at the name. 'Come on, then, home to Timmy.'

Liz was in the water now, by his side.

'It's run itself off its legs,' Cannon said. 'I'll have to carry it.'

Gently, cautiously, talking to the collie all the time, and with a fleeting thought that he wished he'd put gloves on—farm collies he'd known had been a bit inclined to nip if displeased—but he slid his arms under the soaked bundle of fur and lifted.

'Those little…' Liz began with feeling. 'Is it hurt?'

'Not sure,' he said as he waded towards the sea and a less steep climb out, adding, 'At least we'll have the wind behind us on the way back.'

'You'll not be able to carry it all the way, will you?'

'Not sure, or how comfortable it is,' he said. He had one arm under its chest, its front legs dangling and the other under its back quarters, legs tucked up.

'That's about the best you can do,' she said, and as if in agreement Patch turned his head in towards Cannon's chest.

He was glad Liz didn't talk any more, he hadn't the breath. The full-grown dog was a good weight but he managed to carry it all the way back to the stile over into the meadows, then he had to rest.

'Let me get over first and you can pass Patch to me,' Liz suggested.

'Tie the string around its neck first,' Cannon said, resting his arms and the dog on the stile. 'Don't want to lose him now.'

'Poor old boy,' she said, and as Cannon regained his breath he hoped she meant the dog.

'Put him down a minute now,' he said, still leaning on the far side of the stile to take a breather, 'but keep hold of the string just in case.' The dog just lay in the grass and its head moved uncertainly along its foreleg as if it could find no rest, no comfort.

This dog and Timmy needed each other, and Cannon did not want to linger; the warmth that had built up between him and the dog soon ebbed away, and all three of them were wet through.

'You go on,' he told Liz, 'get out of your wet clothes.' She waited until he was ready to pick up the dog again then ran ahead.

By the time he arrived at the pub Liz had one of the big bar pew-seat cushions covered with old towels in front of the Aga, and the kettle was boiling.

'Go and get changed,' he ordered as he laid the dog on the towels, 'then I will.'

While Liz was still upstairs, Cannon made a call to Helen to say they had found Patch and he would return him to Timmy shortly, if she was all right with that.

'Anything to ease the—' The word 'child' hovered but was changed to 'the man's distress'. 'Mrs Riley has been taken to identify the body, her sister is with Timmy.'

IT WAS CANNON who an hour and a half later came back from the Riley house feeling traumatized. He saw that the bar was not over-busy and the normal buzz of conversation was subdued. He guessed there'd be all kinds of speculations being made. He was not anxious to be drawn into any of them. He showed his face at the entrance to the bar; Liz saw him, nodded, and left Alamat in charge.

'So...' she said, assessing how he looked.

'It was awful. Like having your heart cut out,' he said. 'For a start the dog got out of the car himself as soon as I opened the door. He was a bit stiff but he walked into the house past Mrs Riley's sister and went into the lounge. Timmy was slumped on the settee, a picture of misery. The dog went to him, licked his hand then climbed up on to the settee by him. Timmy, well… he just beamed, then told the dog off, wagging a finger at him schoolmaster-style, his arm around his neck, loving him all the time. Told his Aunt Christine that Patch wanted his tea.

'We all went into the kitchen and while Timmy and his aunt found the dog food, Patch went to his water bowl and had a good long drink. It was then I noticed something hanging from his mouth.' He put a hand into his pocket and pulled out a plastic bag; inside it was a black thread about four inches long. 'It was fast between his front teeth.'

'What are you thinking?' Liz asked.

'Well, if someone attacks its master I would think the dog would have a go.' He held up the bag. 'This could be from the attacker's clothing.'

'It could be from that boy's clothes who said it had bitten him,' Liz said, examining the thread. 'Though that doesn't look like a material used for a boy's clothing these days, looks more like a linen thread.'

'I'll mention what you say,' he said as they both pondered the forensics and the protocol of evidence in plastic food bags collected by a civilian even though he was an ex-Met inspector. Liz commented that if the dog had bit the assailant he should hopefully have the teeth marks to prove it.

'Then,' he said, pausing to draw in a long breath and exhale sharply, 'I was just leaving when Mrs Riley arrived back. Timmy overwhelmed her with his talk of

Patch and how he had been for a long walk on the beach and been late for his tea. His aunt tactfully took him to fill up the dog's biscuit bowl. Mrs Riley told me she would have known her Niall anywhere by his hands, good hands, she said, hands that worked and loved.'

'Oh dear.' Liz went round to him, leaned over and tenderly put her arms around him.

'You'd think,' he said, 'we'd get some immunity to emotion, all that we've seen in our time.'

'Heaven help us if we ever do,' she said quietly.

'I keep wondering what else I can do?' he said.

'All you can do now is ring Helen, tell her about this—' she pointed to the plastic bag '—and if you don't want to face the curious lot in the bar, Alamat and I will manage.'

'Well…' He turned and caught her hands. 'Well… that's… Thanks.'

'Ring Helen while I'm still here, see what she says.'

He got through on her mobile quite quickly but he did not do much talking, more listening and making a few exclamations of surprise. When he rang off he sat without speaking.

'What's happened?' she demanded.

'Helen's been taken off the case, and suspended from duty,' he said.

FOUR

'IT'S MY FAULT, must be,' Paul said. 'I overreacted last night in the pub.'

'Having friends who run licensed premises has always been an issue to the police,' Cannon said, making a gesture towards his still-empty bar, 'plus the murdered man being a customer.'

'*And* I did walk our dog along the same stretch of beach much earlier than you were out running,' Paul added.

'Our spaniel would be far more interested in the water than smelling anything out in the dunes,' Helen said, 'and as far as the police are concerned it's a matter of expediency.'

'You say that, but what if the newspapers pick up the fact you've been suspended?' Paul asked angrily. 'What will they make of it?'

'They could of course make just as big a story if Helen was kept on the case,' Liz reflected, and they all fell silent before being brought back to the present by the sound of the front doors opening and closing.

Alan Hoskins pushed his way through the swing doors in clothes that would not just blend with the marshes but looked as if they were made from the very greens and browns of the landscape. His pullover was Fair Isle of long-faded browns, nondescript khaki cords, greenish jacket and all telling much of his long status as a solitary widower. His hair, in contrast, as he pulled off an ancient check cap, was snow-white, and his weathered cheeks clean shaven.

'Hello, what are you lot plotting?' he said, then looking at Helen added, 'Should've thought you'd be raking in the overtime.'

Helen sighed and looked at Cannon who pulled a wry face. 'Contrary to appearances, I'd trust him with my life.'

'We both have in the past,' Liz added, and Helen told him the situation.

Hoskins frowned, dropped his gaze and looked like he was about to say quite a lot but then changed his mind.

'Pull the man a pint, landlord,' Paul said, putting his hand in his pocket, 'then I think it's best if we go.'

During the evening's trade, Cannon was to shake his head and say many times that he had heard no more and knew no more, but he also became quite convinced that Hoskins knew something, sitting in his pew seat at the far end of the bar and for once saying very little.

The regulars decided to set up a fund for Mrs Riley—'the least we can do'—and asked Cannon to put a beer glass on the counter, and as this began to fill with fivers and pound coins, Cannon noted that Hoskins put into the glass but did not drink his normal amount of pints. He refilled the old boy's tankard and found himself impatient for the rest of his customers to leave. Hoskins was invariably last.

'So?' he said, as he finished collecting glasses from the bar. Liz, who had raised her eyebrows and drawn attention to Hoskins several times during the evening, moved closer on the other side of the counter.

Hoskins cleared his throat. 'You know I'm out and about quite a lot,' he said.

'Keeping an eye on the wildlife in the area,' Cannon said. 'Yes, we know. Go on.'

'Aye, well, the biggest estate in the area is now in the hands of the Highams. They're brewers *and* going into wine-growing down south, I hear. There's two sons and a daughter, one son away, the other not long married but following his father in the business. The young daughter's at home.' He paused then added, 'There's been some strange things going on up there. I *would* have said it was village kids or someone who resented a wealthy man coming into the area and having a lot to say about local affairs. He goes to all the council meetings,' he added significantly, as if this was the height of interference. 'But now Niall Riley's been killed that puts a different light on things, and I wonder if he'd seen something, or someone, he wasn't supposed to. Those dunes where he was found, at the far side of Sea Lane, border the Higham estate.'

'Not something many would know,' Cannon began, 'though the police would…' but Hoskins had not finished.

'Then their gamekeeper came to see me,' he added.

'The Higham gamekeeper?' Liz was surprised. 'He's said to keep himself to himself.'

Hoskins nodded. 'Ford, Dick Ford. He knows me well enough, of course.'

Cannon also nodded. He supposed anyone who lived in the area knew Alan Hoskins. A good many relied on him for a cheap meal of rabbit when their money was low. When crows or pigeons needed thinning out, the local farmers and landowners were not above paying for his services. He would not be sought out by gamekeepers at this time of year, when everything that ran on or flew over their land would be preserved for official shooting parties.

'Ford asked me if I'd keep a lookout when I was over that way. They'd had several strange things happen, both on the estate and near the house. For a start the house dogs have gone missing: twice they were found locked in outhouses on the estate, and then once they had been tied up to one of those big stone urns in The Grange gardens. Mr Higham was not amused; he enjoys walking his dogs when he's at home. Everyone was questioned but none of the men, or the family, admitted knowing anything about it. I felt with Ford asking me to keep a lookout I could spend more time up there without worrying, so I did, but…' He paused, half shrugged, half shuddered. 'The strange thing was *I* felt watched. I never saw anybody, mind, but it was strange.'

'I would have thought Higham would have contacted the police,' Liz said.

Hoskins shrugged. 'Ford was very uneasy, then today he comes to see me again, this time with a bag in his hand. He still follows the old practice of having a gibbet outside his cottage, a wire where he hangs the corpses of any crows he shoots. They used to say it was a warning for other predators to keep away. I think it's to show the gamekeeper's doing his job.'

'So this bag?' Cannon queried, wanting to offer him another drink on the house, but he had to ride his bicycle home and there had been one or two mishaps in the past.

'He brought something he'd found on his gibbet to show me. It was an old doll dressed like a man and someone had not only strung it up by its neck but had gone to the trouble of making it look as if it had been shot through the heart.'

'How had that been done?' Liz asked.

'The hole must have been burnt through with a metal rod,' Hoskins said. 'It was a neat job.'

'What happened to the doll?' Cannon asked, this lining up in his mind with the black thread from the dog's mouth as possible evidence.

'Ford took it back—he intended to show it to Mr Higham when he got back. He was down in Kent apparently buying more land.'

'So?' Liz questioned when they had seen Hoskins off and locked up.

'And so—' Cannon tried to divert her '—to bed, I should think.'

'And tomorrow morning's run will be?' she persisted. 'As if I didn't know.'

'If Alan Hoskins thinks he is being watched I would say the chances are he's right. I've never known his instincts let him down, have you?'

She searched for an answer that was not completely on Cannon's side, that might keep him out of this latest trouble, and then she struggled in his arms.

'Just forbid me to go,' he said. 'That's all you have to do.'

'And have you prowling about like a caged lion?'

'So you prefer the free spirited version?'

'Sit down.' She pushed him towards his chair.

'I find tea an aphrodisiac,' he warned.

'Good,' she said. 'On second thoughts, you can make it and bring me mine upstairs. Look at the time.'

THE FOLLOWING MORNING she watched him from their bedroom window as he set off for his run. Somewhat to her annoyance, he turned and waved. Was she that predictable?

He gave her a second wave and set off at a good pace. He wanted to have as much time as possible to explore the Higham woods where Hoskins had felt watched.

As he neared the footpath from Sea Lane to the beach, Cannon could see the blue and white police tape blowing up from behind the dunes. He ran on at the edge of the sea, just keeping beyond the reach of the last ripple as it subsided and drew back. He wondered where the nervy guy with the two Alsatians was walking this morning.

When he reached the area where the Higham estate began, the random pattern of natural pines was replaced by copses of silver birch and larch through which he began to see lawns spaced with even older, more majestic trees, oaks, copper beeches, chestnuts and finally The Grange. He began to have the same sensation as Hoskins. He felt watched.

He moved back and studied the grounds more carefully. He was way out of reach of any security cameras on the house. He could see no one, hear no dogs, but there was a path of a kind. The gamekeeper must walk the woods regularly and possibly kept to certain ways. He went on again and still felt watched. He told himself to do what Hoskins did: trust his instincts.

Suddenly the feeling came over him most strongly. He swung around sharply to see if he could catch someone—and felt a fool. He was alone in these trees, of that he was sure, so why…and then he saw it, a tiny glint from the fork of an ancient silver birch. Binoculars, the light catching a lens?

He moved slowly, looked back, and could still see

that pinpoint of light as if the lens were following him. So now he chose a line which described a circle around the spot, then went in quickly to where he thought the secret watcher might be—but there was no one there. Then he saw the gleam again and located it more accurately in the first division of the tree's branches.

Not a person but a video camera. He *was* being watched, recorded. He moved to the back of the camera: it was a sophisticated affair, up to the minute, protected from the weather. Not, he felt, done by an amateur yet— He turned to look around and nearly jumped out of his skin; a man stood leaning on a tree some twenty yards from him, watching.

'Hoskins,' he hissed, 'you bloody idiot. What are you doing?'

'Could ask you the same,' Hoskins whispered, then asked, 'what've you found?'

Cannon showed him.

Hoskins swore under his breath. 'I knew someone was watching,' he said. 'Come on, let's get out of 'ere.'

He led the way, muttering that he didn't mind keeping an eye out for somebody but damned if he was going to be spied on while doing it and he'd tell Dick Ford as much.

FIVE

For the only time Cannon could remember, the man who walked into the bar of The Trap first that evening was not Hoskins.

Cannon, still in the leather apron he wore for cellar work, appraised the well-built, grey-haired, distinguished-looking man. Springing mass of grey-black hair, in his sixties, probably, but fit and robust. Cannon was himself being as keenly assessed.

We'll know each other if we meet again, Cannon thought, judging that this man would be very much at home in a company boardroom at the head of the table. Then assessing the expensive dark grey suit, cashmere by the expensive sheen and the way it hung, he mentally amended that the boardroom would be that of a top company listed on the Stock Exchange.

'Good evening,' Cannon offered tentatively, with the underlying question of 'What does such as you want here on the dot of opening time? Can I help you?'

At that moment Hoskins pushed his way through the swing doors into the bar. The man turned to look at him, then back to Cannon. 'Yes,' he said positively, 'I think you can. My gamekeeper told me Mr Hoskins, who he described to me, would be your first customer. My name is Alexander Higham.'

'So…' Cannon took off the leather apron and hung it behind the cellar door, which he locked (a brief memory of the man who had fallen down those steps and been shot dead like an injured dog by a fellow villain in his mind). He hung up the key as was his wont, and walked around the counter into the bar. 'What can we do for you?'

'Ford also told me that you were an ex-Metropolitan man,' Alexander Higham said. 'Can we talk? I badly need impartial advice and help.' He glanced from one to the other. 'And I'm prepared to pay for both.'

When there was no reaction from either he added, 'As a stranger to both of you I felt this was my only hope, the one approach I could make.'

'Money don't buy everything,' Hoskins muttered.

Higham's self-assurance deserted him for a second; he swayed a little, grasped the back of a chair, then pulled it out and sat down. 'No, believe me, I have learned that the hard way,' he said quietly, spreading the fingers of his well-manicured hands wide over the small round table, staring down at them as he went on. 'I am tormented by the fact that a man, who I feel might have been just an innocent bystander, has been murdered on my land.'

'Did you know the murdered man, Niall Riley?' Cannon interrupted sharply.

Higham shook his head, 'But link that with the other things that are happening near my house, I know all this malevolence is aimed at *my* family.'

'Malevolence?' Cannon repeated, sitting down beside him and pulling out another chair for Hoskins.

Higham nodded, looked from one to the other. 'I need someone who knows my estate and the area like the back of his hand.' He nodded at Hoskins. 'And someone with a fresh mind, a trained mind, someone who can think out of the box, and is not fettered by thoughts of expenses and overtime payments. The police here and in other places have been good, diligent as far as their resources allowed, but I have wealth, and I need help, extra eyes and ears.'

Hoskins sat down.

'So these incidents have not just happened here?' Cannon asked the question that interested him most. 'They're not just local?'

Higham swung his head from side to side very slowly. 'I am convinced my family have been targeted in several places. It has been coming to a head for a time, and no one but me seems to see the full picture. When we had troubles at our seaside cottage I overheard a constable say he thought I had a persecution complex.'

'So what happened there?' Hoskins asked with a grunt of sympathy; his dealings with the constabulary had not always been harmonious.

'One of my wife's main interests is her gardens. Around our thatched cottage in Kent she had created a picture-postcard garden—roses, hollyhocks, you know the kind of thing. Holiday-makers often stopped to take photographs. One morning we found that from the front gate right up to the cottage, the garden was devastated but in a strange and disturbing way. Near the front gate one or two choice plants had been uprooted and trampled, but the nearer you came to the house the more plants had been destroyed. It was like a wave of destruction rolling towards the front door. It had a most sinister feel, as if some evil was coming.'

Cannon watched Higham carefully. Surely, he thought, not a man given to an overactive imagination. 'Anything else?' he asked.

'In London I've had quite a number of silent phone calls: you could sense someone listening, even hear them breathing, but no one spoke.'

'You can report them things,' Hoskins said.

'I had the calls traced, but they came from places like St Pancras station, the Royal Academy, Covent Garden market.'

Cannon was wondering how seriously *he* would be taking all this? An attack on a perfect garden could be local jealousy. Nuisance phone calls, a daily occurrence, and the murder of a man Higham did not know, which seemed more linked to the trouble in Cannon's bar than out on this businessman's estate.

'Anything else?' Cannon asked. 'Anywhere?'

'My car was vandalized,' Higham added, 'outside my home in Islington.'

'London.' Cannon wondered how many cars were daily vandalized in the capital but looking at the face of this disturbed man he also asked himself if, in his place, he too would not be adding up the incidents.

'No other vehicles were damaged, and the gouges and scratches were quite...' An apt description seemed to defeat him. 'I took photographs.' Just at that moment they heard footsteps. They all paused to listen, the swing doors were pushed open and the tall figure of Regional Detective Inspector Derek Betterson strode in. 'I'll let you see them,' he added quietly.

Hoskins got up and went to sit in his usual pew seat near the bar muttering, 'Evening, all.'

'Evening, Mr Alan Hoskins of this parish, Mr Higham and...' The DI included Cannon with a nod.

'Think I have a customer well due for his first drink,' Cannon said and went to the business side of the bar to serve Hoskins. Higham rose, wished everyone good evening and left.

Betterson took in the empty table. 'You won't get rich with too many customers like him, John,' Betterson said and went to lean on the other end of the counter and mouthed 'on duty', adding 'But I'd like a word.'

As soon as Liz came from kitchen to bar, John took the DI upstairs to their private sitting room. Betterson, as so many visitors did, went immediately to the window to look at the wide panoramic view, placing one hand on the handsome brass telescope Cannon had permanently mounted there. 'I always envy you this,' he said, then turning back to him, 'Pity you can't see as far as the Higham estate. I was surprised to see him here.'

Cannon did not offer an explanation.

'He's a powerful, wealthy man and not too impressed with the police at the moment,' he said and left it at that.

'Has there been some development?' Cannon asked.

'The development is that Spier is still missing. We've learnt that he *did* go home last night, one of the neighbours heard him, and his wife finally admitted he arrived swearing revenge on everyone who was in your bar on the quiz night. He went out again before light, with his shotgun, and has never been seen since. We had no idea he had a gun, his wife dropped that out, then was terrified when she had. Mrs Spier is, well, to say the least, in some state of agitation—not sure whether it's because he's missing, or the thought of the mood he'll be in when he returns.'

'Riley wasn't shot,' Cannon commented.

'No.' Betterson shook his head. 'And from what we learned from various landlords, Spier's behaviour here was typical. Too much to say, someone objects, there's a bit of pushing and shoving, an occasional blow and that's about it. Unpleasant but not exactly life-threatening.'

'That was my feeling,' Cannon said.

'*And...*' Betterson said heavily, turning his back to the window, 'there's something strange about this murder. It seemed from the forensic report that the first blow had caused death, and the rest seemed almost to have been administered as punishment.'

'A frenzied attack,' Cannon suggested.

Betterson shook his head. 'That doesn't feel like the right description either.'

Cannon reviewed what he remembered of Niall Riley's body, the head wounds extreme, with much disturbance, deep disturbance, in the sand all around.

'Looked like someone had done a dance around the body,' Betterson added as if seeing the same picture.

'There would have been the dog to contend with,' Cannon said.

'And thank God for that dog. I think it's the saviour for Timmy Riley and his mother, gives them a focus.' Betterson looked towards the coffee-making machine on a small table the far side of the window. 'Does that work?' he asked.

As Cannon made the coffee the DI went back to the window, where like a theatre fade-out the salt marshes were disappearing into the night. 'I know Higham feels threatened by this murder on his land but if he came here tonight asking for your help, I'd say be very careful what you are getting into. I don't like this one, it has a…' He turned back into the room and gave an exaggerated shudder. 'But I'd appreciate it if you didn't mention that I was going all girlie and intuitive about it.'

Cannon grinned at the idea but knew Liz would have said her partner would be the last one to dismiss intuition as a means to bring the lawless to justice. Sipping his coffee, Betterson suggested that it might be a good idea to let the quiz team and their supporters know the situation with regard to Spier as soon as possible. 'The super doesn't want to make a big issue of his disappearance as yet—he feels Spier might be more at risk of doing something completely stupid if he feels hunted, but the more folk are quietly on the lookout for him the better.'

Later that evening Dick Ford came into the bar, closely followed by Michael Bliss, who waited his turn to be served as Ford handed a small canvas shopping bag over the counter to Cannon.

Hoskins watched with raised eyebrows. 'Heard of poacher turning gamekeeper, but not the other way round.'

'Don't worry,' Ford replied, 'it's nothing in your line of business, but I do have a message for you. Mr Higham would be pleased if you would go and see him tomorrow sometime.' Ford looked at Cannon too as he spoke.

'Ah!' Hoskins exclaimed 'And I want to see him about having hidden cameras in his woods.'

Ford was denying all knowledge of any cameras as Cannon glanced into the bag which was too full to hold just photographs. He noted there was a tissue-wrapped parcel and an envelope, before stowing it under the counter. He then tactfully told Hoskins about Spier. The news spread quietly around the bar during the evening.

Hoskins lingered on, last customer as always, and he almost tutted as Liz picked up the bag Ford had brought

and said she would put it in the kitchen. 'We'll get all
finished and locked up before you start looking at that,'
she told Cannon.

'Bossy tonight,' Hoskins commented. 'She'll not
want you involved, but will you go and see Higham?'

'I'll let you know tomorrow,' Cannon said. 'I'll take
my morning run your way.'

'I'll have the kettle on,' Hoskins said.

Cannon saw him out, watched the red rear light on
his ancient bike waver away into the distance, locked
up and hurried to complete the usual end-of-day check
of his cellar and bar.

In the kitchen Liz had the tea ready. Her face was set
to disapproval and the carrier bag stood centre table.

Cannon sat down, looked at the bag and exclaimed,
'I'd forgotten all about that! Let's see *who* brought it in?'

'I am *not* amused,' Liz declared. 'You and Hoskins
have been itching to know what's in it all evening.'

'And *you* might just be,' he ventured.

'If it meant you would never be involved in anything
dicey ever again, I'd ram it into the Aga this second.'

Cannon pulled the bag to him and took out first the
tissue-wrapped parcel. It was, as he had half expected,
the doll from the gamekeeper's gibbet line. Without
touching it he turned the doll on the paper, viewed it
from all angles, as he told Liz what he knew. As Ford
had said, it was an old rag boy-doll dressed in trousers,
shirt, tie and jacket, and a string made into a perfectly
formed noose was drawn tight around its neck. The
burn driven through the breast looked realistically like
a shot through the heart at close range.

'That could have been done with something like a
heated knitting needle,' Liz said, sitting down next to him.

'So this is…' he began.

'A frightener,' she stated with conviction. 'A real frightener.'

Cannon now took up the brown A5 envelope and tipped out two photographs. One was of the near side of a black Mercedes with obvious damage to the front side door. The second was a close-up of that door.

Cannon felt engraved would be a better word than scratched for the damage that spanned the whole of the panel from window to handle. What had been used must have been extremely strong and sharp for the lines went through to the bright silver body metal of the car. There was nothing random, or ambiguous, about the message being given.

'It's like nothing so much as a…' Liz began.

'Stick man, or a cave painting of a hunter stricken by a great blow to the chest,' Cannon finished. 'The arms thrown up and back above the circle of the head…'

'And falling backwards, thrown back by the force of whatever's hit him,' Liz added. 'I wouldn't want to find such a warning on my car door.'

'There's something else about it, isn't there?' Cannon mused. 'A round head, a series of seven or eight sort of confident lines that depict alarm, a body blow…'

'A fatal blow,' Liz interjected dourly.

'Practised on paper, perhaps, and done in situ with…?'

'Something with a very sharp, rigid point. There's nothing vague…' Liz paused.

'In execution or method,' Cannon added.

'Have the police seen these?' she asked, her hand hovering over the doll, then for longer over the photograph.

Cannon shook his head. 'They certainly should, but as Alexander Higham sent them here to me...'

'You must see he does.' She stopped suddenly as if she could have bitten her own tongue off. 'What am I saying?' she despaired. 'No, tell Hoskins to tell him, don't you get involved.'

THE FOLLOWING MORNING Cannon took his run to Alan Hoskins' riverside cottage. The garden was, as always, the picture of good husbandry, some vegetables cleared, runner beans still producing, and inside the kettle was boiling. He arranged to call back at eleven to pick the old boy up and go with him to Higham Grange.

SIX

As they approached The Grange, Hoskins said, 'They reckon Alexander Higham's up for a title.'

'Do they?' Cannon said dryly, adding as he took in the façade of the Georgian three-storey manor house, 'Well, he lives in the right kind of property.'

'Not exactly heaving with life, though, is it?' Hoskins said as they stood for some minutes after ringing the front doorbell. He had hardly uttered the words when something approaching bedlam broke out. A black Mercedes swung into the drive at speed, barely missed Cannon's beloved classic Willys jeep, and swung round to the side of the house. It was closely followed by a police car.

Then there was the sound of several raised voices, concerned and questioning, car doors slamming. Just as Cannon wondered about walking round to see what was going on, the irate and much disturbed figure of Alexander Higham strode round to his own front door, followed by a young policeman from the patrol car, who was having to almost run to keep up with him.

'Well, I hope your superiors don't think I imagined all that!' Higham was almost shouting as he acknowledged the two men who stood at his door.

'Nothing imaginary about that accident, unfortunately,' the constable said.

'Accident!' Higham exclaimed, clearly beside himself with distress and anger.

'We've called your own doctor to come and have a look at you all, and he's on his way. But it was the car in front of you that really had the accident, sir,' the constable said with studied mildness, but his pallor and set features told another story. Cannon thought he had probably left colleagues dealing with something very nasty. 'Once we know you're in good hands we can come back for your statements later,' he added.

'And perhaps we should come back another time?' Cannon suggested.

'No! No!' Higham dismissed that idea, and at that moment the front door opened and a smartly dressed woman in outdoor clothes stood shaking her head. 'We are all fine, Alexander, there is no need for all this fuss.'

Higham opened his mouth as if to make some heated reply but the small woman, who Cannon guessed might be of Jewish descent and was obviously his wife, added, 'I suggest we all go inside.' She included the constable with a gracious nod.

'I'll wait outside, ma'am, until your doctor arrives, then there'll be someone come to take statements when you've all recovered a little.'

'I understand,' she said and led the way inside.

Hoskins and Cannon exchanged glances as Alexander Higham followed his diminutive wife and they brought up the rear of the party. Once in the room Higham turned to his wife as if to question her but she lifted her hands and gently indicated he should lower his level of anxiety. 'Everything, and everyone, is fine. There was really no need for us to trouble the doctor.'

Perhaps a blood pressure check for her husband might be a good idea, Cannon thought as Higham interjected, 'We were taking our daughter, Catherine, to her special school. She was in the car!'

'Yes, and she's fine,' his wife was saying as they heard the sound of another car arriving. 'Probably the doctor,' she said. 'I'll let him in and go up with him. I'll ask the housekeeper to bring in coffee for you all.'

An organizer, Cannon thought. The power, perhaps, behind their successful business?

Once they were alone, Higham first slumped into a chair, head in hands, then rose with all the suddenness of a released spring, strode to the window, then back. 'The car in front of me was a black limousine; it could have been mistaken for mine.'

'Ah,' Cannon breathed. Now he understood. Higham was adding this to the list of personal victimizations against his family.

'I was first to the car. If it hadn't been for the air-bags...' He shook his head. 'I must be some kind of Jonah, a jinx. One man murdered on my estate, now two men, father and son, injured in a car similar to mine!'

'No need to talk like that,' Hoskins said gruffly but Higham hardly seemed to have heard.

'For God's sake, will you help me?' he pleaded.

'Let's establish a few facts,' Cannon said.

'Before my wife comes back then,' Higham agreed. 'I don't want her involved in more than she need be.'

'First, the time and route you took this morning, is that usual?'

'When I'm in Lincolnshire, yes, every weekday. I have an office in Boston. Normally I'm on my own, but today my wife needed to come with me to sign business papers, so we went together to drop my daughter off at her school first. We never got there.'

'Tell me exactly what happened.'

'I'm sure we were saved because just as I reached the first crossroads, the other car came from my right and he had priority. I was close behind him until we reached the coastal road then I dropped back a bit as it twists and turns.'

'How fast were you travelling?'

'Forty-five to fifty, I suppose.'

'And how far behind were you when the accident happened?'

'I saw him turn a corner ahead of me and he must have been some thirty to forty metres in front, but I heard the crash. I braked immediately, went very slowly around the bend and saw—' he paused, looked down, shook his head '—he'd gone up and over the grass verge and hit the great bole of the only decent-sized tree in the area. If it hadn't been for the airbags…' He stopped and looked so devastated Hoskins instinctively got up and put a hand on his shoulder.

'Saved them then,' Hoskins said.

Higham drew in a great staggered breath and, looking up at the old man, said, 'There was never going to be any chance of getting either of them out without cutting and lifting gear. I hope they'll be…but they'll be…' He took a deep breath. 'It seemed like a lifetime before the services got there.'

'Aye, it would.' Hoskins gave the entrepreneur a couple of understanding pats on the back and sat back down again, shaking his head.

'I told my wife to stay in the car with our daughter, while I kept talking to them, trying to keep them conscious. The older man, the driver, was the worst, with the steering wheel and everything. He said a bird flew at his windscreen, a great black bird. I kept suggesting different birds to try to keep him awake, I thought that was what I should do. Whatever I suggested he kept mumbling bigger, bigger, the son muttered yes, and then passed out, but thank God the paramedics were there by then.'

'I once had a black plastic sack fly in front of me, fetched me off my bike,' Hoskins added.

'You should tell the police all your suspicions again and show them these.' Cannon held up the bag containing the doll and photographs.

He shook his head. 'They already think I've got a persecution complex. I can't, that's why I was going to ask Hoskins here to act as a temporary keeper, work with Ford to keep an eye open in the woods and grounds, and I guess I was going to ask you to believe me and give me your advice. But now...'

Nothing convinced Cannon he needed to *do something* more than another's distress. 'Give me permission to show these to DI Betterson, and we'll take it from there,' he said.

There was the sound of voices in the hall and before they were interrupted there was time only for Higham to nod at Cannon and for Hoskins to say, 'Aye, I'm on.'

They were committed and the possible consequences did not quite hit either of them until they were driving away from The Grange.

'What will your Liz say?' Hoskins asked with a chuckle.

'Hmm,' Cannon mused.

'You'd best buy her some flowers.'

'Then she'll definitely suspect the worst,' Cannon replied, 'but on the other hand, I tell you what we will do on the way back—call in at the prof's shop. He was telling Liz about some artist's materials and equipment he had bought.'

'Righto,' Hoskins agreed, then asked, 'Do you reckon I'll get paid for helping Ford?'

'Cash in hand, I would have thought,' Cannon replied. At least there was one who was quite cheered by the morning's outcome.

Bliss Antiques was open but the proprietor was out. Mrs Moyle, an energetic frizzy blonde, widowed in her fifties, who lived next door, was in charge. She told them Michael Bliss was away at a house sale near Norwich then, watching Hoskins who had also come in and was looking at some antique splay-barrelled fowling piece, she said, 'Surely you're not looking for more guns, Alan?'

'Must have been a useful weapon for aiming at a flock of geese,' he said and Mrs Moyle shuddered.

'Ah, your dad always said you were squeamish, Mavis Moyle,' Hoskins told her, 'but the prof has some interesting things, valuable, I'd think, some of 'em.'

'I think he buys too good for a shop like this, he wants more bric-a-brac, but who am I to tell him, he seems to do very well.'

Cannon had gone off to a far corner of the shop where behind several displays of walking sticks in bright pottery glazed umbrella stands he had spotted a dark brown wooden easel. He lifted it up and over into the body of the shop, approved the smooth finish of the wood: certainly it had age, but it was also functional, and compared to the heavy great angular version he had occasionally carried for Liz, this was a pleasure to handle.

'How much is this?' he asked, then seeing the £45 price tag, asked how much she could discount it.

'You'd have to see Mr Bliss about that,' she said.

'I would quite like to take it with me,' Cannon said, ignoring Hoskins' smirk.

Mavis pulled a mobile phone from her dress pocket and tapped in the first contact. From the other end they could all hear the sound of an auctioneer taking bids, then clearly the prof asked who the customer was.

'Mr Cannon, landlord of The Trap,' she said, then gave a surprised, 'Oh! Twenty pounds.' She ended the call and repeated the price. 'Twenty pounds, you must be a real friend.'

Cannon was not sure he could say that, but he gratefully paid the money and left with the easel.

'Old Bliss has a soft spot for your Liz,' Hoskins said. 'I've seen him looking at her, and anyway,' he added, as the easel was stowed in the jeep, 'better than a bunch of flowers.'

Liz was not deceived. Her look was enough to have Cannon protesting that he felt Higham might need a bit of moral support if nothing else, and he was only handing over the evidence to DI Betterson.

SEVEN

LIZ COULD NOT in the end help but love the beautiful dark barley sugar twisted wood of the old easel. It was a joy to handle and so light after the modern heavy white wood model. Not that she'd had much time for leisure activities in the past week, she thought, and having unlocked the front doors she prepared to take charge of the bar once more, while John went on round two of the inter-pub quiz.

She spread the local newspaper on the counter and scanned the main story on the front page.

There was, our reporter understands, a police presence at The Trap public house, Reed St Clements, when the disturbance occurred. Maurice Spier was said to have taunted the son of the murdered man. Maurice Spier has since disappeared.

Detective Inspector Derek Betterson said the police are following all possible lines of enquiry, but they would like Mr Spier to come forward so he might be eliminated from their enquiries. The police will be issuing a further statement shortly.

Interviewed by this newspaper, Mrs Spier said it was most unlike her husband to be away from home.

Cannon, looking over her shoulder, gave a snort. 'Be a few belly-laughs about that from what I'm hearing.

They say he's always going off on some jaunt or other, race meetings, point-to-points, staying over with boozing or gambling mates. Rarely *at* home from what they say.'

'Probably told his wife what she had to say before he cleared off,' Liz guessed. 'Has he got a job?'

He shrugged. 'No idea, but his wife works, early and late shifts at a Boston supermarket.'

'Where've you learnt all this from?' she questioned.

'Unexpectedly from Mavis Moyle, the widow who helps the prof at his shop. She's known Peggy Spier for years, meets her once a month for tea in Boston. I called at the shop again to say I'd pick the prof up to go to The Stump tonight. I'm picking up Hoskins and Paul as well, we'll all go in one car. Then at least I'll know the team's there, even if no one else is.'

'You don't think many of our supporters will go?' she asked.

'Well, not sure I would if I didn't have to, not going to be a cheerful occasion as it is. The group as a whole wanted to cancel the match and we would have done but Mrs Riley got to know and sent a message to say she knew that would have been the last thing Niall would have wanted. Apparently he loved quizzes.'

Liz nodded. 'He did, you know, I've watched him. He listened carefully to all the questions, and by the look on his face knew a good many of the answers,' she said, 'but I suppose he wouldn't volunteer for the team because of Timmy. What a...' She did not find the right word.

Cannon kissed the top of her head and asked, 'Will you be all right here tonight?'

'Alamat will be here,' she said. 'I'll be fine.'

It was still reassuring to Cannon that before he left to pick up his team Sergeant Jim Maddern, in civvies, walked in.

'I'm here for the night,' he told them.

'Officially?' Liz asked.

'Yep,' he said, 'and on overtime.'

'Crikey.' Cannon pulled an impressed face.

'Not only that,' Maddern said, 'DI Betterson will be at The Stump's Shadow keeping his eye on proceedings there *and* Chief Inspector Helen Jefferson is back on duty.'

'Oh, thank goodness!' Liz exclaimed. 'Paul will feel better now.'

'Hope he's got his babysitting sorted out for tonight then,' Cannon said practically.

'Well, you'll find that out,' Liz said shortly. 'It must be time you left to pick everyone up.'

'Want rid of me now you've got police protection?' he said. 'Right, see you later.' He blew her another kiss, picked up his jeep keys from behind the bar and left.

'Thought I was going to have a domestic to sort out for a minute there,' Maddern said and seated himself in the pew seat Alan Hoskins usually used. 'Can see why the old rogue sits here,' he said. 'You can see all, probably hear a lot and say nowt. If it suits you.'

'John doesn't think there'll be many in here or at The Stump,' Liz said.

Maddern shook his head. 'You can never tell. If somebody rallies the troops there could be a lot to supporters turn out for our team, give 'em a bit of heart. Have a feeling it might be slack here though, and—' he stretched out his legs '—that suits me fine. I'll have a pint of coke, please,' he said. 'At least it looks about the right colour.'

He was right about the customers, and in the end Maddern and Alamat took on the only other two customers in a friendly game of darts. The bar mobile burbled from underneath the counter and Maddern paused in the game to listen as Liz answered it. 'John,' she mouthed to him.

'Crowded out here,' Cannon said. 'I should think every one of our regulars has turned up to support us and they've made a real good collection for Mrs Riley. I'll be home as soon as I can. Is everything all right there?'

She told him everything was fine, told Maddern how busy the pub was at Boston and was sitting down to relax when the doors burst open and Dick Ford, Higham's gamekeeper, stumbled in, holding yet another plastic carrier. He took in the empty bar, the police sergeant and made for the counter as if he needed it to lean on.

'Mr Cannon?' he enquired.

'In Boston with the quiz team.' It was Maddern who answered, putting down his darts and coming to the bar, adding, 'You'd best sit down by the look of you.'

Ford glanced at the other two customers.

'Do you want to go through to the kitchen?' Liz asked.

He nodded. Liz signalled to Alamat, who immediately came to the business side of the bar, then led the way into the back quarters.

Ford slumped down next to the table, then with a gasp of revulsion threw the supermarket carrier on to the table.

'What's this?' Maddern asked.

'The latest thing left on my gibbet. I very nearly caught who did it. The dog heard something and I went out. If your lot don't take things seriously soon I reckon my employer will be hanging there next—that's if he's not already dead somewhere.'

'What are you talking about, man?' Maddern said, and pulling the bag towards him lifted one side carefully and looked inside. He pursed his lips tight, then realizing Liz was looking over his shoulder, let the bag close. 'What I see is a stained deerstalker hat.'

'What you see,' Ford said forcibly, 'is *Mr Higham's* blood-soaked shooting hat.'

'And where *is* Mr Higham?' Maddern asked calmly, 'I presume you've been up to the house.'

'Yes, everyone's there but him. He'd gone to a meeting with the headmaster at the daughter's school, they say.'

'They *say*?' Maddern probed gently.

'Well, the last time they were on their way to the school they narrowly missed being killed in their car,' Ford said. 'It'll be something to do with his daughter's safety.'

'It should be easy enough to check he's there,' Maddern said and with almost slow deliberation took a mobile phone from his pocket as he asked, 'So you didn't show anyone at the house what you had found?'

'No, I came to see Mr Cannon. Mr Higham likes him, trusts him, he says.'

Maddern glanced at Liz, who shrugged noncommittally.

'Leave this with me,' Maddern said, indicating the bag, 'I'll see it goes to the correct people.'

'OK.' Ford said resignedly, 'as long as something's done.'

'We'll check up on Mr Higham first,' he said, and made for the back door, phone in hand.

'What'll he do?' Ford asked.

'Someone will be sent to make sure your employer is where you said and the hat will go to forensics. It could reveal important information.'

'I suppose,' Ford said, 'thinking about it someone could have soaked it in animal blood. I mean, like the doll, a fake-up.'

'A frightener,' Liz said.

'Yes, at least you and your partner understand,' Ford said. 'Think I might have a drink now. I mean, I can't do anything else, can I, not tonight, anyway?'

Liz reassured him and took him back to the bar, where they were soon rejoined by Maddern.

'Mr Higham has just arrived back home,' he told them.

'Home?' Ford questioned.

Liz realized the two public houses were not the only places being observed.

Maddern just nodded and repeated, 'He's safely home, and—' he looked towards Liz '—John and his passengers will also be seen safely home.'

Reassured they had locked up securely, Maddern left Liz and Alamat to await Cannon. Liz sent Alamat to bed when they heard the agricultural note of Cannon's jeep approaching.

'Hi,' he greeted her. 'Just seen Alamat.'

'Police escort home?' she queried.

'A discreet presence.' He kissed her cheek, his face cold from the October night. 'And the quiz wasn't nearly as grim as it might have been. The Stump's Shadow won but our customers were brilliant, turned out in force to support us, made me feel quite emotional.' He was expansive, moving around the kitchen, pulling off anorak and scarf. 'Terry Ladkin announced at the beginning that Mrs Riley had wished the quiz to go on, and a collection was made—more than three hundred pounds—and everyone signed a condolence card Ladkin had bought.' He produced the card and an envelope of money from his pocket. 'I have the job of letting Mrs Riley have it.'

'That was heart-warming,' Liz said, then sighed heavily. 'We had three customers apart from Jim Maddern.'

'Betterson was there,' Cannon continued, 'but he was mingling with the crowd. All I got was a curt nod and a meaningful look as I left.'

'Oh, I guess he'll be coming here to see us when he's heard from Jim Maddern.'

'Why?' Cannon was immediately on her case.

'As I said, we had three customers,' she began. 'One was Dick Ford.'

Cannon's casual air left him immediately, and he became grimly thoughtful as he heard what had happened. 'There's one thing I don't like,' he said, remembering other aspects of the evening. 'There could just be a link between Spier's disappearance, Niall Riley and Higham.'

'What do you mean?' Liz asked. 'What kind of link?'

'I was talking to one or two of the locals at The Stump; a couple of them had known Maurice Spier since he was a boy. They were scoffing at the newspaper report. They confirmed he was rarely *at* home and another said he was with his mother more than his wife.'

'His mother!' Liz exclaimed.

'Yes, they say the money his wife earns goes straight into her bank to pay bills by direct debit, but his mother draws her pension in cash, so when Maurice gets short...' He left the rest unsaid.

'Charming man all round,' Liz said, 'but what's that got to do with Niall Riley and Higham?'

'This second chap, Russell, has a bit of a yard, sells ship's spares. He said he often gives Spier a lift when he's going to work, drops him off along the road to Boston, then Spier walks through the edge of the Higham woods as a short cut to his mother's. If Spier hasn't thumbed a lift back during the day he waits at the same spot for Russell at the end of the day.'

'So the link is?' Liz asked.

'Riley's killed on one edge of Higham's land, and the last time anyone seems to have seen Spier is when Russell dropped him off at another side of the Higham estate.'

'Mrs Spier said her husband did not go home on Monday,' Liz reminded him. 'So where did he spend that night?'

'When I asked the same question, Russell shrugged, said Spier often played poker all night when he'd got money, or the others would accept his IOUs.'

There was silence as each thought over the facts. 'We know Higham is safely home,' Liz said, 'and you've delivered our team to their homes.'

'Forensics will have the deerstalker by now. You say Ford was convinced it belonged to his employer,' Cannon said, adding, 'but we can say it's definitely not Higham blood.'

'So whose blood is it?' Liz asked.

'Could be an animal's,' Cannon said, 'but certainly meant as another frightener.'

'And the warnings, threats, frighteners—whatever you care to call them—are getting more pointed, more directed at Higham personally,' Liz reflected. 'I'm not surprised he's getting neurotic about it all.'

EIGHT

THE NEXT MORNING Cannon was just leaving to take the collection and card to Niall's widow when the sound of someone dismounting from a bicycle drew him to the front of the pub car park.

'Morning, Alan,' he called. 'Everything all right?'

Hoskins leaned his bike against one of the pub flower tubs and shrugged. 'Not sure,' he said, 'and not sure what I should do, so came to see you. Dick Ford said to go and see him this morning at eleven but his vehicle's gone and his dog and...'

'He'll be out and about on the estate,' Cannon said and couldn't see why Hoskins was so concerned. He consulted his watch: it was nearly twelve. Ford, like Hoskins, lived on his own—Ford a bachelor, Hoskins a long-term widower—so mealtimes were probably very flexible for both. Cannon wanted to arrive at Mrs Riley's *before* he might interfere with their midday meal, yet with just a decent amount of time to fulfil his commitment without haste.

Hoskins scowled and kicked at a loose stone.

'Something else bothering you?' Cannon asked.

'The dog's lead,' he said, 'it's on the floor outside the shed where it sleeps—with the collar still attached—sort of stretched out full length.'

The image from the sand dunes was vivid in Cannon's mind; an icy chill ran over his back.

'Isn't that how Riley's dog's collar…?' Hoskins went on.

'Yes,' Cannon said. 'Come on, we'll go back now. Push your bike round the side.'

The gamekeeper's cottage was on a grass-rutted track well into the woods. It must have been built at the same time as the big Georgian house, but while that was grand, this was quaint. It had small, triangular, leaded-light windows, was thatched with Norfolk reeds and, Cannon thought, if it was as quaint inside it must be hell to live in. Even from the outside it had the air of a place occupied by a man on his own. The wood-stack was ordered and neat but from a clothes-line strung from two trees hung an assortment of washing—large garments thrown over it and smaller pegged on to it—and all anyhow.

Cannon tried the door, tried to peer through the windows, but it was obviously a while since they had been cleaned. Hoskins prowled around the outplaces. They finished up together looking down at the collar and lead. Just as Hoskins had said, it was stretched out to its fullest extent, the collar still fastened as if, like Patch, the dog had slipped it and fled. The difference: there was no battered corpse holding the lead.

'That's more laid out than dropped,' Hoskins stated.

Cannon growled agreement.

'Ford asks me to come and see him at a set time.' Hoskins shook his head. 'It's not like him, and I don't like that!' He pushed a foot towards the lead. 'Then there's the doll and—'

'Yes,' Cannon agreed, 'and quite a few other things.' He looked back at the deserted cottage and another cold sensation ran over his skin. All this was confirming his—and Betterson's—feelings. This had the hallmarks

of what in his official days he would have called a far
from straightforward case, and which now he labelled
weird, bloody weird.

'Come on,' he said, 'we'll have a look round for Ford.
Do you know the track Spier would have taken through
the estate as a shortcut to his mother's?' he asked.

'Thought we were looking for Ford,' Hoskins said.

'Combine the two,' Cannon answered, leading the
way back to his jeep. Ever since he had heard of Spier's
shortcut he had itched to walk it; now he had an excuse.
Ford, after all, could be anywhere.

Hoskins directed him to the north side of The Wash.
'It's along 'ere,' he said, as soon as Boston appeared
on the signposts. 'Keep right. This side of the estate
stretches as far as this road, then you can walk through
to Sutdyke. Spier's mother still lives on her own in the
same cottage where he was born. Whatever her son
does, or wants, Mavis Moyes says she's always pleased
to see the lad. He's the only relation she has in the
world.'

Cannon was always aware how lonely Hoskins' life
could also be. The Trap was a big part of his life, and
for this reason Cannon had long ago stopped resenting
the fact that not only was Hoskins his first customer
of an evening but that he was invariably the last, often
finally leaving with a small parcel of something from
the kitchen Liz had found for his supper.

'Ah!' Hoskins exclaimed in annoyance as they
rounded a bend. 'The police are 'ere.'

Cannon drove slowly past the police tape blowing
from one side of a hedge bordering a footpath. 'Looks
to me as if that bit of tape got overlooked,' Cannon said.
'Think they've been and gone.'

'Drive on a bit in case,' Hoskins said. 'There's another way in.'

A hundred yards further on he indicated where Cannon should park. 'You'll get in behind that group of trees; it's like advertising "Here's John Cannon" when you're around in this thing.'

'You speak of the vehicle I love,' Cannon told him.

'Aye, well, we all 'ave our weaknesses,' Hoskins said as he climbed out. 'Come on.' It was all he said as he led the way; the one place the old poacher did not chat was in the woods. Long practice had given him speed and stealth and Cannon had difficulty keeping up as he followed along a virtual tunnel of low-hanging branches. He became so dazzled by the low sun glinting in and out through the canopy of autumn leaves he almost walked into the back of Hoskins when he did stop.

They had reached the main track, and it was clear to both of them that the police had made a wide and thorough search here, for the undergrowth either side of the track showed evidence of disturbance. Cannon was pretty sure they weren't going to find any nasty surprises as they set off along this pathway. He had too much respect for Betterson and his men to think anything, or anybody, might have been overlooked.

He was wondering how long it might take to walk Spier's shortcut, and whether he should phone Liz, then was relieved to see that the trees were thinning and soon he could see a road beyond.

'Mrs Spier lives at the first cottage we come to,' Hoskins said as he climbed the stile out of the wood, and indicated the row of small white terraced cottages on the edge of Sutdyke village. 'Are you going to knock at her door?' he asked.

'The police will have interviewed her,' Cannon said, 'and if they found no trace of her son and we've not found Ford…'

'Well, I'm not coming for nothing,' Hoskins said. 'There's one of the best fish and chip shops around these parts at the other end of the cottages. Greeks, they are, know how to cook. Reckon I could eat my lunch as we walk back.'

'OK,' Cannon agreed, 'you walk on.'

'Want some?' Hoskins asked.

Cannon opened his mouth to refuse and then caught the smell of the shop. 'Some chips then,' he said, 'please.'

Hoskins went ahead but got no further than the small garden to the side of the first cottage. He turned and beckoned urgently to Cannon, who frowned then hurried to where Hoskins was pointing over the gate into the garden. A golden retriever stood tied to a line-post. It was in some distress as it had obviously gone round and round the post trying to get away and the rope that tied it now had no slack. It stood trembling, back arched, tail between its legs.

'That's Ford's dog,' Hoskins said.

'You sure?' Cannon questioned, but was already opening the gate to go to the dog's rescue. 'All right, old lad, keep still,' he said.

Before he got to the post, the back door opened and an elderly woman came out. She was slightly stooped but Cannon would not have described her as likely to be put upon by her son or anyone else. Her iron-grey hair had that uncompromising basin-cut look, and her manner he would have described as aggressive. 'Is it your dog?' she demanded.

'No, but we think we know who it does belong to,' he said.

'What's it doing tied up 'ere?' Hoskins asked.

'That's what I want to know,' she snapped. 'Heard the thing barking early on, didn't realize it was in my garden.'

'Have you told anyone?' Cannon asked. 'Asked your neighbours?'

'Them!' she said. 'No.' Her eyes slid away from Cannon's and she shook her head, adding, 'Thought I'd wait a bit until it calmed down then let it go.'

'You would know Dick Ford, Higham's gamekeeper,' he prompted.

Her eyes came sharply back to him, then she looked at the dog again. 'Is it 'is?'

'Bounder?' Hoskins enquired of the retriever, as he opened his pocket knife and began to slice through the rope. It looked up at him and whined. 'It's Ford's,' he said. 'We'll take it back to him.'

'So you've not seen Dick Ford?' Cannon asked.

She shook her head. 'No one, I've seen no one,' she insisted.

'Is there any news of your son?' he asked.

'What d'you know about my son?' she demanded.

'That he's missing,' Cannon said mildly.

'He'll turn up,' she said, tossing her head as if dismissing both her son and Cannon, then promptly went back inside, slamming the door.

'That's told you,' Hoskins muttered.

'Not exactly the anxious mother, is she?' Cannon commented as they closed the garden gate. 'She probably bullied Maurice, now he bullies others.' He took the rope. 'Go and get your dinner, but I won't have chips; be more than we can manage, dog *and* packages of fish and chips.'

Cannon walked slowly back towards the stile into the woods. The dog was still trembling. 'You're all right now, old chap,' Cannon reassured him, but Bounder's tail remained well down. He explained they had to wait for Hoskins, who lived on his own, and was glad of the chance to buy fish and chips for his main meal of the day. The dog sat down but stared in the direction of the woods, leaving no doubt which way it wanted to go.

Hoskins came back already eating from his polystyrene box of goodies. He offered it to Cannon, who took a chip and said, 'The dog seems keen to go on.'

'Ford never goes anywhere without his dog. It's either at his heels or in his vehicle waiting for him,' Hoskins said.

'So why was he tied up in Mrs Spier's garden? Who would do that?' Cannon wondered.

'The same sod who'd stretch out the dog's collar and lead like it was an exhibit,' Hoskins said vehemently, adding, 'somebody sick in the 'ead.'

'We'll take the dog home first,' Cannon said, 'then... well, I suppose continue looking for Ford if he's not there.'

'Ring his boss on your mobile,' Hoskins suggested.

'Could do,' Cannon supposed.

When they reached the cottage again, both gave exclamations of satisfaction as they saw Ford's Land Rover was back in its shed. 'Thank goodness,' Cannon said.

'Come on, Bounder,' Hoskins said, slipping off the rope and letting the dog go. 'Where's your master?' It ran straight to the cottage, snuffling urgently at the bottom of the door, whining, then barking.

Both men approached the door expecting Ford to open it any second as the dog's barking became louder, more insistent. It began to attack the bottom of the door with its claws, glancing back at them from time to time as if saying, 'Come on, come on, what are you waiting for? There's no time to lose.'

Cannon reached over the dog and tried the door. 'Still locked,' he said, 'but if Ford's anywhere around he must have heard us by now.'

'Someone's been around,' Hoskins said, nodding towards the side of the cottage and the gamekeeper's gibbet line. 'There's something on that that wasn't there when we called before.'

Cannon didn't wait to inspect the new exhibit and as the dog looked expectantly up at him he shoulder-charged the door. The old mortise lock didn't give but the wood of the frame gave a loud crack, split, fell inwards, and he and the dog were inside—Cannon on hands and knees on the doormat and the dog crouched next to him.

The moment was like a hiatus, a vacuum, then facts went through his mind like photos finger-flicked across a screen: Ford's Land Rover back in its shed; a locked door; a dog tied up at the home of a missing man, and that dog now frantic to get inside the cottage. Cannon felt speculation and knowledge fuse. At the same moment the dog startled him by suddenly yelping as if it had been kicked, then leaping over the splintered wood and disappearing into the room beyond the kitchen. Cannon followed, into a kind of small, shabby parlour.

Dick Ford was sitting in an armchair, eyes open, his blood making a great central flower on his cream check shirt. For a second Cannon thought of the doll made to look as if shot through the heart—but this was not a bullet wound. The dog went to its master, whined pitifully, then lay at Ford's feet, not at all at ease as Cannon moved nearer to put his fingers carefully to Ford's wrist, though he knew death when he saw it. This man had been dead some hours, probably before Hoskins had called to see him at eleven o'clock.

His heart must have stopped pumping almost immediately, Cannon thought, and from the blood splatter there was little doubt that Ford had been murdered where he now sat. A noise behind him made him turn to see Hoskins standing some feet away looking first to the gamekeeper, then to a line cut deep right across the shabby old brown fitted carpet. Cannon had not noticed it as he and the dog had come into the parlour. He went back now, seeing the sweep of the cut and where the soiled surface had parted the lighter fawn underneath. He stepped carefully over it, taking Hoskins' arm as he swayed slightly and asked, 'He's...'

'Yes, before you called the first time I would say. Nothing we can do.' He turned the old man back towards the kitchen.

Hoskins looked back over his shoulder. 'Bane of my life,' he said, 'but he didn't deserve that, no one does, and that line, what's that about?'

Crossing the line, going too far, were the phrases that came to Cannon's mind. Had Ford gone too far, found out something he should not? But why had his dog been taken and tied up at the home of a missing man? Had Spier taken it there? A lot of questions to be answered. 'I'll ring the police,' Cannon said.

'What's going to be the end of all this, John?' Hoskins asked.

The use of Cannon's Christian name always meant
Hoskins was very deeply affected. He phoned the police, began to report all he knew to the station sergeant,
who was superseded by an inspector who said help was
already on its way and to remain where they were. As
Cannon explained in his next call to Liz, there was little
option but to do just that.

'If we could coax the dog out of there it would be
easier for the police,' Cannon suggested.

'If there's another collar and lead anywhere we *might*
have a chance of pulling it out,' Hoskins said. 'It ain't
going to leave 'im willing.'

The sound of police sirens gave them no time to do
either. 'They've diverted a patrol car,' Cannon guessed.

The patrol officers had done no more than look into
the cottage and get a brief account when scene of crime
officers arrived to secure the site. They asked Cannon
and Hoskins if they'd mind sitting in the patrol car while
they waited. 'DI Betterson is on his way.'

Taken out of the immediate zone, Hoskins suddenly
gestured towards the side of the cottage. 'Forgot about
the new exhibit on the gibbet line,' he said.

'It's your side,' Cannon said, 'can you see what it is?'

Hoskins opened the car door a fraction, leaned out
and stared. 'It's…' he began.

'Yes?' Cannon asked.

'Another stuffed toy,' he said, 'a fat clown thing,
dressed like a joker, bright colours, looks new.'

NINE

DI BETTERSON THREW the jester doll down on The Trap's counter.

Cannon looked at him and raised his eyebrows. 'So not the one from Ford's cottage,' he said.

'Several supermarkets and garages around Boston have the things on offer. One of the patrol officers had this one in the back of his car to take home for his son.'

'So that narrows the field,' Cannon risked gently.

'Yep,' Betterson agreed with weary good nature, 'our murderer shops locally. Could we…' He nodded his head towards the stairs up to the private quarters.

'Sure, you go up, I'll just tell Liz, she's in the kitchen.'

'Don't get more involved, John,' she pleaded.

'I was the first to find Ford's body,' he reminded her.

She scowled at him. 'You make your statement like a good citizen, then.' She waved a dismissive hand. 'And away.'

'When Alamat arrives let him take over in the bar and come up.' He headed towards the stairs. 'Always did like to have you in on crime conferences in our Met days.'

Her scowl deepened.

'By my side,' he added, 'as always.'

'Right,' she said huskily.

Upstairs he indicated the kettle and cups. 'Coffee or tea?' he enquired.

'Coffee, please,' Betterson said. 'I wondered if you'd mind just telling me what happened today, and I'll get a formal statement taken later.'

He listened intently as Cannon began from the time Hoskins arrived on his bike near lunchtime, and asked no questions until he came to where they had walked the track to Sutdyke.

'So Ford's dog was tied up outside Mrs Spier's cottage, and you talked to her?' he asked. 'What was your impression of the woman?'

'Felt a slight sympathy for Maurice after meeting her,' Cannon said. 'She was at once aggressive and defensive, I thought.'

'She's apparently helped her son out of a few scrapes and a good many debts,' Betterson said.

'I'd believe that,' Cannon said. 'She wasn't giving much away about him. She could be hiding him,' he suggested.

'We've got that in hand, but no sign so far,' Betterson said, 'but now let's get to Ford. How, when and where you found him, and what were your impressions, your feelings about how it might have happened?'

'Been giving it some thought.' Cannon gave an ironic laugh and looked sympathetically at this still-serving police officer. 'Well, as you know these things are not easily put out of your mind.' He drew in a deep breath, held it for a moment, then began his story, particularly remembering the dog's yelp, its grief. 'It seems to me,' he said, 'that Ford was stabbed where he sat. He could have known his killer and been at ease in the chair until the blow was struck—and whatever was used to strike that blow also slashed the carpet, something long and sharp. It suggested a kind of sword or rapier, not things that people carry around.' He lookcd up at Betterson.

'The slash in the carpet was done by the same weapon,' Betterson confirmed, 'and after the murder. Ford's blood was in the carpet fibres.'

'Forensics must be having quite a field day,' Cannon said.

'Plenty of exhibits and sites for them to go at but whoever our joker is, is clever, careful,' Betterson said. He looked directly and searchingly at Cannon. 'But there's one bit forensics have discovered I'd like your opinion on.' He paused as both heard Liz coming up the stairs.

Finding both men looking directly at her as she entered the lounge, she asked, 'Wrong moment?', and turned to leave.

'No, no, not for you, Liz,' Betterson said. 'Close the door, sit down.'

'That makes it sound official,' she said but did as he asked.

'This information is still under wraps as far as anyone else, particularly the press, is concerned,' Betterson said. 'The deerstalker hat which, as Ford told you, *does* belong to Higham…' He paused long enough for them to know the revelation would be startling. 'But the blood on it is that of Niall Riley.'

'Niall Riley,' Cannon repeated. 'So when our murderer attacked Niall Riley he already had it with him!'

'I've seen Alexander Higham,' Betterson said, 'and he says it could have been missing for some time. It was kept in a small open hunting lodge on the estate, where they serve breakfasts or luncheons when they have a big shoot.'

'But…' Liz began as Betterson's mobile burbled.

'Higham will have apoplexy if he doesn't calm down,' he added as he reached into his pocket. He took the call, listened, snapped, 'Hold everything until I get there.' He rose. 'Thanks for the coffee and this informal chat.'

'Spier?' Cannon asked.

Betterson pursed his lips and nodded, but whether it was confirmation or goodbye Cannon was not certain.

Cannon saw him out, quickly checked Alamat was OK, found the normal evening demand for bar meals had not begun, and ran back upstairs. He needed to come to terms with this new info from Betterson, find some strands to grasp and follow.

Liz sat waiting for him. On the table she had placed a large piece of the white card they used for notices in the pub and three biros: red, blue, green. 'I know you will neither hear what customers are saying to you in the bar, nor sleep later, until you've gone down every back alley of this whole affair,' she said, indicating the card and biros. 'But do you want to go this far?'

'The old bubble logic,' Cannon said with a brief laugh, but picked up the red biro used for case certainties, the green being for suppositions and blue for impending action. 'Seems a bit presumptive,' he said.

'DI Betterson came to hear your presumptions,' Liz said.

At the top left-hand corner of the card he drew a red circle and in it wrote 'Higham's troubles' then in the middle of the paper two more circles and in the first wrote 'Niall Riley murdered day after 1st quiz night' and in the second 'Dick Ford murdered day after 2nd quiz night'.

Liz watched without commenting as he added a smaller circle under each of these two. Under Riley's bubble he added 'Spier goes missing' and under Ford's 'Ford comes to Trap with deerstalker soaked in Riley's blood'. Under that he wrote 'Ford's dog tied up at Spier's mother's cottage'. He turned to see a stern critical look on Liz's face. 'You are thinking?' he asked.

'You specify the two quiz nights, but you do not specify that Higham's troubles started way before either of those events,' she said.

'Right.' He turned back and added 'both before and after quiz started' under 'Higham's troubles'.

'Long before,' Liz specified.

He shrugged and added the word. 'There's a link we're missing,' he stated. 'All these events are tied together by…what?'

'It's usually something we know but haven't *seen*, haven't realized the significance of,' Liz said.

'I suppose I ought to put Hoskins in. It was his instincts that led us to finding the camera in the tree, which no one seemed to know anything about, *and* which disappeared before anyone else could see it. Then he made the connection between the dog lead in Riley's hand and the lead laid out outside Ford's garage.' His hand hovered as if about to draw another red circle.

'No, don't,' Liz said, 'it feels like you'd be…'

'What?' he questioned.

'Putting him in the frame,' she said, then added quietly, 'to be the next victim.'

'Heaven forbid,' he said.

'But the facts are,' she asserted, 'he's been around on the Higham estate more than Riley ever was, and probably nearly as much as Ford was. He has to be vulnerable.'

'Not a word I would normally associate with Alan Hoskins,' Cannon said.

'Look,' Liz urged, 'say Ford and Riley were both killed because they accidentally saw something or someone they shouldn't, then Hoskins must be putting himself at terrible risk. He's in those woods all the time,' she said.

'He was asked by Higham to help Ford,' Cannon stated.

They were silent for a moment, then Liz said, 'I also think we should withdraw our team from the quiz.'

Cannon looked at the grim facts he had written down: two murders, one after each quiz night. 'I didn't really want to carry on with the second but Mrs Riley *wished* us to,' he reminded her, then tutted. 'And I still haven't taken the money and card to her.'

'No, and we still haven't begun to understand what's really happening.' She indicated what he had written down so far. 'And won't do until we understand *why* Alexander Higham is being targeted. How much longer is he to be tormented before the coup de grâce is administered? Shouldn't we talk around that?'

Cannon did not voice his thought that for someone who had told him to make his statement and be away, she had changed her tune.

'All this mischief,' she went on, 'his garden dug up in Kent, his car vandalized in London, his dogs shut up or tied up at The Grange, a man near retiring age with a dependent wife and disabled son murdered on the edge of his land, now his gamekeeper. There must be clues in all this we are missing.' She looked fiercely at John, repeating 'must be'.

'One thing keeps coming back to my mind, over and over,' Cannon said, 'though it doesn't supply any answers.'

'What is it?' she asked.

'It's that deep cut across Ford's carpet, a kind of…' He stood up and swung his arm with force at full stretch, as if making a sweeping cut. 'I can't think of anyone being able to make such a straight deep cut with anything other than a—' Cannon swung his arm again '—a sword, a rapier.'

'A carpet fitter's knife would do it easily enough,' Liz suggested, 'but…'

'The weapon was also capable of dealing a single fatal blow to the heart.' Cannon paused then pointed at her, a direct gesture, amounting to an appeal; like he had often made in their Met conference days. 'And remember the graffiti, the drawing on the car, there was something about that…'

Liz was silent thinking about this. 'I know what you mean,' she agreed. 'Sure swift strokes, such as if I was working on a big canvas, I might have stepped back and used an extra long brush for.' She demonstrated what she meant.

'Yes,' he said, 'a possible connection, but where does that get us? It's not easy to conceal a sword, or even a long knife anywhere, let alone cart it around, use in London then in Lincolnshire.'

'I suppose forensics would have no trouble in proving the same implement was used to do both things,' she said.

'I guess Higham had his car resprayed long enough ago, though if they knew what they were looking for...'

'All a bit outside our area these days,' she said, then shook her head, 'and *I'm* the one who is supposed to be glad about that!'

They both started as the bell from bar to lounge rang, the signal that the pub was getting busy and the person behind the counter needed some help.

They rose as one, aware they had completely forgotten that Alamat was alone and probably trying valiantly to cope with bar and kitchen.

Their arrival was greeted by an ironic cheer from customers waiting to be served. It was with a pang of concern that Cannon noticed Hoskins was not in his usual seat, and knew if he did not turn up he would have to go and see if he was OK. However, with the majority of those waiting served, the bar door opened again and Hoskins walked in. He was late, Cannon thought, but after the events of the day perhaps it was surprising he had turned out at all.

Cannon watched him thread his way through to his usual pew seat next to the bar, and as soon as he could, made his way to him. 'The usual,' he said from force of habit, more than a need to ask, and reached for Hoskins' tankard from the shelf above his head.

'No,' Hoskins said. 'I'll have a brandy.'

Cannon looked at him in concern. 'You feeling all right? Nothing's happened, has it?'

Hoskins shrugged. 'You'd better have one on me tonight,' he said. 'You've drawn me plenty of free pints in the past.'

'Come into money?' Cannon asked.

To his surprise, Hoskins nodded.

'Had a message to go up to the big house,' he said. 'Mr Higham's in bits about Ford—the police had not been long gone.' He put his hand in his pocket and pulled out a small roll of notes. 'He's asked me to act as temporary gamekeeper,' he said, 'keep an eye on everything in the woods. Cash in hand every week.'

TEN

FROM THE MOMENT Cannon saw the roll of notes in Hoskins' hand, he felt he was probably on a losing wicket. Then when the old boy lifted the brandy glass to his lips and said, 'Poacher turned gamekeeper, what-ho!', he knew it.

Cannon had still followed him out to his bike at closing time and held on to the handlebars while he put the facts to him again forcibly.

'You think I'm going forget Dick Ford sitting in that chair,' Hoskins protested, 'then there's Niall Riley, both hard-working lads all their lives. If I can do anything to help catch whoever murdered them I will,' he declared, adding, 'and I tell you another thing, if it's one man done both, he killed 'em for very different reasons.'

'What makes you say that?' Cannon asked, taken unawares by the judgement.

'He were mad with Riley, punished and beat 'im, but just wanted rid of Ford, one blow and off,' Hoskins said, finally mounting his bike. He rode away but still had one more thing to say, calling back, 'Anyway, no one knows those woods like I do.'

WAKING THE NEXT MORNING, Hoskins' words were the first thing that came into his mind. 'I'll go and see Higham,' Cannon decided out loud. By his side, Liz stirred.

'Good morning to you too,' she said sleepily. 'So see Higham about what?'

'Taking Hoskins off his payroll.'

'He'd never forgive you,' Liz said, 'being paid to gamekeep over a patch he's poached for years!'

'I'd hate to find him…' He went no further on that, deciding instead, 'Perhaps a better option might be to walk over to see Paul and Helen. I can tell Paul we've decided to drop The Trap team from the quiz and talk to Helen about Hoskins. The police would then at least know what he's doing.'

When he arrived at the bungalow tucked behind the sand dunes, he found Paul looking as casually elegant as ever in green cords and sweater, though he was clearly in charge of his son; the washing machine was spinning its load, and there was a large sketch pad on the table. Nothing, it seemed, was being neglected.

'Ah!' He greeted Cannon with a bow. 'To adult conversation, welcome,' adding to his attentive son, 'We've acquired a helper, young man.'

John Paul was just as delighted to see the visitor and tottered towards him, arms raised. Cannon swept him up and raised him high.

'No wonder you're such a hit with him,' Paul said, then asked, 'Coffee?'

'Helen on duty?' Cannon wanted to know.

'All hours. This man Spier being missing is muddying the waters. They have around-the-clock surveillance on the mother and wife, but you'll know what that's costing in slender resources.'

'They just have to find him and rule him out,' Cannon said. 'I certainly wouldn't put him down for Dick Ford's murder: it was just too sophisticated.'

'That must have been a terrible shock for you and old Hoskins,' Paul said, taking John Paul. Then looking at him more searchingly, he asked, 'So what brings you here this early on a working day?'

'One, to tell you that I feel we should drop out of the quiz,' he said.

Paul pursed his lips and nodded. 'And the important thing?'

'You know me too well,' Cannon said and told him of his concerns about Hoskins.

'The only comfort I can offer is that I understand Higham is hiring more private security, and thinking of sending his wife and daughter off to stay with his son who lives and works in Oslo.'

'Is he going himself?' Cannon asked.

Paul shrugged. 'Can't imagine him letting them travel out alone, he's very protective of that daughter of his. Like Riley was with his son. Strange that, both having disabled children.'

Cannon frowned as a thought flickered but for the moment refused to be caught and kindled. Then as young John Paul struggled in his father's arms, wanting to go back to him, he remembered what it was. Taking the baby boy, who squealed with laughter as Cannon raised him arms high and waggled him about, Cannon knew it was the mention of disabled children sparking the memory of Liz's story of the brothers, one disabled and the other winning cups at a swimming gala and deliberately leaving them behind.

Giving John Paul another hoist into the air, he had to raise his voice above the child's laughter as he told him, 'Your daddy's a lucky chap, and unless he's forgotten he's going to make me a cup of coffee.'

'So *that's* what you came for,' Paul said, and had just clicked on the kettle when the front doorbell went again. 'My morning for early callers,' he said and went to answer it. Listening, Cannon heard another man's voice, surprise in Paul's greeting—surprise and welcome. 'Come in, come in, I'm really pleased to see you again. How are things going with you? Come through. I've another friend here.'

The young man who walked in was a tall, well-developed young man with a mass of black hair cut very short, probably, Cannon thought, to stop it curling. Cannon knew he had never met him before yet there was something familiar about him.

'John, this is Toby Higham,' Paul said. 'Toby, John Cannon, landlord of The Trap public house.'

'Ah! Yes, if I'm in this country long enough we must become better acquainted.' The young man's smile was disarming, and there was no mistaking whose son he was; as age mellowed him he would be the image of his father. The bearing, the self-assurance were already there.

'Toby came and looked over my shoulder when I was out on the marshes painting,' Paul said and nodding at Cannon added, 'He works in the arts, currently at the Academy in Oslo.' He turned back to Toby. 'You are still there?'

'Very much so, working on a music and digital photo-paintings production for Norwegian television at the moment, quite excited about that.'

'You will gather he is not into landscape and water-colours,' Paul told Cannon, then turning to the young man asked, 'Good of you to look me up. Coffee?'

'Please. I have to admit I'm using you as a retreat.

I just had to get out of the house for a bit, away from my father. Talk to someone about something other than murder and mayhem.'

Neither men answered.

'Sorry,' Toby Higham apologized, 'in the circumstances that was in very bad taste. It's just that all my life I seem to have been living in one or other of my father's crises.'

'How far back do these crises go?' Cannon asked.

'Oooh!' There was impatience in Toby Higham's exclamation. 'My father's just that kind of man. He was more relaxed, more fun, I suppose, before Catherine was diagnosed with a problem, but since the moment she was, he's spent his life—all our lives—trying to compensate, as if it was his fault, *or* our fault!'

'Compensate?' Cannon queried.

'Yes,' Toby confirmed vehemently, but gave no further explanation.

'But the incidents involving the police, did they start when your sister was…diagnosed?' Cannon asked.

'No, no,' Toby said, 'those started, I should say, about the time I graduated from East Anglia University, but then I went on to Oslo University to study there, so really I only *heard* about the occurrences. I didn't experience them first hand, just suffered them at a distance.' He shook his head. 'I know I should be more tolerant, but my father is a stubborn man. I wanted him to let Catherine come to Oslo to live with me; she has a gift for music and colour. Her speech makes her seem a much less clever girl than she actually is, and when she's focused her movements are so much better.'

'Her trouble is?' Cannon asked.

'She has a type of cerebral palsy,' he replied. 'But

she could be a help to me in what is fast becoming a sideline to my television work; between us we might develop new aids to help so many disabilities that fall within that general heading. However, my father always thinks he knows best but…' Now Toby raised clenched victorious fists. 'But he has finally agreed I should take my mother and sister back with me. He will, of course, travel out with them and I intend that he as well as them will have a proper holiday in Norway, as extended as I can make it, *and* I'll make sure he sees what it could offer Catherine.'

Toby Higham left soon after and Paul returned from seeing him out with a quizzical look on his face. 'What do you make of all that?' he asked.

'My old mum would have said father and son are too much alike ever to get on. My old man would have said they wanted their heads knocking together, hard.'

'And both would have been right,' Paul said. Scooping up his own son, who was falling asleep on the floor with his head on a blue teddy bear, he added, 'I hope I do better.'

Cannon grinned, 'I think you'll do all right, and I'll come and knock your heads together if and when necessary.'

'Good,' Paul said. 'I'll put him in his cot, then another coffee, or something stronger?'

'No, I should go. I might call to see the prof and tell him of our decision about the quiz.'

Paul gave him a nod of agreement. 'Has to be right, I'm afraid.'

BLISS ANTIQUES WAS being supervised by its owner, who looked over his glasses as the old-fashioned doorbell he had set up bounced on its spring. He was working over a packing case at the far end of the shop, and came forward carrying a walking stick in each hand.

'Good morning, John,' the prof greeted him, 'I hope you're not bringing more bad news.'

Cannon shook his head.

'And the easel was suitable for Liz, I hope? If not...'

'Ah no.' Cannon dismissed any idea of dissatisfaction. 'It was perfect, she loves it. No, it's the quiz.'

'We're dropping out,' Michael Bliss guessed, adding, 'Well, I suppose in the circumstances it was inevitable.' He carefully put the two walking sticks down on a glass-topped counter.

Cannon saw that one had a carved bone figure of an old-time barrow boy as a handle. The figure of the boy formed the top part of the cane and his barrow the handle.

'Oh, what an attractive thing,' he said, extending a hand towards it, asking permission to pick it up. He found the piles of vegetables and fruit on the barrow were carved into smooth shapes that fitted so very comfortably into the palm of his hand. 'My father was a Cockney fruit and veg man,' he said, 'lots of lovely ackers, he used to say.'

'A man after my own heart then.' The prof grinned.

'I could almost believe it looked like the old man when he was younger. How much do you want for this one?'

'I've only just bought a collection at a house sale. The man had been a serious buyer, he had some nice pieces.' He led Cannon over to the packing case inside which was a collection that made Cannon exclaim in delight.

There were sticks with the heads of dogs, ducks, horses, parrots, old ladies, a pool ball, carved horns and antlers.

'I'm not sure about pricing yet,' the prof went on, 'and to be honest I just picked these two out because the carving on both is of such high quality.'

Cannon looked at the second one. The handle of this was made up of the carved spread wings of an eagle, talons stretched to grip the cane and amber eyes staring down. 'It's a sea-eagle,' Michael Bliss said. 'I saw them once on a trip to northern Norway, always said I'd go back.'

'So these two are going to be expensive,' Cannon said. The eagle was if anything a finer bone-carving than the costermonger, but it was this one Cannon was reluctant to leave. 'I really like this,' he told the prof. 'Would you let me have first refusal when you have priced it?'

The prof promised.

'Did you know that the Highams are all set to go to Norway?' Cannon said as he was leaving.

'Really!' the prof stood with the two sticks in his hand again. 'When's this to be?'

'Soon, I think, I've just met their son Toby.'

'Toby.'

He seemed to snatch the name from Cannon's lips.

'You know him?' Cannon asked.

Michael Bliss turned away, taking the two walking sticks and placing them back in the packing case, but picking up another to show Cannon. 'Toby,' he said, displaying the terrier on the top of this stick, 'Punch and Judy's dog.'

'Right,' Cannon said, knowing a diversionary tactic when he saw it.

'So,' HE DEMANDED of Liz when he reached home, 'if Michael Bliss knew Toby Higham, why didn't he just say so?'

Liz shrugged. 'Well, I'd never heard of Toby Higham, we've lived here longer than the prof, and you say this Toby lives in Oslo anyway. I don't see the problem.'

'It was the way he behaved, the way he said "Toby", his reaction to the name, then he fishes out this walking stick, it was ludicrous.'

'John!' Liz's exclamation was quiet but meaningful. 'This man's an academic, no telling what avenue his mind was going down. You're not in the psychiatrist's chair. If you have serious concerns you should tell Helen or Betterson, but I think with this latest murder they are looking for more positive leads.'

He said no more but when Liz was busy serving all-day breakfasts for two regular customers, lorry drivers back from delivering loads of vegetables to the southern markets, he went out on to the front step with his phone. He sat on one of his bench seats, admiring the display of mauve and pink miniature Michaelmas daisies and pink dahlias in the big round barrel tubs, and quickly brought up the site for the university Toby Higham had attended. He made a note of what he thought might be the best sources of information, then rang the porters' lodge where, in his experience, parcels, letters and all the gossip of a university often resided. He got through very quickly and was pleased to hear the voice of an older man announce, 'Jenkins, head porter.'

'I wonder if you can help me,' he said. 'My name is John Cannon and I am trying to trace a professor friend of mine. I believe he taught at your establishment some ten years ago.'

'Well, I've been here for thirty so it is possible. I've a good memory.'

'The professor's name was Michael Bliss,' Cannon said.

There was a chuckle at the end of the line, but to his surprise the porter said, 'No, no one of that name, I'm sure of that sir, no, not Bliss.'

Jenkins asked him if there was anything else he could help him with, wished him good afternoon and rang off.

Cannon was left wondering what the man had found amusing, realized that it could be nothing at all to do with his phone call but then, as if wanting to find some fault with the man, consulted his watch. It was *just* after midday.

'Pedant,' he judged.

ELEVEN

THE SENSE OF DISCONTENT, unease of having not quite understood the significance of things, stayed with Cannon like a knot in his mind he could not untie.

He stood out on his front step at opening time that night watching the sky, wondering that everything could still be so peaceful, look so beautiful. He watched the clouds become undershot with pink and gold from the lowering sun, and wondered if Dick Ford had liked the autumn? A gamekeeper's busy time before the quiet of the winter. He could have wished he had known the man better, and as the sun dipped to the horizon and its passing glory increased, he asked a silent question. 'I wonder what you saw that made it necessary for such a swift execution?'

The sun lowered and as the colours faded Cannon's more immediate concern returned. How had Alan Hoskins fared during his first official day as overseer of the Higham woods?

Then he gave a low humph of satisfaction when, as if on cue, he saw the very man on his bike hove into view. He stepped down from his front step to meet him but before Hoskins could come anywhere near the pub a white van came from the road behind him. It swept in front of the bike, much too close in Cannon's opinion. The driver got out and raised an arm but whether in greeting or attack Cannon did not wait to see. He shouted and ran. The open door obscured his view until he reached the vehicle and slammed it shut.

'Aah!' he said as he recognized the young man talking animatedly to Hoskins as Callum, an apprentice at a local boatyard. He had first met Callum when Hoskins had taken him to the yard. A case when local cruisers were being bought and used for criminal purposes.*

'HELLO, YOUNG MAN, you swung in a bit sharp and stopped quickly, I just wondered if everything was OK?'

'Hello, Mr Cannon, I've just come to tell Mr Hoskins about his…rabbits,' Callum said. 'I wasn't sure what to do.'

'Rabbits?' Cannon questioned.

Callum nodded.

'You can tell us both what's happened,' Hoskins authorized, adding, 'Young Callum here takes a few *rabbits* once a fortnight to a butcher in Sutdyke for me.'

Callum took up the story. 'I popped over in my lunch break, and that detective was there, the tall chap I've seen quite a few times making enquiries about things.'

'Detective Inspector Betterson,' Cannon suggested and Callum nodded.

'Yes, that's him. He was asking the butcher about a woman who had been to the shop. The butcher took no notice of me so I didn't know whether he was supposed to buy things from just anyone.'

'The detective was asking what this woman bought, but then DI Betterson realized I was there, and said to serve me first.'

'So?' Hoskins asked.

---

* Deadly Serious

'I bought some steak,' Callum said. 'The rabbits are still in the van.'

'He lives on the premises,' Hoskins began. 'It wouldn't take us long to drive back there now.' He looked at his young friend and with a nod urged him to do just that.

'OK,' Callum said, the faintest hint of reluctance in his voice.

Cannon guessed he had more attractive plans for the evening, and reached out to take Hoskins' bike from him. 'Drop our mutual friend back at the pub afterwards,' he told the young man. 'I'll park his bike for him.'

'Thanks, that'll save a bit of time,' he said as Hoskins relinquished his bike.

'Go on, let's see you ride it,' Hoskins challenged.

'Clear off and sell Higham's rabbits and whatever else you've poached,' he told him, refusing to admit he had never learned to ride a bike. His dad had told him where they lived in the East End that it was better to be a 'foot soldier' and so he had been until a Mini, the first motorized love of his life, with a Union Jack painted on its roof, had come into his life. He waited until the van was out of sight, then put one foot on a pedal and scooted back to The Trap.

Hoskins walked into the pub three-quarters of an hour later. Once ensconced in his corner pew-seat at the end of the counter, the bar was quiet enough for Cannon to give him his full attention.

'So what did you find out from your butcher friend?' Cannon asked.

'Quite a lot,' Hoskins said. 'The police have been watching Spier's wife and his mother ever since Maurice went missing. Suddenly the mother starts using two butchers. She goes to her usual one for her bits of stewing meat, a chop or a chicken breast, but then goes on to my chap and buys sausages, best steak, pork chops, liver, the works.'

'So she's...'

'Either feeding an army, or her son, Maurice,' Hoskins confirmed.

'So it shouldn't be hard for the police to find out where he is,' Cannon said, frowning. 'Should think by now...'

'They should have 'im,' Hoskins added. 'We'll hear sooner or later.'

It was sooner, as everyone in the bar was alerted by the sound of a loud bang and breaking of glass.

'Somebody hit something.'

No one denied the comment.

One or two, including Cannon, made moves to go out and see, but before anyone reached the doors they were flung open. Cannon blinked as if to be sure of what he saw, as a slightly stooped but hard-looking, grey-haired woman burst into his bar. She immediately focused on Hoskins and made directly for him. Hoskins got to his feet defensively, as the woman he and Cannon had last seen in her garden denying all knowledge of the dog tied up to her line-post brushed aside men twice her size to reach him.

'What've you done with my son?' she demanded then, stabbing a bent forefinger, included Cannon: 'And you. Tying up a dog in my garden so you could come snooping around.'

'What you talking about, woman?' Hoskins asked.

'I'm talking about my son, Maurice, what've you done with him?'

'What have *I* done with him? I think it's what you've been doing with him!' he exclaimed.

'What'ye mean?'

'Where've *you* been hiding him, and feeding him best steak and sausages and stuff?'

'How d'you know?' Mrs Spier was disconcerted for a second, then launched herself at Hoskins, arms flailing. 'You tell me where he is! What you done with him?' she screamed. 'You came on to my property snooping around, you'd no business—' She stopped as the sound of a police siren wailed swiftly in from the distance and stopped outside.

Cannon glanced around; everyone in the bar was as rapt as if they were watching a good crime drama on TV. With excellent timing, the doors swung open and Betterson, and Maddern in sergeant's uniform and greatcoat, came in, both big, experienced men. Their authority was almost like an extra presence. As one they came towards the old lady.

'That was a silly thing to do, Mrs Spier,' Betterson said, 'driving off like that. You're only adding to your troubles.' He looked her up and down. 'You're not hurt, are you? We'll get a doctor to check you over at the police station.' Then he turned to Cannon. 'She's demolished one of your big flower tubs.'

'I'm not going to no police station!' Mrs Spier shouted.

'I am afraid you are,' Betterson told her, 'and at the rate you're going we'll need an extra long charge sheet.'

Mrs Spier suddenly launched herself at Betterson. 'You find my son!'

'If you hadn't hidden him in the first place he might be safe in a nice comfortable cell,' Betterson told her, as he tried to catch her flailing arms. 'Look, lady, you'll only finish up hurting yourself. You've hidden a wanted man, resisted arrest, crashed your car, cost us time and expense—' Then as she caught him a good sound slap across his face, he threatened the use of handcuffs and Maddern came to his aid.

'Come on, Lily,' Maddern said, 'we don't want to take you to the station in handcuffs,' but she still violently shook off his hand when he tried to take her arm. He merely took hold a little firmer and said loudly, 'Lily Spier, you're making an exhibition of yourself, and none of us will find your Maurice while we're wasting time here.'

Lily Spier looked up at Maddern. 'He's all I've got,' she said.

'Let's get on then,' Maddern said briskly, nodding down at her, and she allowed herself to be led outside.

Cannon followed, thinking Maddern was probably worth several recruits with top degrees and a good many others thrown in.

His flower tub had split with the impact, soil and dahlias were strewn over the ground and the bonnet of Mrs Spier's car concertinaed.

'It doesn't look as if she even attempted to brake,' Liz said. 'It's a wonder she managed to get out of the car.'

'Thank God for airbags,' Cannon muttered, kicking some of the soil and plants to one side. 'I'll get a brush or this lot will all walk in.'

'What do you think they'll charge her with?' Liz asked.

'They'll be spoilt for choice,' Cannon replied.

THEY WAITED FOR news of Maurice Spier being apprehended—but nothing. The daily gossip in the bar hard-

ened on the opinion that Maurice was dead because
he was not smart enough to evade the kind of police
raids and searches that were said to have peppered the
whole area. The newspapers ranted on about lack of
progress in the case of the two separate murders, and
for want of better material repeated the gory details of
each death with much speculation, over which Cannon
tutted and swore.

To his relief Hoskins said he was keeping strictly to
the woods around The Grange, making sure 'the boss
sees I'm on the job'. He told Cannon that the family
were preparing to leave for Oslo, though the police had
been paying plenty of visits to The Grange.

'They'll probably be liaising with the Norwegian
police,' Cannon said.

'So you think Higham will take trouble with him?'
Hoskins asked.

'He's targeted everywhere, or he thinks he is, according to his son who lives in Oslo.'

'He said he'd met you. I explained you were ex-Met,'
Hoskins said. 'Spit of his old man, who by the way
wants to see you before he leaves. He said could you
make it tomorrow afternoon about three.'

'I suppose,' Cannon said, keeping any eagerness
from his voice; at last a chance to ask questions, to *do*
something. He had fretted that he had seen neither Paul
nor Betterson since the day Mrs Spier had been taken
away from his bar, and no one seemed to know for certain whether she had been charged, released on bail, or
kept in custody. Paul was difficult to approach because
he did not want to make matters any more complicated
for Helen but this summons to The Grange gave him
the impetus to make another call en route.

Liz was quiet when he told her of Higham's summons, but when he said he proposed to go to see Mavis Moyle at the antique shop, she wanted to know why.

'Mavis is a good friend of Maurice Spier's wife, who would surely know if her mother-in-law was in custody,' he explained.

'You can't just walk into the shop and ask her that!' Liz said.

'No but I can go in and ask after a walking stick I saw there and get chatting.'

'A walking stick?' Liz protested. 'You've got a couple of walking poles you never use.'

'No, this wouldn't be to use.' He described the stick in some detail.

'Oh, I see, it'd be like a family memento for you,' she said, appreciating his enthusiasm. 'Well, it's your birthday at the end of the month— let me buy it for you.'

'I would really like to have it but it could be expensive.'

'For you no expense shall be spared.' She smiled at him.

'Thanks, Liz,' he said huskily. 'What would I do without you?'

The question was rhetorical but Liz replied that he would probably still be in the Met. 'You retired to nurse me back to health.'

'A question of priorities,' he stated.

'I shouldn't really…' she trailed off.

'What, object if I go in for a bit of amateur sleuthing,' he guessed.

'Something like that,' she admitted.

He folded her protectively in his arms. 'I'd do the same again,' he said, and added, 'it's high time we had a holiday, somewhere scenic where you can paint. Once this business is tied up…'

'No, no, John Cannon, I know you. I'll believe in a holiday when it happens,' she said, then in businesslike tones added, 'and if you're going to pull in the shop and The Grange, we'd better have a quick snack now.'

THE SHOP WAS locked up but there was a notice suggesting the caller try Ivydene, the next-door cottage. Mavis Moyes answered his knock with the shop keys in her hand. 'I was just going round, if you wanted something from the shop,' she said with a smile. 'You're becoming quite a regular.'

He laughed. 'I didn't expect to be this way again so soon but I wanted to ask you something, and I was keen to buy a walking stick I saw the other day. Will Michael be here later?' he asked.

'No, I found a note and the keys through my letter-box first thing this morning. He mentioned an extended buying trip. The thing was I had a dentist's appointment, just a check-up, so I stuck a note on the shop door before I left, only just got back.'

'Does he often do this sort of thing?' Cannon asked.

'He's certainly done it before, a time or two, I suppose. I think he hears of promising sales and off he goes.'

'He's lucky you're free to step in.'

'Mr Cannon, he trusts me to put down the exact time I spend in the shop and he pays me ten pounds an hour no questions asked, trust on both sides. I'm not going to let him down, am I?'

He followed her to the shop, where she undid the door and deactivated the burglar alarm, saying as she did so, 'He usually leaves me detailed instructions on the counter here.'

She made her way to the main counter and picked up a sheet of paper from under a millefiori paperweight. 'Do you want to have a look round for your stick while I read what he has to say?'

The message looked fairly long and Cannon drifted off in the direction of the box the professor had been looking through.

The lid was closed, and when Cannon lifted the lid the first stick he saw was the one with the Jack Russell terrier head. 'Toby,' the prof had explained. Once more Cannon ruminated on the name, on the way it had been said, but was diverted by the fact that what he could not see was the stick he was so keen to own, or the one with the sea-eagle handle.

He looked around. On a back wall beneath a selection of sporting prints, there were several large old umbrella stands, and tall pottery jardinières, in which there were many walking sticks all with labels giving details of materials, age and price of each stick.

They included some very nice sticks indeed. He could see how a man might become a collector. He soon realized that the older items with the more competent renderings of brass, or amber, metal or bone handles were in two particular stands and the prices ranged from £30 to £100. These were handsome things, and one or two had regimental badges and mottoes on them, such as a retired military man would esteem. He lifted them out one by one, weighing them in his hand. There was much weight in the carved hard wooden handles of some; Irish shillelaghs came to his mind. Those with brass heads of ducks and horses were heavy, while those with bone or horn handles tended to be lighter. He was particularly attracted to one he found right at the back, a long dark wooden stick, the wood scrolled and carved up to a broad silver ring with an escutcheon and initials. A handsome and very heavy stick considering it had no metal but the circle of silver. He wondered what kind of wood it was, but this one had no label.

He was attracted to those that had age, and the highest price tags. He could almost hear Liz commenting, 'Well, of course,' but he could not see 'his stick'.

'Found what you were looking for?' Mavis called. 'Hope so because it sounds as if Mr Bliss could be gone some time. He says I'm to take my wages out of the till each week so...'

'Must be an important sale,' Cannon said, still happily rummaging, 'does he say where it is?'

'Could be anywhere, perhaps more than one. He goes further and further afield but he sells all over too. America, Canada, and he says China are fast reclaiming their antiquities.'

'Doesn't look as if I'll get my walking stick until he comes back,' Cannon said.

'Wait a minute, he's got an office, he could have put it through there. We can have a look.'

'Please, if it's only to put a note on it reminding him I'd like to buy it,' Cannon said.

The office was lined with shelves and these were full of books and papers. 'I think most of this is to do with his university days,' Mavis said. 'He told me he would not have retired so soon but for an awful car accident he had,' she added as she looked into the corners by the side of books cases and cupboards.

'He's certainly made a complete recovery—mentally and physically,' Cannon said.

'That's true. He can manhandle some quite hefty antique chairs and things.' She paused, then exclaimed as her hand found a stick on the top of a cupboard and lifted it down. 'There,' she said, 'and it has your name on and...' She peered closer at the stringed tag. 'The price of fifty pounds.'

'I'll take it,' Cannon said.

'Great,' Mavis said, 'good first sale. I like to do well when he leaves me in charge. By the way, what did you want to ask me?'

The question seemed awkward, rather blunt, but Mavis answered readily enough. Mrs Spier, she told him, had been given a warning about her behaviour but was released the same evening she had driven into his flower tub.

'And her son, Maurice?'

She shook her head. 'No one's heard or seen anything of him. Poor Lily, his wife, is living on tenterhooks. He seems to have dropped off the face of the earth.'

Cannon climbed back into his jeep wondering how Mrs Spier had explained her purchases at the second butcher, and began to wonder if the gossip that the man must be dead might not be right.

He put his foot down as he reached a decent stretch of straight road. He had no wish to be late, and he was anxious to get back to Liz and show her the walking stick.

An approaching car flashed its lights at him—then again, and again—then left them full on. Cannon slowed and stopped as he recognized Betterson's car. He waited as the DI pulled off the road into a gateway, then walked over to the jeep.

'Trouble?' Cannon asked.

'My trouble is we can't find Maurice Spier. Your trouble may be somewhat different when you've seen Alexander Higham. I've just come from there.'

Cannon shrugged. 'How did Mrs Spier explain the trip to that second butcher?'

'Oh, she still had the steak and stuff in her deep freeze. Her son had been with her. When she realized he had disappeared she showed us where he'd been hiding. Over the years he had made himself a sweet little hidey-hole under the garden shed. He'd dug out and lined a space with carved zincs just like an underground war-time Anderson shelter, re-laid the wooden floor with a trap-door under an old mat. His mother knew he was desperate not to go to prison, was terrified of having to serve his suspended sentence, but she never expected him to clear off. How long he'd been gone before she returned with the shopping she's no idea. She thought he was just asleep in his bolt hole. It was only as time went on that she investigated and found he had really gone, taking most of the clothes and his shaving kit.'

'So that was when she came raving over to The Trap. She knew Hoskins and I had been to her house, she put two and two together and made five or six,' Cannon said.

Betterson nodded, then cleared his throat. Cannon looked at him expectantly.

'What I am going to say is unofficial,' Betterson said, scowling at what he obviously thought was going to be an impropriety. 'I know you are going to see Alexander Higham, *and* I know what he is going to ask of you... I just want to say I hope you'll take it on.'

'So, are you going to tell me what it is?' Cannon asked.

Betterson shook his head. 'No, best you hear it straight from Higham but—' he pulled a pen from his breast pocket '—you got something I can write on?'

Cannon produced a receipt for diesel. Betterson took it and, leaning on the jeep bonnet, wrote down a series of numbers then handed it back. 'That's my mobile number, you can reach me any time. Take it with you.'

'With me?'

'Yes, keep it handy.'

'So where am I supposed to be going?' Cannon asked.

'You'll know soon enough,' Betterson said. 'I must get on.'

TWELVE

It was Cannon's turn to scowl as the front door of The Grange was opened by a man who was the epitome of every security guard ever featured in a gangster movie.

'Mornin',' the suited giant said and on hearing Cannon's name showed him into Alexander Higham's study. Cannon went to look out of the French windows on to a sweep of back lawns until he heard the door close, then he grinned and wondered if you hired such men by the kilo.

He was not alone many minutes. The door opened and Toby Higham came in with a handsome, dark girl of about sixteen on his arm.

'Mr Cannon, we meet again,' Toby Higham said enthusiastically. 'This is my sister, Catherine.'

The girl smiled, her shoulder and arm jerking in an uncontrollable spasm as she said, 'I am very pleased to meet you. Toby's friend Paul says your partner is a painter.'

Cannon smiled. 'You're very well informed,' he said, thinking that in her speech there was just a hint of the way Timmy Riley split his sentences.

She laughed. 'Toby keeps me up to date. We're all going to Oslo with my brother.' There was another convulsive twist of her shoulder. 'I am so looking forward to it all.'

They all looked back to the door again as it was

thrown open recklessly wide, hitting a bookcase standing behind it as Alexander Higham strode in.

He seemed slightly disconcerted to find the three of them obviously already acquainted, but came forward, hand outstretched to Cannon. 'So pleased you've come,' he said, though no look of pleasure replaced the anxiety on his face. 'So you have met my younger son and my daughter, good, good.' Then turning to them, he said, 'Your mother needs Catherine—I think it's a matter of clothes to pack, et cetera.'

'I hope to see you again soon, Mr Cannon,' Catherine said as her brother led her away, Toby nodding enthusiastically in endorsement of the sentiment.

'Sit down, John.'

The use of his first name and the fact that Higham did not take the desk seat but one alongside his visitor made Cannon wonder even more what was going to be asked of him.

Higham cleared his throat. 'I have just been given DI Betterson's official blessing to leave with my son, Toby, and take my wife and daughter to Oslo.'

Cannon waited.

'His murder enquiries seem to have reached a standstill,' Higham added.

Cannon still made no comment.

'I have a proposal to put to you,' Higham went on.

Cannon raised his eyebrows.

'You are aware how troubles, attacks, near fatalities and now murder have followed my family about,' he said.

'I can understand how you must feel,' Cannon agreed.

'I will be honest with you, John, I've made it my

business to learn quite a lot more about you, your career, your partner and why you are here keeping a public house.' Before Cannon could react, he went on. 'This is why I want you to come to Oslo and keep an eye on my family. However much surveillance the Norwegian police may or may not provide, I'd like someone there who knows me, who's met my family, who has a kind of personal interest in my case.' He paused and leaned towards Cannon. 'And I think you do.'

Cannon's interest had more to do with a widow and disabled son, with the image of O'Reilly battered to death as he walked his dog, and a gamekeeper stabbed to death in his cottage—but he sensed this man pleading for help was more than just a single link in a chain. He was more catalyst in a chain reaction. Cannon needed to unravel that chain, follow it link by link back to its beginning and on to its bitter end. 'You could say I've a personal interest in *justice* for everyone,' he said mildly.

'Just come and be a member of our party, keep a watchful eye on things. I am more than willing to pay the expenses for you *and* your partner to join us. I'm sure there'd be time for your partner to paint. Norway is a pretty scenic country at any time of year. My family do not keep late hours, the duties would not be onerous; in some ways it could be like a holiday.'

Cannon gave a brief ironic laugh: murder was never a holiday.

'No expense spared to keep my family safe,' Higham hastily added. 'If you need to hire more help at your public house…'

Cannon found himself breathing slightly faster, hooked by the old excitement of a deadly puzzle he might help solve. He wanted desperately to respond to

Higham's appeal immediately but he shook his head. 'You must give me time to…well, for a start talk to my partner.'

'Of course, but we leave the day after tomorrow. I'd like to think you would come very soon after that.' Then he added as if it might be an extra incentive, 'Toby's home is within walking distance of a very good hotel. I always have security men on duty at night. It would be daytime activities I would mostly need your help with.'

Cannon found himself gifted with another personal mobile phone number and the offer of an immediate cash advance, which he refused.

'Later, then,' Higham said.

He was back at The Trap by five and let himself in by the back door. All was quiet; he called but there was no answer. He went to the stairs to their private quarters. 'Liz!' he called up. 'I'm back.'

Silence.

There was no one upstairs. Then he heard a noise in the kitchen and hurried back there. Liz was just closing the outer door.

'Where've you been?' he demanded.

She raised her eyebrows in surprise. 'Just to see Alamat, he's got problems with the showerhead in his bathroom. It just needs—'

He stopped listening. 'I couldn't find you,' he interrupted, wondering if some of Higham's acute state of anxiety had rubbed off on him.

'So!' she asked. 'Where is it?'

'What?'

'This marvellous walking stick,' she replied, watching him carefully.

'Oh! I've left it in the jeep.'

'So you're so taken with it you've forgotten about it already,' she said.

'No, it's what's happened since,' he said, and sat down. This all needed a lot of tact and diplomacy.

AS OPENING TIME APPROACHED, Liz had gone through 'but we can't', 'surely not', 'you say Betterson wants you to go' and 'you say this daughter is...'

'A really nice, obviously very intelligent, girl. I can understand Higham's protectiveness.'

'Yes, of course, it's his child, but...' She rose from where she had sat next to him and went to stand with her back to the sink, regarding him, he felt, with enough distance for cold judgements to be made.

'She knows you paint, that you are an artist,' he added.

His attempt at blarney brought a look that almost made him cringe.

'You want to go,' she stated.

'If anything does happen, after I've been asked, I'll always feel I might have prevented it had I been there but I shan't go unless you do, I've made up my mind about that.' He paused then launched into appeal proper. 'Two heads, two lots of eyes, professionally trained, so much better than one. And his son and daughter are into the arts, it could be an opportunity to paint, a real opportunity...it could be a kind of holiday.'

Her ironic laugh echoed his own when Higham had said the word. 'A holiday!' she was repeating as the back door was politely tapped and Alamat came in.

'Ah!' he exclaimed. 'You are going to have that holiday you are always talking about—good! I have a friend who works in a restaurant in town, afternoons, but she needs extra hours to earn more money to send home to nurse her sick brother.'

This was all news to Cannon and Liz.

'A girlfriend?' Liz questioned and their invaluable Croatian blushed and tried to shrug his shoulders nonchalantly, but it did not quite work.

'Well, as you say, everything possible. You like to meet her?'

'Very much,' Cannon said.

THE IMMEDIATE CONCERNS of opening and running the pub took over and neither Cannon nor Liz realized that Alamat had telephoned his girlfriend, until a woman in her late fifties walked into the bar. Alamat lit up like an old 150 watt bulb, replaced the empty glasses on the table he was clearing, and rushed to greet her.

'This is Bozena,' he said, bringing her to the counter, 'we have known each other over two years. Bozena means divine gift,' he added.

Alamat's penchant for analyzing words and sayings was occasionally embarrassing, Cannon thought, as he shook hands with this pleasant, broad-faced, smiling woman, who was exactly the same height as her fellow Croat. She greeted Cannon with the information that she was learning more English.

'Alamat learns me.'

The teacher looked about to correct her but instead said, 'Bozena is a very good cook and cleaner.'

It was only later when Cannon offered to run Bozena back to Boston that they realized Alamat was entertaining her for the night. 'We'd better get that showerhead fixed,' Cannon whispered to Liz as they met at the optics. She gave him a warning nudge but grinned.

Later, when the two had gone to Alamat's quarters, Cannon sipped his tea thoughtfully. 'We've missed a few things under our own noses,' he said. 'They're like a pigeon-pair, alike in size. I'll have to tell him, he'll like that saying—and I never realized he blushed so easily.'

'And I never realized I could…well, be steered willy-nilly into doing something I feel is against all common sense, outside our responsibility, unnecessary, ridiculous,' she said, 'but just look what I'm doing!'

She was stacking sketchpads, pencils and colours into a neat pile.

'Just don't say anything,' she warned him.

'I don't need to,' he said, but rose, put his cup and saucer into the sink, took her hand and led her out of the kitchen, switching the light off as they went.

'There'll be a lot to do if…'

'Tomorrow,' he said.

THIRTEEN

IT WAS RAINING when they landed in Oslo just before eleven, gaining an hour on UK time on the journey. The end of October, and Cannon had expected to see some snow and ice. He wondered if global warming was responsible for there not being any.

As soon as they had collected their cases and reached the arrival hall, they saw Toby Higham waving to them. He came forward, shook Cannon's hand and kissed Liz twice, three times—'one for luck,' he said—then took her case and replaced it with the upmarket department store carrier he held. 'It is for you,' he said, 'both of you. Open it when you get to your hotel. They are the same as the very first thing I bought when I came to Oslo. You'll see, you'll be glad.'

He whisked them into a taxi he had waiting. 'It is a long drive to the city centre,' he said, 'about forty kilometres, but I can fill you in on the situation.'

'The situation?' Cannon queried. 'Has something happened?'

'Only my father,' he said.

'Just at the moment I have an ongoing project with children's art and a television company. I set a theme and children send in their work. Usually this results in a programme on the work but this time it has all become far more meaningful. The latest one based on the theme of "father" has resulted in a programme for children, an exhibition and a late-night programme based on what a psychiatrist sees in their pictures. I want to take my sister to the opening of the exhibition and your arrival may just make it possible to do this. My father is still paranoid that someone is going to attempt something to harm Catherine.'

'When is this exhibition?' Liz asked.

'This afternoon,' Toby told them. 'The official opening is at three but I've just come from there and I shall go straight back when I've seen you to your hotel.'

'I'd like to see the children's work,' Liz said.

'Of course, we'll both be there to escort Catherine,' Cannon said.

'That's wonderful!' Toby's enthusiasm and his chatter, full of information about the old city of Oslo, its many museums, its centres dedicated to Henrik Ibsen, which Cannon immediately felt he'd like to visit, and the Edvard Munch museum, which Liz was particularly interested in, passed the journey very pleasantly.

The roads were wide and modern from the airport, passing through newer suburbs before reaching the old city, where they glimpsed the parliament building, the cathedral and the docks before arriving at their hotel.

'Everything to go on that,' Toby emphasized as they booked in at reception and he handed over a bank card. 'So, I will go and be back to pick up at 2.15. There will be refreshments at the exhibition and my father would like us all to eat at my house this evening. Is that…?'

They both nodded.

'I'm sorry it is all such a rush,' he added.

'We don't mind that,' Cannon assured him.

'At least we are starting with some art,' Liz said when they had been shown into an elegant room with a large sitting area, a balcony overlooking dignified old stone buildings, and a huge double bed with a large quantity of enormous square pillows.

Cannon sat on the edge of the bed then leaned back. 'Wow,' he breathed appreciatively, 'these are the most comfortable pillows in the world! Liz, try them!'

She sat on the other side of the bed and followed suit. 'You're right,' she said. 'You know, it could be a holiday. We could have left Higham's troubles in England. Holiday from murder,' she said.

His head pressed into the great down pillow, his laugh was hopeful but still ironic. 'What's in the bag he gave you?' he asked.

Liz pulled the looped silver cord through so she could open the bag. She drew out two very stylish broad-brimmed hats and looked at the labels. 'They're rainproof,' she said. 'I see what he meant by being the first thing he bought when he reached Oslo but they're rather…' She put one on at a rakish angle.

'Very nice. You'll probably need it this afternoon, but what about grabbing a coffee and a sandwich before we're whisked off to wherever—it could be a long afternoon.'

TOBY ARRIVED BACK for them at 2.15. He looked flushed, excited and a little put out. 'My father's in the car with my sister. He insisted we all ride together, and I've just insisted they stay in the car while I fetch you. I have a VIP opening the exhibition. I can't afford to be late.'

Liz was ushered into the back seat next to Catherine. Higham reached across his daughter to shake hands. He was clearly delighted they had both arrived, but the conversation was quickly taken over by Catherine, who was excited not only about being in Oslo with her brother but about going to his exhibition. This made for a few extra breaks in her speech but her enthusiasm was catching.

'We must stay together to see everything,' Liz said. 'Perhaps we will learn a lot from each other.'

'Yes, yes,' Catherine agreed. 'I...love talking... about...painting.'

'And doing it?' Liz questioned.

'Yes!'

Cannon thought it sounded like a friendship forming.

Accompanied by Toby, they were all allowed in by a side entrance before the general public were admitted. The curator of this museum of childhood came to meet them. He was a surprisingly young man: small, slight, pale faced, black beard, very welcoming.

Catherine exclaimed aloud as she saw the main hall where there was a huge shout of colour from the assembled children's work. She went straight to one picture which showed in bold outline the back of a man with a boy, walking together, their arms around each other. Liz was by her side as the girl lifted her arms to it in appreciation and joy at the closeness of father and son. She looked back to her own father. 'Just like us, Pa,' she said.

Cannon was aware that the television crew were already in place. They were busy, absorbed in their own affairs, in a separate universe looking at everything and everyone through dispassionate lenses, receiving instructions from directors. He wondered how far afield these broadcasts were transmitted. Were they filming at that moment?

He went to stand behind Catherine and Liz, between

them and the cameras. Higham's tormentor had followed this family about before; whoever it was did not need to have any of his possible victims located by a television broadcast.

Three o'clock approached quickly enough, the public was admitted and assembled in the main hall, and cameras and Toby awaited their guest celebrity.

Cannon had ascertained that the lady was a minor but popular royal. She was certainly glamorous, he thought, as the dark-haired sylph-like young woman glided in, arm outstretched to Toby, who bowed then kissed the gloved hand.

The crowd greeted her with something approaching rapture. Cannon and Liz listened politely to the speech in Norwegian but her enthusiasm for the project was obvious in any language.

The presenter now walked into camera shot and began to speak to Toby in English, the whole country's second language.

'Mr Toby Higham, I think we could say this is another successful art project you have organized for children all over Norway and beyond. At this time of day we will have a lot of young viewers, and—' he directed his remarks to the camera '—be patient, children, for we will soon be showing you many of the pictures you have sent in and which have been hung in these magnificent rooms. First, though, I want to ask Toby here—' and now his gaze went back to Toby '—just how he makes these exhibitions work so well. So tell us…'

The camera was now on Toby, who was confident and completely unselfconscious. 'The children will know,' he said, 'that I set a theme, a subject, which I ask them to illustrate. In this case it was just one word, "father", but what happens is the children turn the word into a question. "Father?" In their pictures they then attempt to answer that question.'

'It has brought a very wide range of work.'

Cannon thought the presenter was now a little cautious, and could imagine some pictures might raise issues too sensitive for afternoon viewing.

'Indeed it has,' Toby agreed.

'There is to be a programme in our later schedules, I understand.'

'That is correct,' Toby said, 'and many of the pictures you see here today will form part of a travelling exhibition on our arts bus, which will visit as many schools as possible. Schools can apply for a visit through our project address, or website.'

The presenter bowed towards the celebrity who, joined by Toby and several officials, began to make her way around the pictures in the main hall. Double doors to other rooms were now opened and visitors were free to go where they wished. Some were obviously looking for particular drawings, others had children with them eager to find their own work.

The afternoon wore on, the crowd began to thin, the celebrity departed and Cannon and Liz found themselves with Catherine and her father alone in the refreshment room. Toby had left them there to go and thank the curator and all those who had helped hang the works and have a short conference with the television director. Liz and Cannon were then to be driven back to their hotel and picked up again in time for a late dinner with the Highams. Toby's wife and his mother, who they learned had opted to watch the occasion on television, would be waiting to welcome them. So it had all been live, Cannon registered.

Higham was more relaxed now the crowds had gone. He sat with his arm around the back of his daughter's chair. Catherine was full of talk, impatient with her own inability to chatter as quickly as she wanted. 'So many…drawings…of fathers,' she said, 'tossing their children up in the air…reading at…bedtime.' She turned to her father with a smile. 'You have done all…those things.'

Higham's arm slid from the chair-back to hug his daughter. Cannon glanced at Liz as he blinked away a ridiculous threat of tears, but her face was impassive, even a little remote, which surprised him.

There was a sudden flurry of activity in the doorway and Toby burst in, looking a completely different man to the composed, assured individual who had left them fifteen minutes before. Cannon rose to his feet and heard Higham whisper, 'Something's happened.'

'Toby?' both men questioned.

'Yes.' He acknowledged their concern. 'There has been an incident.'

'Has someone…?' his father began.

'No, no, it's one of the pictures, one of the largest drawings, but it's very disturbing. No one saw anything.'

'But are we able to leave now.' Neither Alexander Higham's words nor his manner made it any kind of question.

Their footsteps and voices echoed eerily in the empty museum as Toby led the way out. The curator was standing in the main hall looking disturbed and shaking his head as they walked towards him.

'Such a thing,' he said, 'so unexpected. We do *not* want this kind of publicity.'

Higham walked on determinedly, the curator scampering to keep up.

'It must have been done so quickly and, one might say, so expertly.' By almost leaping in front of Higham, he diverted the man from the exit to the vandalized picture. 'One of the pictures we were most pleased to exhibit, so big and bold, such a pity, and whoever did it must have taken the…with him.'

Higham stopped as if struck, pole-axed, before the drawing Catherine had so admired, the picture of father and son walking away from the viewer. Only now the father was missing; the son walked alone.

'And whoever did it must have taken the—' the curator waved a hand at the missing oval '—with him. There's no trace, we found nothing, and *no one* saw anything.'

'Someone with…a disturbed mind,' Catherine said. 'How sad.'

Cannon went closer. It was indeed expertly done; had a template been laid over the picture a more perfect oval would have been difficult to remove, and the mounting board behind was deeply scored by the sharpness of the instrument used. Cannon recollected Higham's vandalized car and the sweeping cut across the gamekeeper's carpet.

He glanced at Higham, who looked so stricken he might fall to his knees. Cannon moved quickly to his side, held his arm, led him a few paces towards the door and said in a low voice, 'Bear up, don't let your daughter see you upset.'

'He's here, isn't he?' Higham whispered. 'He's followed us.'

'Yes, I think so,' Cannon agreed.

Higham's gaze shot to Cannon's face, and his lips parted, shocked and surprised that someone should so readily agree with him. 'Oh, thank God,' he said, 'thank God you're here. I began to think I was deranged.' He looked as if he might have opened his heart, said so much more, but Cannon shook his head.

'Not now,' he advised, 'this evening.'

'This evening,' Higham repeated.

The ride back to the hotel was uncomfortable, restrained, Catherine looking continually to her father, who was silent. The way he kept putting the back of his hand to his lips then shaking his head suggested that his mind was working overtime.

'Do we keep running?' he suddenly asked, but seemed unaware that he had spoken aloud.

'I like it...*here*,' Catherine said, 'with Toby.'

'And we've promised to show each other our paintings,' Liz intervened.

'Will you bring some this evening?'

'Perhaps tomorrow would be better,' Cannon said. 'You'll have more time.'

'OK.' Catherine beamed at Liz. 'Tomorrow.'

Cannon was quite pleased to get back into the privacy of their hotel room. 'It feels like sanctuary already,' he said, stretching out in one of the armchairs. 'Will you use the shower first?'

'Looks like it,' she said. 'we've only an hour and a half.'

'Hmm.'

'John, you won't forget we're going out!'

'No,' he said abstractedly, and sat staring into space.

She watched him closely. She could see this was going to be one of those moments she called his epiphanies, when something struck him so forcibly he just stopped functioning in the present. She had seen him do it many times in their Met days: during meetings, at crime scenes, in hospitals interviewing victims, and in mortuaries. She shook her head, went into the bathroom, showered and was sitting at the dressing table when he said, 'The loving father obliterated, cut out with something as sharp as slashed Dick Ford's carpet.'

'You honestly believe this picture being destroyed is something to do with the Highams being here?' she asked.

'The loving father obliterated, the devoted dad destroyed,' he said, 'like Niall Riley, murdered, bludgeoned to death. Yes,' he said, 'I do.'

'It could surely just be a local feud, even parental jealousy...' she suggested.

'Some sort of parental sin more likely,' he said. 'I wondered about the expression on your face when Higham's daughter was listing all the things in the pictures they had shared.'

'Ah! No.' She shook her head at the idea it was anything to do with Higham or his daughter. 'For some ridiculous reason I suddenly remembered that family I knew as a child, the one whose son competed in the swimming gala and left the cups he'd won behind the door at the pool.'

'Another father who cherished his disabled son to the detriment of the normal,' Cannon mused. 'That's not a ridiculous reason for remembering.'

'Another?' Liz questioned that. 'Niall Riley had only one son, and Dick Ford was not a father.'

'No, but Higham is, and has a disabled child.'

'Yes but his sons do not seem disadvantaged in any way whatsoever,' Liz said, 'and you'd better get ready.'

'We never met the other son. I don't even know his name. Isn't that odd?'

'Not really,' Liz said. 'He runs the London office of Higham Associate Companies, he is like his mother and his name is Jacob.' Then obviously quoting someone, she added, 'Bit of a runt compared with the other son.'

'How?'

'According to Hoskins,' Liz said, adding, 'we've now less than an hour.'

'Thought you were going to shower first.'

'I have,' she said patiently.

When the time came they were ready but Cannon was hot and fussed. 'I could do with a walk,' he said.

'You certainly won't have time,' she said as their phone rang and reception told them Mr Toby Higham was waiting for them.

The evening was hard work and it was impossible to ignore what had happened, though an attempt was made as Liz and Cannon joined the party and all became properly acquainted, even with Toby and Karen's dog, a friendly white terrier called Munch. Karen explained that when he was a puppy he was a scream so they called him after the Norwegian painter Edvard Munch, whose famous painting, 'The Scream', was owned by the Oslo Museum. The dog was a welcome distraction. They had, however, only just been shown to their places at table when the telephone rang.

'I better answer it,' Toby said. 'You serve, Karen,

I'll keep it as short as I can.' He came back to the table looking if anything grimmer than ever but insisting that all was well and nothing else untoward had happened.

'Thank goodness for Catherine,' was Liz's reaction when they again reached the privacy of their hotel bedroom. 'She was the only one not watching and worrying about her father all the time. Know what, I'm whacked, feel as if I've been here a week, not flown in this morning.'

At that moment Cannon's mobile burbled.

'I don't believe it,' Liz complained, 'now what?'

'It'll be Toby, he said he would ring me.'

Cannon sat in one of the armchairs and Liz, with the air of one determined to see the day through to its bitter end, sat down in the other.

Cannon put the phone on speakerphone so Liz could hear. 'Thought you should know at once that it was the curator who rang me earlier tonight. He *has* informed the police but in the circumstances they have come to an agreement to keep the matter under wraps for the time being. They do have a local mischief maker who might just be responsible; they'll look into that first. They have also had information about our—' Toby hesitated to find the right words '—family troubles, from the British police.'

'You've told your father?' Cannon asked.

'I have, but this latest thing has hit him hard. I'm not sure how much more he can take. He talks about the net closing in on us.'

'I do believe we have to take extreme care,' Cannon said. 'Are you happy with your night-time security?'

'They're experienced men my father trusts.'

Reassured on this score, Cannon went on, 'I always

take an early-morning run when I'm at home. I intend to do that tomorrow, all around the area, keep my eyes open and get my bearings.'

'You could finish here, shower and breakfast with us,' Toby said. 'I could collect Liz and a change of clothes for you later. I understand Liz and my sister have arranged to have a viewing session of each other's works.'

Cannon looked at Liz, who nodded at him.

'Yes, OK, that'll be fine.'

FOURTEEN

CANNON PICKED UP a brochure for the city from reception on his way out the next morning, then headed for the harbour just at the end of the street.

He ran unhindered along the edge of the docks, between mooring posts and in front of the offices and warehouses belonging to various shipping lines. The city and its affairs, the sea and all its busyness, were very much part of each other.

He finally paused under a castle rampart to check where he was. 'Akershus Fortress and Castle,' he read, learning there was also a Resistance Museum and an Armed Forces Museum within its precincts. Then he decided he must drop the tourist role and head back to the residential area where Toby lived.

But all was novelty, the expanse of this enormous fjord, the docks, the liners, then his way lay more inland past the imposing City Hall and into Rosenkrantz Gate. Leaving the National Gallery on his left, he was soon near Toby's home.

He reached the quiet street with individually styled detached houses either side, a much older residential development to that they had seen on the way from the airport. Newer was, as everywhere, more standardized, more uniform—the key to keeping prices down.

He walked the last hundred yards, checked his watch—just after eight—but when he came in sight of the house, he frowned, then hurried forward more urgently. Three schoolboys, about twelve or thirteen, satchels over their shoulders, stood looking with extreme interest at the entrance gates to Toby's home. There seemed to be some game of dare going on, two egging the other on.

He drew nearer and could see something quite large was pinned, or rather pinioned with a knife, to the gates. Even as the boy reached a hand up to take the hilt of the knife, Cannon shouted, 'Don't touch it!' They had been so engrossed they had not seen him coming. Startled, now they ran.

Now it was Cannon's turn to stop and stare, shocked by not just what was on the gate but the implication of it being there. He stood before the oval of the father cut from the museum drawing. It was held to the gates by conventional pins, but a knife had been driven into the back. Cannon found himself thinking that if not deflected by the ribs the blade was accurate enough to have penetrated the heart.

If they were to keep things quiet, this needed screening quickly. He did what he could, opened the gate and pushed it right back so that unless a passer-by stepped into the driveway the drawing would not be so easily seen—but if this was on the route to a school more must be done. He went to the house and rang the front doorbell. Toby came quickly. 'Thought it might be you. Had a good—'

Cannon beckoned him urgently outside and to the gate.

As soon as Toby saw the drawing he gasped in horror and disbelief, his hand too going up towards the knife.

'Don't touch anything,' Cannon warned. 'The police…'

'Yes…of course, I…'

'It's already been seen, three schoolboys were eyeballing it when I arrived,' Cannon went on, 'but if we could put something in front of it now, that would help.'

Toby hesitated then said, 'I've got some long canes and fine netting in the garden shed.'

'Better than nothing. Fetch them while I stay here. Where are your night security men?'

Toby looked around, consulted his watch. 'They would have had to pass this so they can't have gone.'

At that moment two men came from the back of the house. Toby and Cannon waited for them to reach the gate and take in the drawing skewered to it. Toby explained where the drawing had come from.

'I heard nothing in the night,' the taller of the two said, 'and I was at the front.'

'It's just what Mr Higham dreaded. The family's been followed 'ere,' the other said in awed tones. '*This* I don't like.'

'Did you work for Mr Higham in Lincolnshire?' Cannon asked, and they both nodded.

'This'll about do the old boy in,' the taller judged.

'We're going to cover it as best we can. Perhaps you could help,' Cannon said as two teenage girls walked along the far side of the street looking curiously over at the group of men.

Cannon took up a kind of casual patrol near the gate while Toby went further into the garden to phone the police. The two men did a fair job of erecting a freestanding screen and offered to stay on until the police arrived to make sure nothing was touched.

It was all accomplished smoothly until Alexander Higham wondered what the activity was in front of the house and came out to see. He walked from the front door, firing questions at them. Toby tried to forestall him but he pushed aside one end of the cane and mesh screen and soon saw for himself. He staggered backwards, turned, walked two or three strides and was violently sick in the shrubbery.

Higham's wife, Trude, who had stood watching from the doorway, now came running to her husband. There was a confusion of questioning and explanations. Cannon and Toby ushered the couple back into the house, leaving the security men to re-erect the screen. Trude took charge of her husband much as if the big man was another of her children. 'Sit down, Alex, I'll get a damp towel so you can wipe your hands and face. You'll feel better.'

'We've made a big mistake coming here. We've brought trouble here with us. We must move on,' Higham said and looked at Cannon as if requesting his support.

'Let's deal with this first,' Cannon said.

'The police are here, sir,' the tall security man popped his head in to say.

'Toby and I will see them outside first,' Cannon said, 'you sit still for a time.'

'I want to talk to them,' Higham said, 'they must know everything.'

'From what DI Betterson told me, they already do,' Toby said. 'You stay here, Father, please.'

Higham was far from happy but Trude arrived back with the towel. He took it perfunctorily, wiped his hands and face, pushed it back into his wife's hands and told her to go to Catherine. 'I don't want her upsetting.'

The two policemen had obviously been briefed about the situation and one stayed outside while the other came in to see Higham.

'So your local trouble-maker,' Toby asked, gesturing him to sit down, 'you are sure it is nothing to do with him?'

'Our local offender has one of the best alibis we have ever known.' The officer answered Toby with the merest suspicion of a grin. 'He's in hospital having his appendix out.'

'Well, that's certainly ruled him out,' Cannon said with a brief laugh.

'I see no reason for amusement,' Higham said and, positively glaring at his son, added, 'I see no reason even for the question. This…person…has obviously followed us from England and is intent on destroying my family.'

The emphasis always on his daughter, or his family, made Cannon reflect that it had been Niall Riley, a father, who had been brutally beaten to death. It seemed the only definite link. He gazed thoughtfully at Higham—fathers of disabled children—devoted, over-protective fathers—not unlike Liz's memory of two boys, the disabled being cosseted but much to the detriment of the other. His eyes switched to Toby, so like his father in looks—did he feel disadvantaged? Did he bear a real grudge against his father?

After a short interview with Higham and much radio contact with his headquarters, the officer told them he and his partner were detailed to stay at the house until a senior officer was available.

After a phone call to the hotel, Liz arrived by taxi. Cannon went with her and Catherine into the conservatory, where he told both of them exactly what had happened.

'So this is…aimed at my father?' Catherine said.

'I think so,' Cannon confirmed quietly.

'Well…' she answered, 'it is…why you are here.'

He nodded.

'And…let's be practical…you came for breakfast, I believe…'

CATHERINE AND HER mother made sure all had breakfast. Afterwards, while any thoughts of outings of any kind were curtailed, Liz and Catherine went to sit in the conservatory and made an effort to compare scrapbooks and ideas. Cannon took the opportunity to talk to Toby, who was alone in the kitchen.

'Tell me,' he said, 'have you or your wife had any kind of trouble since you've been in Oslo?'

'No, never!' Toby exclaimed. 'Quite the opposite.'

'And you must forgive me for asking this but I think it could be relevant.' Cannon pushed the door closed and sat down. 'Have you ever resented your father's overwhelming devotion to your sister?'

'I…' Toby frowned then sat next to Cannon. 'This sounds dreadful but I did at one time because I honestly couldn't see it was necessary. Cathy was Cathy, I love her, have always loved her, as she is.'

'So when exactly was this, this one time?'

'It was, stupidly enough, when I was at university. It was just that when I went home the situation hit me afresh each time. I felt my father was suffocating Cathy. She's so bright, has always wanted to be independent, make her own life. I was hoping this stay with us would enable her to do just that, but this is the worst start there could ever be.'

'So when you were at university did you talk about the situation to anyone?'

Toby pursed his lips then gave a short humph of laughter. 'Yes, I remember coming home and being so fed up with my father's attitude I really messed up work I had to do for one particular tutor. He asked me what was wrong and I told him in no uncertain terms, I'm afraid.'

'What was this man's name?' Cannon asked.

'Unusual name. Professor Heaven.'

Cannon felt as if he had been hit in the chest. 'Heaven,' he repeated. 'Do you have any contact with this professor now?'

'No, no, not since I graduated. I came to Norway soon afterwards,' Toby said, 'never seen him since. Why?'

'It's just that we have an ex-professor who comes in The Trap at home. His name is Bliss.'

'Heaven and Bliss. I suppose that's about as risible as our local suspect having his appendix out,' Toby said.

'Yes,' Cannon agreed, remembering the university porter's laugh when he had inquired after a Professor Bliss.

FIFTEEN

CANNON FOUND THE opportunity to have a concentrated session on his iPhone in the afternoon when Toby and his parents were having a 'heated discussion' in the parlour. Liz and Cathy were sketching a still life, an orange vase next to a rustic basket of pinecones. Not Liz's forte, he thought, but Cathy had set up the exercise in the conservatory and both were totally engrossed.

He walked to the far end of the garden where there was a small copse of silver birch and conifers, brought up the information he wanted, and was soon through once more to the porter's lodge of Toby's old university but not to the same man. This man had a much deeper, gruffer voice, and when he enquired after Professor Heaven the response was totally different: the tone was sympathetic, the manner almost reverential.

'He left the university some years ago, sir,' the porter said, 'very sudden and very tragic it was too.'

'If you are able to tell me any more…' Cannon ventured carefully.

'It was common knowledge, sir, so I see no harm in repeating it. The professor went home mid-term because his younger brother died very suddenly. He attended the funeral then had a terrible car crash on the way back.' His voice fell. 'He never came back to us.'

'So Michael Heaven never taught again?' Cannon now ventured the Christian name. The habit of people who changed their surnames, at the same time keeping the same first name, was well known to the police.

'No, sir, that's right. Terrible head injuries he suffered. In the end the college had to clear his rooms. As I say, he never came back, though as far as I know he did make a recovery of sorts.'

Probably resurrected under a new name, Cannon thought, as he thanked the man and rang off. Then he consulted the contact list he had on his phone and checked the time. It would be roughly an hour earlier at home, so if he rang Bliss Antiques it should be within normal opening times.

He paused before making the call to decide his tactics depending on who answered. He knew he would be relieved if it was the professor, relieved to kick his growing suspicions into touch. He'd always got on well with Bliss, an interesting man to talk to, knowledgeable, an invaluable member of the defunct quiz team.

He pressed the green button and waited. It was quite a few seconds before the sound of the phone ringing out came, and quite a few more before the phone crackled into life and Mavis's announced: 'Bliss Antiques.'

'Hi, Mavis, John Cannon.'

'I thought you were in Norway,' she said.

'I am, but I need to speak to the prof if he's around.'

'Well, he's around, but somewhere in East Anglia is the nearest I can tell you,' Mavis said. 'I've had deliveries from sales in Boston and Lynn.'

'Could you give me his mobile number?' he asked.

'Sure, hold on.' She gave him the nine-figure number, he thanked her, hoped she was coping and said he would pop in to see her in a fortnight when they got back.

'I hear Alamat and his lady friend are coping very well,' she told him. 'They say the place is like a new pin.'

'Oh, right, thanks,' he said and decided he wouldn't tell Liz the second part of that message; she could be very sensitive on such matters.

No time like the present, he thought, and immediately tapped in the new number. It took about the same length of time to begin ringing out but rather longer for the same voice to answer.

'Mavis?' he enquired.

'Yes,' she said, rather wearily, he thought. 'His mobile's here at the back of his desk drawer. Wonder I even heard it.'

'So he's not actually spoken to you since he left?' he asked.

'No, he usually does, but as I said, I've had some of his purchases delivered, and before he said he might go directly to London. If he "achieved his goal" was the way he put it.'

'What did he mean by that, do you know?'

'I took it to mean if he managed to buy the right things he could sell at a good profit in the City; it's one of the things he does quite regularly.'

He thanked her again, rang off, and found himself thinking that a man like the prof would be too canny to make a call that could be traced if he was about some mischief—or murder.

He was putting away his phone and walking back to the house when Toby erupted from the back door and came towards him, his face furious. Behind him he could see Liz and Cathy in the conservatory, looking up, distracted by this sudden violent action in front of their windows.

'It's my father,' Toby said without preamble, 'you'll never guess what he now wants to do. What he thinks is a brilliant idea?'

'No.' Cannon turned back with the younger man towards the trees. He had always found out in the open was a good place for people to talk. 'So what is this idea?'

'He wants to take my mother and Cathy back home at once. He says he will feel safer in an environment he knows, can deal with matters better there. Cathy will be devastated and my mother is for once refusing totally either to tell Cathy, or to go. She says that if trouble is going to follow them it's best to stay put and deal with it here where they have us to support them, the security arranged and the police all alerted. I don't know what we're going to do, and in addition to all that we can't find the dog.' He gave an ironic laugh. 'As they say, it never rains but it pours.'

At that moment Cathy came hurrying to them. 'Auntie Karen says…she can't find… Munch,' she said, adding, 'I let him out into the garden ages ago. Is it my fault? Does he not…be let out?'

'Yes, of course,' Toby reassured her, 'we've made sure the garden is dog-proof, but come on, we'll all look round. We'll find him. Don't worry.'

Cathy became more and more distressed as they looked and called.

Higham vetoed any of them going out into the streets to search.

'That will not include Karen and myself,' Toby stated.

'And I'll go,' Liz said.

'I want to help,' Cathy said.

'You help by staying here with me and your mother, and John,' Higham said equally firmly.

'I was...the last one to see Munch. I...have to go.'

'No!' Higham exclaimed. 'No.'

'You...' his daughter said with as much vehemence as her father, 'try to make me...a prisoner. I *am* going.'

Higham looked as if he had been struck.

'Cathy can come with Karen and me,' Toby said. 'We're hardly going to let anything happen to her.'

'My daughter is under my protection—' Higham began.

'I shall soon be...eighteen...and able to please myself.'

Higham looked as if there were other measures he might resort to, but even as he was reminding her she was not of age yet, Toby said, 'Come on, Cathy, you call his name and I'll whistle. We'll start in the garden just in case he's asleep under a bush.'

Cannon watched Higham's face; from the man's expression there would be repercussions from this mini-rebellion.

There were sadly no results from the search for Munch, though they scoured the neighbourhood. Cathy came back in tears. 'It is punishment for being disrespectful,' she said.

'Nonsense!' Her mother vetoed the idea. 'The dog's probably got himself a lady-friend somewhere.'

'He'll probably come home when he's really hungry,' Toby said. 'Come on, Cathy, no more tears. It will soon be time for Liz and John to go. What have you got arranged for tomorrow?'

Cannon was remembering the last time he had seen someone so distressed over a missing dog—that had been Timmy Riley. Now it was Cathy Higham. And the link? An over-devoted father?

'A punishment for being disrespectful!' Liz repeated Cathy's words as they walked back to their hotel that evening. 'The girl's been over-protected; she knows little of normal life as far as I can see.'

'And does she have the talent her brother thinks she has?'

Liz stopped walking and took a folder from under her arm. 'We've swapped sketchbooks. We're going to give each other a crit about our work.' She opened the book at the last page worked on, the still life set up that day.

'Well, that looks pretty good to me…' he began.

'Yes, but look at the background she's sketched in,' she said.

'Like cloud effects, yes, if those were in, say…' He frowned then added, 'Well, they're kind of more the sort of thing you do in your landscapes.'

'And they'd be spectacular but she's never done landscape. She's been restricted to the art at her special academic-slanted school. They had an art teacher come in, who she said was about a hundred, and they did still life and botanical studies. She copies with amazing skill but she also has imagination like Toby. She needs an outlet.' She fanned through the pages and he saw that every still life had been given a background, each botanical study of leaves, flower and root had the suggestion of a garden behind it.

'I can see what you mean,' he said, 'but we are here to help keep the family safe, not improve Cathy's art.'

'Having seen her work and enthusiasm, I feel it's a mission,' Liz replied. 'My mission if you like. Devotion is all very well in its place, but when it gets out of all proportion it's maudlin, wrong!'

Cannon sighed. 'I'll just be glad when this dog is found,' he said. 'It's getting too familiar: lost dogs; dogs shut in sheds; dogs tied up to garden urns and line-posts.'

'So what are you going to suggest the family do?' she asked.

'As soon as we get to the hotel, I'm going to have a talk to Betterson.'

Once the DI was free to talk, Cannon brought him up to date with events, after which there was a moment's serious silence. When he told him of his suspicions that Bliss and Heaven might be the same professor, there was a longer silence.

'I'll look into it—discreetly, I think,' Betterson said. 'Work forward from the date of the brother's death; we know his name would be Heaven. Only ever come across the surname once before,' the DI added. 'A romantic novelist my mother used to read.'

'There's something else that's bothering me,' Cannon heard himself say, and until that moment he was not sure he had seriously intended to voice this concern; it was more theory than fact.

'Go on,' Betterson said.

'First there was the strange figure drawn on Higham's car in London, then the wound to Ford's chest, the slash across the carpet, and now this. A drawing cut out so cleanly while it was mounted on a board on a wall, not easy to do. I…' He hesitated but he'd gone so far now he told himself he might as well finish. 'Bliss has a large collection of walking sticks in his shop, one I thought seemed heavy for its slender shaft, much heavier that the others. I didn't think of it at the time but now I'm wondering if it could have been a sword-stick. This could be the way a blade was carried undetected around London, Lincolnshire, perhaps even here in Oslo.'

Again there was a silence, then Betterson said, 'But if it was used to cut out the father in the drawing, Bliss would have had to get it through customs, and it could not have been still in the shop when you last went there.'

'No, not the same one,' Cannon agreed, 'but there was another that *was* there, a great heavy beast of a stick, like an Irish shillelagh…'

'Christ!' Betterson breathed. 'You're thinking of Riley?'

'It was distinctive,' Cannon went on, ignoring the query. 'The whole stick was in dark wood, heavy, very polished as if with regular use, a businesslike…'

'Weapon,' Betterson finished for him, 'and you want me to find it and let forensics…'

The line crackled, cut out for a moment then came back, and Cannon added hastily, 'See if you can trace where Bliss is now through these sales Mavis Moyle says he's been to,' Cannon said.

There was another slight pause, as if Betterson was weighing his own position and Cannon's suggestions and value out there at Higham's side. 'OK,' he agreed, 'but you keep me informed of anything new your end, *anything*.'

'Of course,' Cannon said, sensing that now he had a proper 'professional' understanding with the DI. 'We can go forward on that.'

SIXTEEN

HEART-THUMPING ALARM was Mavis Moyle's reaction to the noise that woke her. She sat up and listened. Nothing, but she had certainly not imagined it, or dreamt it. Had it been the sound of glass shattering? She frowned; no, it had been more like something falling, rattling down, and even as she listened the noise came again. She slipped out of bed and went to the front window of her cottage and peered cautiously out.

The moon was behind cloud but the white van parked outside Michael Bliss's shop stood out very clearly. Even as she watched, the large dark shape of a man passed along the side of the van. The back doors were open and he disappeared for a moment. She could hear the sound of objects knocking together as he loaded them into the vehicle. He emerged, retraced a few steps, bent to scoop something up from the pavement he must have dropped, turned, put this into the van, then went back towards the shop.

So the antique shop she was in charge of was being robbed, but why hadn't the alarm gone off? As she reached for her phone, she was racking her brain to make sure she remembered setting the alarm—it was something she did quite automatically. The thought made her stomach turn; surely she *had* gone through the procedure?

She reached for her mobile, pressed 999 and asked

for police, whispering, for the man she had seen could be one of several, a gang.

'The police are on their way,' she was told as soon as she had given the address and circumstances, then she was asked, 'Are you safe?'

'I'm in my bedroom next to the shop,' she told the calm, reassuring woman on the other end of the phone.

'Stay where you are and keep away from the windows,' she was told.

'Damn it,' she breathed, when she had disconnected, 'I should see as much as I can, I owe it to the prof.'

Then she heard an engine starting up, and rushed back to the window in time to see the van moving away. Now she pushed the curtains aside, trying to see the number plate, but all she could make out was that it had an advertisement on its side, bold black letters made into a square with an exclamation mark at the end of the first three words and below a question mark at the end of the second three words.

'Oh! No!' she exclaimed. She knew exactly what it said without being able to see the words. 'Hire a Van! With a Man?' The prof often hired a van liked this, and with a man if he bought large objects. What she had seen being reloaded could have been packing materials—and she'd sent for the police! She went downstairs as fast as she could. She slipped her feet into her outdoor shoes, unlocked the door and stepped outside. A first bird piped that dawn was breaking, and in the distance she heard the siren of a police car. The air was chill, a promise of winter coming. She went back and put an outdoor coat over her pyjamas, and waited.

She soon realized that the police siren she had

thought was hurtling to answer her call was in fact moving away, towards the main road.

Slowly she walked down her garden path to the front gate and noticed there was a light on somewhere in the back of the shop. It *must* be the prof come home specially to receive this early-morning delivery. But why on earth this early? Was he up to something he shouldn't be? She smiled at the thought. She would pull his leg about it and tell him off about his hired man making such a clatter.

She was surprised to find the shop door wide open, pushed right back, but because the light was coming from his office, and convinced it was her employer, she called out, 'Hello! Mr Bliss! It's Mavis.'

Her words hit a blank wall of unresponsive silence, but she called again and walked through the gloom of the shop towards the office. She could see things had been moved, but this often had to be done if something large was delivered.

'Mr Bliss?' she enquired at the office door.

The office was empty but the main switches to the shop were here, and she flicked the whole lot on and walked back into the shop proper—and gasped.

BETTERSON HAD A lot to tell Cannon the following night when he rang. 'Are you sitting comfortably?' he asked.

'Couldn't be more so,' a pyjama-clad Cannon said, lying back on his great square pillow, being handed a glass of wine from the mini-bar by Liz.

'Sorry it's late but I've been waiting on some forensic results.'

'Sounds ominous,' Cannon said. 'What's happened?'

'Bliss's antique shop has been raided.' He told Cannon of the robbery and what Mavis Moyle had seen.

Once more Cannon beckoned Liz to come and listen, switching to speakerphone so they could both hear.

'It was hardly burglary,' Betterson went on. 'Whoever did the job had a key *and* the code to the burglar alarm. The last prints that should have been on those buttons, Mavis's, were all smudged; someone with gloves on had switched the alarm off.

'The shop's been stripped of all the jewellery items, and again these were in locked cabinets, which had been unlocked with the keys. Then…' Betterson paused to draw breath as if to impart the most important piece of news. 'Then, although there were plenty of other more portable objects that could have been taken, the other collection that has gone is the walking sticks you asked me to look at—every last one.'

Cannon sat up and put his drink down. 'The walking sticks,' he repeated.

'Not one left in the shop, and Mavis Moyle said there were a lot, and in several different places.'

'But it wasn't Bliss himself Mavis thought she saw?' he asked.

'No, a big man, she said, and the forensics that have just come have proved her right.'

'How?' Cannon wanted to know.

'Mavis told us Bliss is a regular customer with this van hire company. We've been to see them, and found Bliss had phoned to say he would probably be making internet bids on some items in Boston and Lynn, as there were big house sales in both places. He wanted a careful man with the van, he said, as there were items of Georgian glass and mirrors he hoped to buy. These incidentally were still in the shop but then they had a call saying a van was needed overnight and it would be collected.'

'Was the call from Bliss?'

'The young chap in the office said he thought so, but wasn't certain because the phone was crackly.' Betterson paused before adding, 'But we know now who picked the van up.'

Cannon waited; Liz strained closer to the phone.

'The office chappie said they were quite busy when this big fella came in, and he remembered him standing with one hand up on a small shelf near the door where they keep the phone directories. Forensics got a beautiful set of prints.'

'And?' Cannon said.

'The man who collected the van was our friend Spier. We've issued a warrant for his arrest and—' Betterson was interrupted and quickly ended the call with, 'Have to go, possible sighting of the van. Will be in touch.'

'Spier!' Cannon exclaimed after Betterson had rung off. 'Spier?'

'Who had an argument with Riley on quiz night, and who possibly tied up Ford's dog at his mother's house,' Liz said. 'This alters things.'

'Some things,' Cannon amended, finishing his wine quickly as if to get something out of the way. 'Maurice Spier, who's got plenty of brawn but not too much up top,' Cannon said, 'and who obviously is in England and not here cutting up drawings or kidnapping Toby Higham's dog.'

'But who it seems has keys to Bliss's shop and cabinets, so to have these he must have…what?

'Been given them by Bliss.' Cannon suggested.

'Or attacked and robbed Bliss…or worse. Having done two murders one more can hardly seem to matter,' Liz said.

'But Spier is certainly not the man who has followed Higham from Wales, to London, to Lincolnshire and now to Norway to keep him scared to death.'

Before Liz could answer, Cannon's mobile went again.

'Have they found the van already?' Liz wondered. 'That was quick.'

The call was not Betterson, it was Catherine, in tears.

'What's the matter?' Cannon asked. 'Take your time, talk slowly.'

She tried but it was in a series of rushed and broken phrases that would have made little sense to anyone who did not know the circumstances.

'A friend of Toby's lives…near open ground and…a cemetery…says there's a dog barking…sounds…in… distress. My father says…could be…any dog…says no one is to go and… I…' She sounded so distraught she could hardly breathe and in the background Cannon could hear raised voices, then she gasped, 'But Toby says he is going…now.'

'No,' Cannon said quickly, 'tell Toby to wait, I'll go with him. I'll be there in ten minutes.'

He pulled on joggers and top as he told Liz what had happened.

'Shall I come?' she asked.

'No, I'm ready and off. Stay put. I'll keep you informed.'

For a capital city Oslo, he thought, was quiet at nights, or at least quiet in the streets he ran through.

One or two people leaving restaurants, a late bus and one or two cars, that was all.

One of the security men greeted him at the gate and Toby was waiting for him on the doorstep, clearly not very pleased. Karen was holding Catherine's hand in the background and in the lounge he could hear Trude Higham talking to her husband.

'Let's go,' Toby said and, turning to nod at the two women, closed the door behind himself.

'It's a colleague from the Art Academy who rang me, he says there has been a dog barking continually from the direction of the cemetery. He's never heard a dog in that area before and thought it might just be Munch.'

'Is it far?' Cannon asked as they ran.

'Five minutes,' Toby answered. 'I'm sorry Cathy rang you at this time of night.' As if to underline his words, a church clock chimed out midnight.

'Seems like the ideal time to be in a graveyard,' Cannon said as he saw the outline of a spire, iron gates and a wall at the end of the road.

Toby stopped running, bent over and gave a short, ironic laugh. 'God, my father gets me so uptight,' he said.

'I got on better with my grandfather than my old man,' Cannon said, starting to run slowly on again. 'My grandfather was a policeman; suppose that's why I joined the Met.'

'And left before your time, I understand,' Toby said, catching up with him. 'Why was that?'

'Long story, tell you sometime,' Cannon said. 'In the meantime, how do we get in here? Will it be locked up for the night?'

'Not sure but I know the wall is quite low at the back

around the older part of the burial ground.' He stopped and stood quite still. 'Listen!' he said. 'Hear anything?'

Cannon listened. 'I hear something but it doesn't sound like a dog.'

'It sounds like something in trouble, that's for sure,' Toby said.

'And it is coming from the direction of the grave-yard,' Cannon said, 'and isn't there a park of some kind?'

'Yes,' Toby said, pulling a torch from his pocket and leading the way once more. 'The colleague who rang me lives near the park.'

As they reached the stone wall some distance from the chapel, the low sound came again, strange, thin, like a person keening for a lost soul. 'Glad you insisted on coming,' Toby murmured appreciatively.

Gee, so am I, Cannon thought, as the sound increased dramatically to something between the howl of a wolf and a banshee and the hairs prickled on the back of his neck.

He followed Toby over the wall and as they began to pick their way between the long dead, his ears strained for any sound, any repeat of that awful cry, but the only noises now were those they made moving through the grasses.

'So how do we go about this?' Toby asked, shining his light all around the many old gravestones which made elongated dense shadows, confusing reality with imagination.

'I would say you shout your dog's name as loudly as you can,' Cannon advised, 'or whistle him if that's how you usually call him.'

Toby stood and gave a tootling double-note whistle,

then they stood and listened. He turned and repeated the call in a different direction and again they listened. When he turned so his call went towards the chapel, they was a response. A single bark.

'That's Munch,' Toby said and whistled again. Again the single bark.

'He obviously can't come to you,' Cannon said. 'Come on, shine your torch, let's get off this humpy ground to a path.'

The round pool of light Toby shone at their feet and the outline of the chapel spire just visible against the midnight sky was all they could see. Huge monumental stones and sarcophagi continually blocked their direct passage, but eventually Toby's light fell on the pale gravel of a path.

Toby whistled again, and again the bark *and* a keening whine, but it was much closer, more urgent, anxious. They hurried forward close under the ancient chapel wall, and here they realized were railed-in family vaults going back hundreds of years.

Cannon started as the dog barked again; it was so close. Toby shone the light, and almost beneath their feet they saw there were steps down to a heavily railed crypt, and tied low and tight to the inside of the stout iron bars was a small white shape. The dog had freedom only to stand or sit.

Toby swore and, passing the torch to Cannon, crouched as best he could on cramped steps and tried to free the dog. Talking to Munch all the time, he assured it that the bastard who had done this would suffer, and if only he could unknot the rope Munch's ordeal would be over.

'Let me,' Cannon said, passing the torch back as To-by's anger made him hasty and clumsy.

It was not easy as the dampness of the night had swollen the rope since it had been tied, but bit by bit Cannon pulled the hemp freer, slacker from the thick ironwork. The moment it was done Cannon pushed his hands through the railing and lifted the dog up high enough for Toby to reach over and take him. To rid the dog of the rope, Toby undid its leather collar. Cannon took rope and collar and saw there was a label tied to it. He angled it into the beam of the torch. The writing was smudged with the rain and was in Norwegian.

'*Dod hommer*,' Cannon sounded out. 'What does that mean?' he asked.

Toby repeated the words in little more than a whisper. '*Dod homme*: death comes.'

SEVENTEEN

'BUT THIS IS the same thing over again!' Higham raged. 'Our dogs were tied up to the stone garden urns, then shut in sheds, now your dog is found in a burial vault. Don't you all see whoever this man is, he's here, determined to…to…'

To send you mad, Cannon silently supplied, and at the rate he and you are going he'll succeed.

'We can't stay,' Higham declared, 'we're only endangering my son, his wife, and…' He paused to look at Karen, who had Munch on her lap. 'May I tell Liz and John?'

She nodded and smiled. 'Of course,' she said.

'Our coming grandchild.'

Liz was the first to exclaim and congratulate the parents-to-be. Cannon followed and shook Toby's hand.

'So I intend we leave immediately,' Higham went on.

'For where?' his wife asked.

'For home!' he exclaimed. 'Where else?'

'We came here because you wanted to be away from *home*,' she argued. 'We came to give Catherine a chance to expand her horizons. You've also brought Liz and John here away from their business for two weeks. Now you talk of going home.'

'I refuse to let my family be a sitting target for this maniac,' Higham stated loudly, 'and do you doubt he knows where we are? So! Let's hear someone else's ideas.'

'I want to see more of… Norway,' Catherine said from the doorway, 'and you're shouting, Daddy.'

Higham was at once full of contrition and tried to lead her towards a seat, but she resisted.

'No… I'm…glad you woke me. My idea, my…great wish is that I want to stay…and go with Toby on his bus.'

Had she said she wished to go on a mission to Mars she could not have caused Higham more concern. 'On his bus? On his bus!' he exclaimed. 'For God's sake! So where's he supposed to be going on this bus?'

'All over,' Catherine said expansively, 'and I can go with him. He says so.'

'And while Toby is away I am staying here with Karen,' Trude announced.

'Oh!' Higham now threw up his hands, glared at his son. 'So this has been discussed?'

'My job is taking me, with driver and bus, up to the extreme north next week, to Kirkenes. Then as we drive back south we have a list and will call at the schools and colleges that have requested the touring exhibition. We already have quite a demand, and Cathy would be invaluable to me.'

'Next week?' Higham said. 'I'm not waiting here for a week. I'd like to get away, get Catherine away, tomorrow.'

'Could I make a suggestion?' Liz, who had been listening carefully, said quietly. 'When John agreed to come I understood there might be an opportunity to sketch and paint.'

'That…is what… I want to do,' Cathy put in rather dramatically. 'I want to be an artist.'

There was a slight embarrassed pause before Liz went on. 'So I looked at what Norway has to offer. What it does have is a very stylish ferry service running along the coasts and up many fjords from Bergen northwards.' She smiled and nodded at Toby. 'They say it is the most beautiful coastal voyage in the world. I would love to see part of that, as I am sure Cathy would.'

'Look!' Toby burst in with enthusiasm. 'Liz, John, Cathy and Father could fly to Bergen tomorrow, catch the ferry and meet me in Kirkenes. Then Cathy can transfer to the bus, you two and Father could stay on the ferry for the return trip, and we could all meet up in Bergen before you fly home.'

'Our return tickets are from Bergen,' Higham said, adding doubtfully, 'but not happy about this bus idea. Though the thought of getting away tomorrow would be very good.'

'It would be better than staying here and looking over your shoulder all the time,' Trude Higham urged.

It was in the end agreed but only after it had been decided that Karen and Trude should take Munch and travel to Finland to stay with her parents rather than remain in Oslo. Toby immediately undertook to make all the travel arrangements, and Karen to telephone her parents.

IN THE SETTING sun the quayside at Bergen was an artist's delight. Lined with a long terrace of steeply gabled four-storey wooden buildings, each painted in different shades—white, cream, brown, orange, terracotta—and their ground floors converted into shops and cafes. Even

Higham relaxed enough to wish they had more time there before the Hurtigruten ferry they were booked on arrived.

'Perhaps when we come back,' Cathy said as they arrived at the ferry's terminal and saw their boat, more liner-like than ferry. She turned excitedly to her father, took and held his hand as they boarded and waited in reception to be directed to their cabins.

Cannon's mobile burbled as Liz was exclaiming over the canopied double bed, saying, 'Toby said it was the better-class cabins that were available at short notice.'

'The only ones,' Cannon replied, adding as he looked at his phone, 'It's Betterson.'

There was no preamble from Betterson this time; he spoke briskly as if to a colleague. 'We've ascertained Michael Bliss has a second home. On the coast, posh end of Skegness, a seafront first-floor apartment. We've looked around, made enquiries, got a search warrant.'

'And?' Cannon heard himself prompt the DI.

'Spier's prints are all over the place. I would say he's been living there.'

'Spier?' Questions were multiplying in Cannon's brain. 'Living, or hiding out, in Bliss's flat? He also hired a van in Bliss's name and had the keys to the shop and jewellery cabinets.'

'Yes,' Betterson confirmed, 'but we found one other thing of far more significance, far more incriminating than your suspicions about the professor's name.'

'More damning?' Cannon found he was breathing faster. 'Don't keep me in suspense,' he said.

'In a closet in the bedroom we found the professor's academic gown. One of the forensic boys noticed that there was a thread pulled. They took it away, and the thread you found in Riley's dog's teeth is an absolute match. Under a microscope the torn edges, well, there's no doubt.'

'So was Bliss actually wearing it at the time Riley was battered to death?' Cannon tried to picture the scene. Then he remembered the road accident. The 'great black bird' that had caused the limousine in front of Higham's to crash. Had that been someone wearing, or flourishing, this same black academic gown? 'And why would he do that?' he asked aloud.

'We've a lot still to prove,' Betterson said before delivering his final piece of information, 'but I can tell you it was definitely Bliss who flew from Gatwick to Oslo, we have him on airport CCTV. The Norwegian police have been brought up to date.'

'As you have about what's been happening here, I presume,' Cannon said.

Betterson confirmed this and as the *Nordsol* ferry gave a loud departing blast on its siren, he asked with some curiosity, 'Where are you?'

The explanations given and the call ended, Liz and Cannon went on deck to watch as the ferry, using a combination of side and forward thrusters, moved slowly away from the quayside and made her way along the middle channel out and away from Bergen.

Liz raised her gaze from the crowded properties on the quaysides and streets to the hills beyond, the green pastures, the wooded slopes, the higher peaks where snow shone bright white, golden-edged with dying sun. Cannon watched her affectionately and knew tomorrow would see her sketchbooks out. Meanwhile he leaned on the rail and fell to making a series of mental logic bubbles.

One. Spier goes to Bliss's van hire company and takes away a van. *Two.* Spier clears the shop of walking sticks.

No, he stopped himself, I'm doing this from the wrong man's point of view.

One. Bliss arranges for Spier to pick up the van. *Two.* He gives Spier the shop keys.

No, no, no. He scowled down at the waters swirling past the ship's sides as they picked up speed. No, before that.

One. Bliss takes Ford's dog and ties it up in Spier's mother's garden. *Two.* With Spier thoroughly implicated in both murders, he offers him help in the form of a hidey-hole in his Skegness flat. *Three.* He tells Spier to fetch the hire van, gives him the shop keys, tells him as long as he clears the shop of all walking sticks, he can help himself to whatever he chooses, even gives him the keys to the jewellery display cases. Bliss, he concluded, had now reached the point where he did not care how much it all cost.

Cannon growled quietly to himself. Perhaps Liz's idea of bringing Higham on this ferry might be saving his life. He glanced over to her, then over to the scenery she was watching so avidly. Lights were appearing in houses, and along the roadways near the coast. Some specks of brightness looked incredibly high and inaccessible, as unreachable as Cannon found understanding what was motivating Michael Bliss, this seemingly mild academic.

Cannon had known him best as the most valuable member of the quiz team. A quiet man who, it seemed to Cannon, spoke when spoken to, listened a lot, dropped in the odd sagacious remark. A pleasure to have in the bar.

First he needed to be *sure* whether in fact Michael Bliss was Professor Michael Heaven, Toby's former university tutor. Had something Toby told his tutor about his father triggered some vehement hatred to the point of murder? Perhaps what he needed to know was far more about Professor Heaven's background. Betterson said he was doing this but Cannon itched to be on the spot doing these enquiries himself. He promised himself he would find out—sooner or later he would uncover the truth. He would fully understand.

'Time to go below, I think,' Liz said, but they stood on at the rail, and she asked, 'So what have you concluded?'

He was about to deny even thinking about the case but as she raised her eyebrows at him, he said, 'I need to know all about Toby Higham's relationship with his university tutor, Professor Michael Heaven.'

Rather against his will, he found himself explaining the two names and the porter's laugh. 'But didn't Toby ever meet Professor Bliss when he was visiting his parents?' she asked.

'I got the impression the only person Toby ever got to know was Paul because of his painting,' Cannon said, feeling that he had underestimated Liz when he had expected her to ridicule his idea. 'Toby certainly never came to the pub.'

'No,' Liz agreed.

'I have Betterson looking into the professor's background,' he mused.

'Then isn't that all you can do?' she asked, adding, 'Shall we go in, it's getting chilly.'

Once back in their cabin he sat on the side of their bed wondering whether he should phone Toby, see if there might be more he could tell him. He glanced at his watch. He shook his head; too late for a casual call.

'Why the head shake?' Liz asked as she stood before him, already in that ridiculous nightshirt, embroidered with a baby bear cuddling a toy bear, surrounded by stars and a new moon way up on her shoulder.

'It can wait,' he said. 'I love you.'

'You mean there's nothing you can do until morning,' she said matter-of-factly.

'It can wait,' he repeated, 'and I do love you, more than you'll ever know.'

'And I love you,' she said, going to him, her voice very low with a threat of a tear as she added, 'And I do know.'

Gently the two of them kissed, slowly falling back on to the double bed in their superior cabin.

EIGHTEEN

THE *NORDSOL* MADE two stops in the night, and Cannon was awake for both of them. He slipped from their bed, curious to watch the procedure of docking and loading in the night-time.

The first stop was Måløy, which seemed a sizeable place. He remembered reading that Rolls-Royce Marine had interests there. It was no doubt a busy port in the daytime but not much was happening at half past four in the morning.

The only lights were those mounted high on the sides of the warehouses and reflected on the black waters in glittering, shortening lines as the distance between ship and quay diminished. Three or four men moved about their work, catching ropes thrown from the ship, pulling in the heavy hawsers attached to them, heaving them up and over the mooring bollards.

The ship's huge freight doors were lowered down to the quay. Three cars immediately emerged from the shadows of the buildings and drove aboard. A forklift truck, loaded with a mountain of wooden crates, came from the lighted interior of one of the warehouses and was driven into the ship's cargo hold by a separate ramp.

It was slick, efficient and soon accomplished. The ramps were immediately raised, the mooring ropes released, and the ferry resumed its journey.

Cannon was on deck when they docked at Torvik at

half past seven; this was a much smaller but very picturesque port.

He watched a man walk ashore; he wore a black fleece with 'Crew' in large yellow letters on the back. He went across to the open door of an office and came out carrying a very large black portfolio, which he brought on board. This seemed the only business they had in Torvik that morning. No passengers and no cars or cargo.

He was at the rail for a more definite reason when they docked at Ålesund. He knew from the departure boards at Oslo that there were flights from Oslo to Ålesund. If Bliss had found out where they were, it was in theory possible he could have flown to Ålesund to join the ship there—and continue his reign of terror.

Cannon stayed at the rail until they were ready to sail. He watched a family party saying goodbye to an elderly couple.

'Goodbye!' they called as they walked up the gangway. The two children on the quay were in tears but waving energetically. 'See you at Christmas,' the old man called to them.

'I love you, Gramps!' one of the children shouted back.

Cannon cleared his throat, scowling at a threatened surge of emotion.

He had left Liz and Cathy on deck sketching and Higham installed with his iPad and a novel in the panoramic lounge. He decided before he rejoined them he would explore a bit more of the *Nordsol*.

Cannon started by going to the shop. Here he bought a lanyard to hang his plastic cabin card on. This, he was told, had to be zapped if he left the ship at any point, and when he re-boarded. 'That way we know who has gone ashore and who has come back,' the girl in the shop told him with a friendly smile.

'What happens if someone doesn't come back?' Cannon asked.

'The captain *could* delay his ship for a little time but these ferries run on a very strict timetable; if a passenger misses the ship it is up to him or her to make their way to the next port and re-board there. We take no responsibility for missing passengers.'

Thinking of Higham, Cannon felt this was an unfortunate way of putting things, but knew what she meant.

He made his way next to the cafeteria. This he found was a twenty-four hour service, which provided everything from snacks to hot meals for short-distance travellers going from port to port. He served himself with a coffee and sat sipping it, listening to the comings and goings of passengers.

He took the opportunity to make a phone call to Toby, who said everything was 'very quiet with even the dog gone'.

Then Cannon found himself asking something of Toby he had certainly not planned, but that suddenly made so much sense to him.

'Toby,' he began, 'you know I am here with your father and your sister…'

'Yes, of course…' His voice was suddenly wary, as if aware he was about to be asked to do something he probably would not find easy.

'Could you leave your bus to be loaded by someone else?' Cannon asked.

'Well…' Toby sounded doubtful. 'The museum people have a list of what I wish to take but…what do you want me to do?'

'Fly over and find out all you can about your old professor. You could start with your college porter.'

'Old Weaver,' Toby said automatically.

'I need to know all about Michael Heaven's childhood, his family, his younger brother who died while he was a professor.'

'I don't remember that,' Toby interrupted.

'Perhaps after your time but the porter remembers it vividly,' Cannon said. 'You said you talked to this professor?'

'To be honest, he became almost a soul-mate,' Toby said frankly. 'I talked to him an awful lot. He was always ready to listen.'

'Did you talk to him about anything in particular?'

'I usually found myself having a rant when I'd been home.'

'A rant?'

'As I said, it was just the way my father was. He thought he was being kind, but he was keeping my sister a kind of intellectual cripple when she was certainly *not*!'

'No,' Cannon agreed, 'and that's the reason she is in Norway now, to give her this chance of blossoming, but…'

'But?' Toby questioned. 'There is a but?'

'I believe that the man who disfigured the painting at your museum is the professor calling himself Bliss who keeps an antique shop near my public house. I also think he is the Professor Heaven who you complained to so bitterly about your father.'

There was silence as Toby absorbed this. 'You be-

lieve because of what *I* said, he…' He gave an aston-
ished and disbelieving laugh. 'Surely it makes no sense
or…' And now he sounded distressed. 'I hope it doesn't.'

'From the beginning,' Cannon went on, 'there has
been the involvement of a disabled child, the punishment of the father and the murder of anyone who has
got in the way of this *unstable* man's intentions.'

'Unstable,' Toby repeated. 'So did the road accident
affect his brain? You say Professor Heaven never went
back to tutoring.'

'No,' Cannon confirmed and waited.

'You think I should fly back to the UK?' Toby asked.

'I feel this man is not going to give up, he has sac-
rificed too much, so it's urgent. I believe your father's
life is becoming increasingly at risk.'

'But the police…'

'Yes, DI Betterson is doing his best, being hampered
probably by a press demanding he find Spier, by his
expenses for so much overtime and all the red tape of
police work. The Norwegian police are—well, in Norway…'

'So?'

'I want you to fly back to the UK and find out all you
can about Professor Heaven's background. Did he have
a disabled sibling? When did this car accident happen?
Are any of his family still alive?'

'You really think it is because I complained about
my father that this whole…bloody trail of tricks and…'
Words failed him.

'Yes,' Cannon said sharply, 'I do, and if we find
out the facts of Heaven's background we might at least
begin to understand, if murder is ever understandable.'

'OK. I'll do it,' Toby agreed.

Cannon made private thanks, feeling he had recruited a man who would give his entire time, limited as it was, to this one object.

'I'll see you in Kirkenes,' Toby said, adding, 'I'll do my best.'

'So will I,' Cannon endorsed.

He was to remember his promise when they reached Trondheim, the capital of Norway at one time. This surely would be a far more likely place for Bliss to come aboard. There was a much larger airport, more frequent services, and the *Nordsol* was docked from 8.30 until midday.

They would all have liked to have stretched their legs ashore, seen the cathedral, browsed the shops, but knew the wisdom of staying together on board. Cathy shrugged and said 'another time' as they watched the majority of the cruising passengers leave the ship, while others had obviously reached their final destination. Leaving empty cabins to be filled, Cannon thought.

He stayed on the deck immediately overlooking the loading areas and watched for the whole three-and-a-half hours. He saw new passengers, singly or in little groups, two in wheelchairs, came aboard, but no one resembling Bliss. Once they were underway again, he rejoined the others in the lounge.

Higham put down his iPad. 'So?' he asked. 'Do you still think this was a wise move, this cruise?'

'I think so,' Cannon answered, seeing the pleasure leave Cathy's face as her father once more questioned the wisdom of this journey. 'Comings and goings are strictly monitored.'

'Come on, Cathy, let us go to the dining room, get a table,' Liz suggested. 'The men can follow.'

'It's a bit like being in an old walled city,' Cannon told Higham as he watched them go. 'Well, in a way it should be much safer. When we're at sea *no one* can come and go, and when we dock the gangways and loading ramps are like gates, watched over and controlled.'

After lunch Higham went to the ship's library, a quiet place to work on his laptop. He kept in touch with his son Jacob and a close eye on his businesses. Cannon held the door for one of the wheelchair users who followed them in, a benevolent-looking old boy with a mass of grey hair and beard. He was thanked with a nod of the head and a wave. Cannon always doffed a proverbial cap to the disabled who travelled; this ship was well equipped with ramps and lifts but he still reckoned it took some courage.

When they all re-met in the evening, Higham told Cannon he had received a call from Toby. Cannon waited for some impassioned outburst, but Toby had obviously not revealed his new mission.

'Karen and Trude are safely settled in Finland so I feel happy about that,' Higham said, 'but there seems some change of plans about his bus. He has some other work to do, so he's doing that first, then flying up to Kirkenes and leaving another member of the museum staff to come up with the driver.' Higham drew in a deep breath and exhaled in a mighty sigh. 'He also says the Oslo police department are keeping watch on airports, and he's informed them this maniac, who they obviously now *believe* has followed us from England, may have changed his name again?' Higham looked at Cannon as if for some enlightenment, but none came.

'I'll not be at ease until he's caught, whatever he's calling himself,' Higham added.

THE NEXT MORNING, while passengers were assembling for the crossing-the-line ceremony, Cannon was delighted to receive a text message from Toby in the UK. saying, 'Contacted Weaver. Taking him for lunchtime drink. Be in touch.'

Cannon followed the others to the rear upper deck, feeling that with Higham in his sights, Cathy holding her father's hand and Liz holding on to his arm, in a ridiculous state of excitement, he could really relax a little and enjoy the fun.

He had vague recollections of pictures showing liners crossing the equator and people in bathing costumes being well and truly doused by Father Neptune, not a practice they could follow crossing the Arctic Circle. The laughing crowd on this deck were well muffled in anoraks with fur-lined hoods, scarves and gloves.

He could see a long table had been set up, then there was much speculation and laughter as two of the crew came carrying a large covered pan and the captain himself followed brandishing a large ladle.

There was a keen wind blowing but they gathered from what the captain was announcing that Father Neptune might come aboard any moment and they were all to keep a sharp lookout for him. People looked in all directions. Liz thought he might come up the side on 'one of those hoist things they use to paint ships'. Cannon kept his eyes more or less fixed on a set of steps which came up from a working area just to the right of where the captain was standing. He seemed to be thoroughly enjoying himself holding the ladle in the air, then looking beneath the cloth into the contents of the pan with pretended horror.

Then Cannon nudged Liz and drew her attention

to the steps, up which came Father Neptune complete with crown and trident, long tangled hair and beard, dark green robes well draped in seaweed, with water dripping from his green gloves.

'Didn't know you could get green Marigolds,' Cannon said, near enough to both the captain and Neptune for them to hear him.

Now the captain invited all who had never crossed the line of the Arctic Circle before to come forward and 'be properly initiated'—with this he revealed the contents of the pan. Piles of ice cubes. 'There is a reward for all who come,' he promised and indicated trays of glasses with good measures of spirits ready poured being brought to the table. 'And we have one brave gentleman here—' he waved Cannon forward '—who can't wait to be first.'

Liz urged him forward and the captain invited him to kneel before the table. Cannon knelt, felt his collar pulled away from the back of his neck and a large ladle of ice cubes went down his back, followed quickly by another.

'We always give our first initiate special treatment,' the captain informed him.

The crowd roared with laughter as Cannon shuddered and urged Liz to scoop some of the ice out.

The captain beckoned Cathy forward. 'We are very lenient with lovely young ladies,' he said and as she went forward she received just one ladleful, but still squealed and shuddered. The laughing crowd pressed forward to see the fun, some urging others on while others definitely stood their ground or moved to safety. Neptune was being photographed by and with all and sundry. Cannon saw Liz taking pictures of Higham and Cathy on either side of the man from the deep, Higham actually laughing and Cathy proclaiming that this and to go to see the husky puppies in Kirkenes— 'photograph them…then sketch them…'—were the things she wanted to do most.

Cannon realized he had never actually seen Higham laugh properly before and he hoped it would not be the last time. He also thought Neptune's costume might have been 'tailored' for a bigger man but everyone was in such good humour nothing mattered. Hunching his shoulders, he felt that his remaining dose of ice had melted and soaked well down to his underpants. He did wonder if the captain was not enjoying putting ice down his passengers' backs a little too much!

Then slightly to his surprise he saw Cathy urging her father towards the table, and though Higham was protesting, he was laughing, shaking his head but still allowing himself to be taken to the table. Relaxed and happy, Cannon saw how very much alike father and son were. He must do all in his power to help the whole family. The torment had gone on long enough.

The last of the stragglers were being urged forward and for a moment Cannon lost sight of Cathy and her father. A movement near the steps caught his eye again and he saw Father Neptune was leaving the scene; one or two had also noticed he was departing and gave him a cheer. In return he waved his trident before disappearing.

Then Cannon saw Higham, instead of rising from the kneeling position, had fallen sideways and was supporting himself on one hand. Cannon, heedless of those in between, was by his side in seconds, kneeling by him, as was one of the crew members ordered rapidly in by the captain from the far side of the long table.

'No, no,' Higham protested, 'I think someone bumped into me. I lost my balance.'

Cannon had his hand on his shoulder, then as Higham rose patted him on the back in reassurance, only to find a paper under his hand, a kind of post-it stuck to Higham's back.

'What was *that*?' a woman asked.

Cannon glanced at it, shook his head, then pushed it into his pocket.

'What happened, sir?' the captain was now hurrying to enquire.

'Well, your Father Neptune was nearby, I know. I think he touched my shoulder. I looked up at him and sort of toppled over,' he said apologetically, but then as he stood straight felt the ice run down his back and shuddered.

The captain picked up two glasses, tipped one measure of spirits into the other and handed the double measure to Higham. 'Your health,' he proposed.

Higham tipped the glass back and choked. 'Fugh!' he exclaimed. 'Ice outside, fire inside.'

Like the rest of the ceremony, all was good humour again. Liz came to Cannon's side and whispered, 'What's happened? What did you take off Higham's back?'

'Later,' he said.

Higham insisted they all had what was termed 'drink of the day', a different cocktail of amazing colours the bar mixed every day. The drinks that day were a brilliant green, and were consumed among a guessing game as to what was in them. Then Higham and Cathy both decided they must go back to their cabins to change various items of clothing.

'So?' Liz questioned as the other two left the lounge.

Cannon put his hand into his pocket and pulled out a yellow post-it; on it were written the same words as had been tied to Munch in the vault. *Dod homme.*

Neither of them translated the words aloud.

NINETEEN

'THE ONLY PERSON who was near enough to put a note on Higham's back was Neptune—Father Neptune—and—' he broke off and was on his feet.

'John?'

He indicated one of the stewards who had just come into the lounge, a man who had helped serve the trays of drinks on deck at the ceremony.

'I wonder if you'd mind me asking you something,' Cannon said as the man busied himself restacking glasses behind his bar.

'Ask away.' He was a short, sturdy, middle-aged man and reminded Cannon of their laconic postman back home: steady, reliable, not given to idle chatter.

'Who plays the part of King Neptune?'

He gave a short laugh as the question surprised him, then said, 'Oh! Henrick, he enjoys coming up from below.'

'Below?' Cannon queried.

'Yes, he's second engineer. He comes from the engine room, on to the rope deck, then up the steps to surprise you all.'

'So have you seen Henrick since this morning's ceremony?'

The steward shook his head. 'But then I wouldn't,' he said.

'Could you contact him for me?' Cannon asked.

The man shook his head. 'The captain *really* is the only one directly in contact with his engine room. You'd have to go to the bridge and have a word up there.'

'Thanks.' Cannon nodded acknowledgement. 'I'll do that.'

The steward cleared his throat. 'I wouldn't unless...'

'It's a matter of life and death,' Cannon suggested but turned away immediately, his hand going to his pocket for his mobile. Before he was back by Liz's side, he was through to Toby.

'There's been a small, significant incident which I'll ring you about more fully later,' Cannon said, 'but right now I need the name of the most senior police officer in Oslo who knows all about your father—'

'My father?' Toby interrupted. 'Is he...?'

'He's fine. In fact at the moment he knows nothing about the incident,' Cannon told him.

'This "significant" incident?' Toby questioned.

'Just give me a name, Toby, I'll ring you again later.'

The name—two names—were finally given and written down. Cannon rang off, then turned to Liz. 'I'm going to see Captain Anders but I want you to go to Cathy's cabin, find some excuse for you both to go to her father, and all stay together until I come.'

'What shall I tell Higham?' she asked.

'Nothing, but perhaps you should tell Cathy what's happened. She's a sensible lass and she'd be more help to you if she knows,' he decided.

Cannon had a good idea where the approach to the bridge was; he had seen specially privileged passengers who had been invited to the bridge queuing in a corridor. He made his way there. The only notices he could see were Prohibited Area and Crew Only. He knocked at the first and got no answer, the second and it was jerked open so quickly it made him jump. A senior and unsmiling officer confronted him.

'I would like to speak to your captain,' Cannon said, 'about the safety of his second engineer.'

The senior and distinguished-looking officer, who was obviously far older than the captain he had seen dispensing ice cubes down the backs of his passengers, looked him up and down and asked, 'And you are?'

'My name's John Cannon, former London Metropolitan detective inspector, aboard as extra security to other passengers.'

'Passengers on this ship?' the officer questioned, 'needing extra security?'

It was obviously a completely unheard-of occurrence. Though the man only used his finger as an indicator, Cannon felt metaphorically hoisted by his collar to stand just inside the bridge door. 'Wait there,' he was told, 'don't move.'

Several other officers in white shirts, black ties and trousers turned to look at him as the first officer went to his captain, who was standing in front of a bank of television scenes. He was at the elbow of a man watching a screen with a red line, which Cannon presumed showed their course through a particularly complicated group of islands and coastline. What was interesting was that the height and depth of the mountains both above and below sea level were shown. The valleys looked as deep, or deeper, under the sea as the peaks rose above.

Captain Bernt Anders listened, then turned to look at Cannon, who thought the young impish face of the man with the ladle had been replaced by a sterner disciplinarian who ran a tight ship. He spoke to the senior officer, indicated one or two things on screens then came towards Cannon.

'I am concerned about the safety of your second engineer,' Cannon told him

'Step outside,' he said. 'I don't want my officers distracted.'

Once outside the door in the deserted corridor, the captain stopped. 'You mentioned my second engineer,' he said.

'He played the part of Father Neptune, I understand.'

'He always does,' the captain replied.

Cannon handed him the post-it he had preserved in a small plastic bag. The two words were read and the bag returned to Cannon with a slow, questioning look.

'Father Neptune was the only one near enough to have put this on my employer's back.'

'Your employer being the man who fell sideways at the ceremony?' Captain Anders asked.

Cannon nodded then gave him the piece of paper with the two names of the Oslo police officers. 'You can verify what I need to tell you by speaking to one of these men.'

'Why are you concerned about my engineer?'

'Why would your engineer wish to stick a frightener on the back of a passenger he does not know?' Cannon said. 'My fear is that your engineer was not the man in the green gloves and Neptune seaweed.'

'Come back to the bridge,' the captain said, cutting off Cannon's supposition that his engineer might have been persuaded to allow someone else to play his part.

On the bridge the captain spoke directly down to his engine room. 'Henrick, is he on duty?'

'He should have been ten minutes ago,' a tetchy voice replied. 'Just sent a man to his quarters.'

'I need to speak to him urgently,' the captain said.

'Aye, aye, Captain,' the chief engineer answered, 'and I'll be speaking to him myself.'

Cannon made as if to leave, but the captain indicated a seat near one of the computer screens. 'You can wait here,' he said and Cannon made a fair guess that he was just taking precautions in case Cannon was any kind of crackpot. He was not risking a possible lunatic wandering around his ship creating havoc.

Minutes later the answer came that Henrick was not in his cabin, and that no one had seen him since he had gone to get into his Neptune outfit.

'Set up a discreet search for the man,' the captain ordered, taking out the paper on which Cannon had written the name of the Oslo police officers. 'I need to do this in my cabin,' he said to Cannon. He summoned his second-in-command, the officer who had admitted Cannon on to the bridge. 'Look after Mr Cannon here, tell him a bit of how we operate this ship. I'm sure he'd be interested.'

Cannon had learned quite a lot about the screens all around the huge forward-looking windows of the bridge, how they showed not just the outside of the ship but the holds, how the temperature of each hold could be read. He felt there was not much left to chance when it came to the security and safety of the ship. He realized that the man actually steering the ship sat in a very comfortable-looking chair with a lever the size of one used to propel a wheelchair. He was questioning this when the captain came back.

'Mr Cannon,' he began with a more serious but understanding manner, 'I think you should join your passengers wherever they are, and stay with them until we find our second engineer. In the meantime I am having our passenger list checked. There are quite a few people who have cruised with us before, plus a few Norwegians who are well known to us, so if there is anyone aboard for the sole purpose of harassing Mr Alexander Higham that will narrow the field a little.'

'Pleased you've spoken to the police,' Cannon said, 'I didn't want you to think I was another headcase.'

'Well…' Captain Anders sidled his head a little, shrugged, and for a second Cannon saw again the man who enjoyed a joke, relished putting ice down his passengers' backs, but the disciplinarian quickly replaced him.

'It's been suggested that your party, which I understand includes your partner and Mr Higham's daughter, relocate: your partner moving in with the daughter, and you moving in with Mr Higham. We have adjoining cabins on another deck and—' he paused '—we shall have a police presence on the ship as soon as possible. This is likely to be at Tromsø when we dock there tomorrow afternoon. That will leave a day and a half before we reach Kirkenes, where I am told you may now all be disembarking.'

Cannon opened his mouth to say this was not what they had intended, but thought that could wait. There was another question he wanted to ask. 'Have you found the Neptune outfit?' he asked.

Captain Anders shook his head.

'Where that's found might give an idea who actually wore it,' Cannon suggested, 'and there'd be DNA on it.'.

'I am hoping I will find my second engineer and be

told that,' Anders said, adding, tight-lipped, 'Though the police are scrambling helicopters from Oslo in case my man has gone overboard.'

Cannon saw from his face that he thought there would be little hope of a happy outcome if that had happened.

'The whole ship will be thoroughly searched?' Cannon asked tentatively

'It will take a time,' Anders said. 'A ship has many odd corners and angles. At this point I do *not* want to alarm all my passengers but you can be reassured that the last members of the crew are at this moment being informed of the serious situation. The cabin staff have already been detailed what to look out for and to report *anything* out of the ordinary in any of the cabins or elsewhere.'

Cannon itched to be part of the search but he did not know the ship. His job was to be with Higham, and he soon found himself escorted to a cabin on a deck below their superior suites. These were smaller but well appointed, no problem to share with an amicable partner, but Higham might be a different matter.

The post-it preserved in its plastic envelope had made him completely paranoid. He vowed he would not leave the new cabin until they docked at Kirkenes and he had full police protection.

Cannon found himself calculating just how many hours that would be. Perhaps if the police came aboard at Tromsø it was possible they might take Higham into protective custody from there.

One could only hope, he thought, as he watched Higham sighing and throwing himself in and out of chairs and on to the bed.

It was, Cannon thought, going to be hard work for them all before they reached Kirkenes.

THE HOURS WENT slowly by, with all meals brought to the cabins. The *Nordsol* made four brief stops during the night. Each time Cannon was at their window to watch. He saw men in the black 'Crew' fleeces run in and out of lighted offices with packages, a forklift truck brought goods on board at the first stop, but nothing else. No one left the ship and did not return, and no one extra came aboard.

By early morning he began to feel like a caged animal and turned restlessly on the bed. He longed to be running on the beaches of Lincolnshire, to feel the keen east wind taking his breath, even for the rain to be pouring down—anything but this air-conditioned enclosed cabin.

Higham, who he had thought was asleep, suddenly said, 'You're not thinking of going anywhere?'

'No, of course not,' he answered, thinking perhaps it was from Alexander Higham his children inherited their artistic nature, naturally intuitive as to what was right, what was going on in other people's minds.

'Do you think Cathy and Liz are all right? I wonder if they've slept.'

'They'll be fine,' Cannon was saying as their door was given two short, sharp, authoritative taps.

Cannon gestured for Higham to stay where he was as he went to the door. It was the older officer, the second-in-command.

Cannon opened the door and invited him inside.

'Captain Anders requests your presence on the

bridge,' he said to Cannon, adding with some anxiety, '*Now*, sir, if you would.'

'This early!' Higham exclaimed. 'It's not light! Has something else happened?'

'It's all related to the first incident,' the officer replied carefully, 'and Captain Anders has asked me to stay outside the cabins until Mr Cannon returns.'

Cannon pulled on a tracksuit, went into the wash cubicle, made sure he had a pair of plastic gloves in his pocket and left the second officer to his new task.

So I'm having a run after all, he thought, as he made as much speed as he could up the rather grand curving staircases and along the corridors to the bridge.

He had no doubt whatsoever that there had been some significant incident, or find, for him to be sent for well before six in the morning.

Captain Anders, in dripping raincoat, stood waiting for him at the far end of the bridge. He came forward, running his hands distractedly through his hair. He was obviously a man with much on his mind, much to deal with.

There was no preamble. 'I've made a thorough check on your background,' he said. 'In fact, the Oslo police department have spoken to one Detective Superintendent Robert Austin who cannot speak highly enough of you—'

'*Superintendent*,' Cannon interrupted, a smile coming to his lips as the name of his former sergeant in the Met was mentioned. 'He's been promoted again. Chief inspector the last I heard.'

The captain ignored the interruption. 'So I would like you to come and take charge of a crime scene, until our police can come aboard at Tromsø.'

'A crime scene?' Cannon questioned, dread filling his heart once more. Surely not another innocent by-stander in this affair?

'You'll see soon enough,' he said as he unhooked another raincoat and gave it to Cannon. 'You'll need that,' he added. 'I'll tell you as we go.' He led the way off the bridge down an open set of steps towards the bow of the ship which had been lit up by a spotlight from the bridge.

'We've found the Neptune outfit,' he said grimly, 'and my second engineer.' He broke off as they reached the exposed area where the winches were housed, and ropes coiled ready for use in the many ports these ferry-boats called at on their strictly timed, fast-route service.

This deck, like everything Cannon had seen aboard, was tidy, orderly. It was also wet, cold and slippery, for though it was not raining at that moment the wind was whipping the sea spray up from a choppy sea, well dous-ing them every few seconds. The motion right at the bow of the ship was much more noticeable and Cannon had to hang on several times to keep his feet.

The captain led him to where there was a locker. Two crew members moved away along the rail as they approached.

'This is not pretty,' the captain warned as he put his hand to the lid.

'It never is,' Cannon muttered to himself, though all he could see when the lid was raised was rope, roughly thrown in unlike all those on deck, so meticulously coiled.

Cannon caught the smell first, that strange, almost dry, butchery smell of a lot of blood. Peering closer, he could see where it had soaked into and congealed on the lengths of rope that had fallen to the bottom of the locker, but he could see nothing more.

'You have to…' Anders reached in to lift the rope, but Cannon caught his arm.

'No,' he ordered, 'let me.'

'The men have already shown me,' Anders shouted above a sudden great gust of wind and spray.

'Even so,' Cannon shouted back, pulling out the gloves. Anders caught his arm to steady him as an extra dip of the bow brought a wave in and over as high as the bridge windows above them, soaking them, and the open locker.

'Get your men to hold the top, keep out as much water as we can,' Cannon shouted as he bent down and into what he quickly realized was virtually the second engineer's coffin.

Under the rope he lifted very carefully, he could see the wig, the trident, the green robe with seaweed stitched to it, and under that the drained, white face of a man loomed as if he was in truth underwater, but he would never come up from the deep any more, that was for sure. A deep, deep gash gaped right across the front of the throat.

'Look out! Hold tight!' one of the men trying to hold the locker lid warned.

'The weather's worsening!' Anders shouted. 'What do we do?'

'Secure the locker,' Cannon said. 'Put a tarpaulin over it, lash it down as tight as you can.'

The men lifted their hands, acknowledging the task.

'And…' Cannon waved his hand to secure their attention and made a zipping motion across his mouth as the wind roared with ever greater force.

They nodded but both looked to the captain. At the top of the steps back on to the bridge, Anders paused. 'All on the bridge know already, and the chief engineer,' he said.

'How long before we make our next stop?' Cannon asked.

Anders looked at the islands they were passing between. 'About forty-five minutes,' he said.

'And we're there for?'

'Arrive at 0600 hours, leave at 08.45,' Anders said, adding, 'No one usually goes ashore, we just pick up and offload a small amount of freight.'

'Could your man stay with Higham?' Cannon asked. 'I need to be out and about, keeping an eye, and we need to talk to Oslo right away.'

TWENTY

CATHY'S FIRST THOUGHTS were for her father when Cannon went to her cabin with the news.

'I must…go to him,' she said, and when Liz offered to go with her shook her head. 'You stay here with John.'

'I'd like to speak to Oslo,' Cannon said when she had gone.

'I'll get us some coffee,' Liz said, picking up the two thermos mugs, purchased on board for the purpose of fetching hot drinks whenever they wanted them from the cafeteria.

Liz paused momentarily outside the next cabin door. She could hear Cathy's voice raised, sounding more like the parent calming a child than daughter trying to reassure a father.

By the time she had climbed the flight of stairs to the cafeteria deck, she was aware that some order must have been overheard, or some careless words spoken. There were so many more people around than usual at this time, people talking to each other in concerned little groups, some making their way towards the forward panoramic lounge, from which she guessed they might have a view of the bow and the locker John said had been battened down.

There was also a small queue around the coffee and tea bar, as folk picked out their favourite tea bags or coffee sachets. She waited behind a grey-haired old man in a wheelchair who was in turn behind a woman: the phrase 'mutton dressed as lamb' came immediately to Liz's mind. It was a saying Alamat had learned and occasionally brought out at inconvenient moments—but it certainly applied here. The woman's bleached hair was tied up in a vivid yellow and red scarf, and she wore an expensive tracksuit which would have looked good on someone thirty years younger and half the bodyweight. Liz had encountered her before, regaling those on surrounding loungers with tales of her *very* many cruises. Now she did have a captive audience, for unless the man ran at her with his wheelchair he could not turn away.

'Something's happened, you know, something serious. I'm going to take my coffee up to the bow and keep watch,' she said. 'My hubby says they have tied up one of the big locker things there *and* earlier on they had a spotlight on it from the bridge, a special light,' she added triumphantly.

Liz lifted her eyebrows at the excitement in the woman's voice.

'Now let me get yours,' she said and before the man could prevent her she had taken his mug and was waving a hand over the selection of packeted drinks. 'Which do you prefer?'

'I prefer, madam, to get it for myself,' he said and, holding out his hand, demanded, 'My mug, please.'

'Oh! But…' she began.

Liz, aware of others becoming impatient behind her, now stepped forward and picked up the woman's mug. 'There is a coffee here, who does that belong to?'

'That's mine,' she said and took it from Liz.

'Ah good, so if you would now step aside we can all get our drinks.'

'Thank you,' the man in the wheelchair said, and took his empty mug from the woman's hand, threw an Earl Grey teabag into it, took three milks and pressed the boiling-water button, repeating 'Thank you,' then as he turned away, his mug balanced between his knees, he added, 'Again.'

'You must have helped him before?' The next man in the queue, a fit-looking, handsome pensioner, said.

'Not to my knowledge,' Liz said, putting the lid on her mug.

'I was talking to him the other day, comes on these holidays on his own. Takes some pluck, and,' he added conspiratorially, 'I've also learned to keep well out of earshot of our champion cruiser.'

Liz laughed.

'And by the way, I've heard the fuss is all about a stowaway.'

'Really?' she said.

'SO MUCH FOR keeping things quiet,' Cannon said as Liz related the incident. 'I'm trying Toby again. I've already spoken to the Oslo inspector, who treated me with the utmost courtesy, by the way, and as I thought, the stop after Harstad…'

'Tromsø,' Liz supplied, 'two o'clock this afternoon.'

He nodded. 'There's an airport and full facilities for dealing with a body and forensics, and they have arranged for a senior man to come aboard at Harstad, and we are to liaise with them.'

'We?'

'Yes, I told the Oslo chappie that you were my invaluable partner in the Met, and he's obviously old-fashioned because he then went on to refer to you as my wife.'

'Old-fashioned!' she exclaimed, pushing his coffee at him. 'So you are not proposing?'

'Hardly seems the time,' he was saying, when a tired-sounding voice at the other end of the phone repeated, 'Hello, hello.'

'Toby?' he questioned.

'John? Why this hour?'

Cannon told him all that had happened aboard the *Nordsol*. 'Tell me as quickly as you can what you've found out. I need to be on watch when we dock.'

'Certainly the facts of the car accident are true, and Professor Heaven did sustain massive head injuries. They did not think he would survive. I wish I had known, I would certainly have sought him out.'

Liz had moved to the window as the *Nordsol* sounded its horn.

'I've visited the hospital where he was taken and met a ward sister who remembered him because he had no visitors all the time he was with them, and that was several months. She also remembered talking to him before he left about having a wig to hide his head scars.' Toby paused. 'I'm not sure there's much else I can find out in the time I've left. I have a flight back tomorrow. I must be in Kirkenes when my colleagues arrive. There just seems no trace of the professor once he left hospital.'

Cannon shook his head as the call ended. 'I'm certain Bliss and Heaven are the same man.'

''Bliss, Heaven, Evan, Evans,' Liz mused with a sigh.

'What's that mean?' he asked sharply.

'Nothing, wasn't thinking really,' she said, 'just came into my head.'

'Nothing just comes into your head,' he said, 'something triggers it, something always triggers everything.'

'You could be right,' she said. 'It's thinking of fathers and sons, Toby and Higham. I suddenly remembered that Evan or Evans was the name of the family I lived near as a child. The mother and father who had a disabled son and a clever son.'

'Who pushed his swimming cups behind a door instead of taking them home?'

'Yes, that's right,' she said as they gathered up coats, hats, scarves ready to go on deck. 'That family never got their relationships right.'

Cannon had the sensation of a light flickering on his brain. A tiny, bright, intutive flash, like the lights of those improbable-seeming houses they had glimpsed high on the mountain slopes their first night afloat. It felt like a preposterous solution had fallen into his lap. He sat down suddenly on the edge of the bed and gazed at Liz. Surely, surely, he thought, it could not be?

'What is it?' Liz asked. 'Are you all right?'

He opened his mouth but at that moment the side-thrusters of the *Nordsol*'s engines announced docking procedure was underway.

'Come with me,' he ordered and led the way at a sprint towards the bridge and Anders. 'I know from the passenger list there is no Heaven or Bliss aboard, but Evan, or Evans....'

'Wait a minute,' Liz said as the idea that had flitted into John's mind now slipped into hers. She shook her head and began to move again, for the idea had stopped her in her tracks.

Captain Anders handed over the docking procedure to his second-in-command, nodded to Liz, looked questioningly at Cannon and listened.

'We have no passengers due to disembark at Harstad but Tromsø—' he shook his head '—is always busy and most passengers will want to go ashore.'

'At Tromsø there will be a well organized police presence,' Cannon said.

'Yes,' Anders agreed, 'and I'll have them aboard before *anyone* is allowed off.'

Cannon nodded agreement.

'So now we'll have a look at the passenger list again.' He turned away to a computer at the side of the bridge complex, woke the screen and in seconds had first an alphabetical list of crew, then passengers.

This gave details of a party consisting of one Owen Evans, Pamela Evans and James Evans, aged ten years, a Michael Evans, and a Michael Evan.

'Two Michaels,' Cannon said, 'concentrate on them.'

The screen now switched to showing a graphic of the outside of the ship with the decks marked in different colours. The cursor moved down to click on number five, and now they saw the layout of that deck with all the cabins numbered.

'Both on this deck,' Captain Anders said. 'Cabin 546 is a mini suite, right next to the lifts. This is a cabin we often use for anyone needing a wheelchair.' He touched another button. 'In fact, Mr Michael Evan is a wheelchair user.' He switched back to the previous graphic. 'The other cabin is 555, port side further back. Shall we take that first?'

Cannon nodded.

The three of them used the lift to go down two decks,

turned left out of the lift, left again and down the corridor until they came to 555. The captain knocked, twice. The second time a voice called, 'Coming.'

A tall, grey-haired man opened the door; his eyes widened when he saw the captain. 'Are we sinking?' he asked.

'No, sir, you are quite safe,' Anders assured him and directed his gaze out of the cabin window to the quayside of Harstad where they were moored.

Cannon in the meantime gave Anders a very definite shake of the head. This was not their man.

'Ah! I was sound asleep.' The pyjamaed passenger stepped back a little, apologizing, then said, 'But there must be something wrong.'

'We are urgently looking for someone by the name of Michael Evans, but you are clearly not our man. I am sorry we disturbed you.'

'Are you sure?' He spread his arms, appealing for reassurance. 'My wife? My daughter? There's not a message for me from home?'

'No, sir, we just have the wrong Mr Evans. The man we need is known to this gentleman.' He indicated Cannon.

'That's correct, Mr Evans, and it is not you. You relax and have a good trip,' Cannon said, beginning to move away.

'I've come to see the sea eagles,' the man said as he stepped back into his cabin.

'It's a very good outing, Mr Evans,' the captain replied, murmuring when they were out of earshot that he must invite his disturbed passenger on a courtesy visit to the bridge when things returned to normal.

They moved quickly now to the mini-suite but as

they neared the lifts a crew member came to report to the captain that they were ready to lower the freight ramp.

'They are to wait until I'm in the hold to give the order personally,' he said. 'I'll be there shortly.' When the crewman had hurried away, he knocked at cabin 546 but there was no reply.

'Once more, I think,' the captain decided.

'Let me,' Liz said, and taking the initiative, knocked again, leaning close to the door and shouting 'room service' loudly.

Still no response. 'So I think in the circumstances…' the captain said, taking a master card from his pocket, using it in the key-slot and leading them inside.

THE FIRST THING they saw was a wheelchair folded and pushed up by the side of the bed. They paused and both looked towards the shower unit. Anders strode forward and pushed open the door: it was empty.

Liz moved to the far side of the bed, looked down and gasped.

'What is it?' Cannon asked.

Liz bent and picked up a dark grey wig and beard. 'Mr Evan, I presume,' she said, 'who does not need a wheelchair to get about…and who I stood behind in the queue for coffee this morning, and who…'

'Who?' Cannon questioned the pause quickly, sharply.

'Who,' she said, 'is Bliss, and is now Evan…again.' She repeated the word the man in the wheelchair had used to thank her: 'again'.

'And who is now presumably out and about in some other disguise,' Anders said grimly, 'but no passenger is getting off my ship, and he's going to have to eat and go to bed somewhere. Surely we must have him! He's trapped on board. Come on, our police officer needs to know all this as soon as he boards.'

They followed him through a door marked 'Crew Only' into an unpretentious lift and down to the enormous freight-hold. This had an echoing, metallic feel and the smell of welding seemed still to linger. There were several men standing around, all wearing the black fleeces marked 'Crew' in bold yellow letters on the back. One man, with a fistful of papers, detached himself from the group when he saw the captain.

'Sir,' he said, 'we have four extra crates coming aboard for Kirkenes, a delayed shipment the previous ferry should have taken.'

'Right, and I have a police officer coming aboard,' Anders said, looking around. 'You're sure you have no one down here who is not authorized?'

He shook his head, but looked over to Cannon and Liz.

'No, these two are assisting me and the police; they know the man we are looking for.'

'The man who…' the man stopped, 'our second engineer?'

The captain nodded, then ordered, 'Carry on.'

The man moved off to give the order for the freight ramp to be lowered. It was quite a strange experience, for it seemed as if an enormous slice of the side of the ship was giving way, falling slowly, letting in the bright reflected light of day and snow. Above the dockside buildings they could see where fences had been built across the hills to prevent the weight of heavy snowfalls coming down on the town. These hills were sparsely covered with broken snow as yet, but on the higher reaches lay thick blankets of unbroken white.

Cannon moved forward, walked on to the ship end of the ramp, but he was waved away as a forklift truck began to move from inside a building and along the quayside with a long unwieldy crate protruding a metre and a half, or more, either side of the forklift.

A second truck followed with a similar load, both trundling slowly towards the ramp—and behind this walked a man with a small medical-looking case. He was certainly not young. Cannon thought he looked more like an office man than an active police officer, or he might even be the local doctor? He kept a very sensible distance behind the vehicles.

Some of the crew were detailed to steady the ends of the loads as the ascent up the ramp and into the hold began.

As these first two crates reached the interior, the man with the case made his way towards the captain, but Cannon moved around him, wanted to be where he could see all. There was too much activity and too many men moving about for his peace of mind. Nothing like a melee of vehicles, and men, for a suspect to disappear, and this murderer desperately needed to get off the ship.

He watched as the crew were forced to both guide and steady the second lot of unwieldy loads. 'No wonder they were left behind,' he heard one man grumble. 'I'd leave the bloody things given half a chance.'

Even so, Cannon thought they managed very well. Then just as he was about to relax, when the trucks were both back on the quayside, the crew all back in the hold, and the ramp being raised, Cannon saw a man in a black fleece with the hood up pressed up against a warehouse wall. The man half-turned to take a fleeting backward look towards the *Nordsol* before moving rapidly away and revealing the large yellow *lie*—'Crew'— on his back.

'Stop!' Cannon bellowed. Many faces turned his way but nothing, and no one, stopped. The ramp end was well clear of the quay. He saw its angle was rapidly steepening.

'Bliss is on the quay!' he shouted as he ran up the increasing slope, scrabbled, scrambled. He heard shouts of alarm at his back. Eat your heart out, James Bond, he thought, as he hurled himself in a sideways leap between the narrowing 'V' between ship's side and the ramp.

Many things crowded the moment and his mind—the sight of Liz's horrified face, approval from his policeman grandfather, hearty Cockney blaspheming from his father—and as his raised arm scraped metal going the opposite way the horror that he might not make it before the freight door hermetically resealed itself back to the side of the ship.

TWENTY-ONE

CANNON LANDED IN a crashing heap, fighting to suck air into lungs that had lost capacity. He rolled over on to his knees, fighting for the breath of life, strength to get up, at the same time trying to see where Bliss had gone. Then his view was obscured by the truck drivers who came running to him.

'Police!' he managed to gasp and, lifting a hand towards the building, 'Stop…man.'

There was no one to be seen. Cannon stabbed a finger in the direction he must have gone, and the younger of the two set off in a run in that direction, but was back as Cannon at last managed to get to his feet and take something like a normal breath. 'No one,' he reported, 'but the taxi drove off. He could have taken that.'

'*The* taxi?' Cannon repeated, the implication doing much to restore his breathing. 'You mean there are no more? Have you got a car?'

'A scooter.' The young man shook his head, adding as Cannon looked towards the other driver, 'Ola walks to work. We wouldn't catch them on my scooter but if I could take you to the taxi office, two brothers run the taxi and car hire business. I think they are always in touch by radio.'

Cannon nodded. 'I must catch that man.'

'Come.' The young driver beckoned and ran around to a small car park, where his scooter stood quite alone.

'Something bad happened on board?' he asked as he swung on to his bike and made room for Cannon on the pillion seat. 'Ola said that there was a police doctor waiting to go aboard. I'm Lars, by the way.'

'Cannon, John Cannon,' he replied. 'And yes…a death, a sudden death.'

Lars shrugged his shoulders as they roared at full throttle, but no great speed, along Harstad's quiet streets. 'Police do not chase men for a sudden death,' he said.

'No,' Cannon agreed, 'but I can't say more.'

'I understand,' he said, 'so we chase a suspect.'

Cannon did not answer.

There was no sign of the taxi, and not many other cars. Cannon was relieved to see that the office Lars pulled up in front of had a light on, and a man looking out of the window was already on the telephone.

'I know the brothers well,' Lars said and preceded Cannon into the office, bringing the taxi owner straight to the urgency of their visit with a mouthed 'police', then as the man put down the phone Lars added aloud, 'It's the man who's hired your taxi, Mr Cannon here needs a car to go after him.'

Looking startled, the man said, 'That was my brother on the telephone. He's on his way to Tromsø with a passenger who says he needs to go to see a very sick relative quickly.'

'And you do have a hire car?' Cannon asked, reaching for his mobile.

'I do,' he said a little cautiously.

'I'd like to hire it, now,' Cannon said, pressing the first contact on his phone.

'It is *very* urgent,' Lars urged. 'Very…'

'Fill in that form, there'll be a full tank of petrol. How will you pay?'

'Card,' Cannon said.

'I thought you just took a car if you wanted one,' Lars said.

'You watched too many TV crime stories,' Cannon said, taking the card machine from the businessman and punching in his number, as Liz answered her mobile.

'Bliss has taken the only taxi and is "speeding to see a sick relative in Tromsø",' Cannon told her. 'I'm following in a hire car.' He listened for a moment, then said, 'Road blocks, I would think. There can't be many alternative routes in this terrain.'

'I'll fetch the car round,' the owner said.

Cannon took his receipt from the card machine; Higham would pick up this tab eventually, he hoped. Then he picked up a business card from the desk, read name and telephone number to Liz. 'Contact this man when I've gone, he'll give you the numbers of the taxi and the hire car I'm taking.'

'They're both black Toyotas,' Lars supplied.

'You heard that?' Cannon asked.

'Black Toyotas,' she repeated. 'OK.'

He sensed the 'be careful'.

'I'm all right,' he said aloud.

'OK,' she repeated and rang off.

'I wonder if there's a road map here?' he asked Lars while they waited.

'Sure.' Lars referred to a pile of papers on a side table and pulled some stapled sheets out. 'There you are,' he said, 'a map and detailed instructions. Four hours, fifteen minutes driving,' then flipping the pages over, added, 'and there's a hiking route—take you forty-six hours, twenty-five minutes to walk.'

'Right!' Cannon said drily, as he took the four sheets and the business owner returned holding out keys.

'I hope I'm doing the right thing,' he said.

'You are,' Cannon reassured him, 'just radio your brother and tell him to let you know as soon as he's dropped off his passenger, say you have another fare waiting. When you are sure he's alone, ask your brother to tell you as much as he can—exactly where he put him down, what time, what his passenger said, if anything, then report all he tells you to this number.' He had put Liz's number on the bottom of another business card.

Lars left the office with him and pointed him on his way. 'It'll be the main road—the only road in parts.' Cannon shook his hand as he climbed into the car.

'The snow chains are fitted, you'll be glad of those as you get towards Tromsø—they've had a good fall of snow already,' Lars said. 'Godspeed.'

'Thanks.' Cannon felt strangely touched by the unexpected blessing, but then concentrated on the driving. He had already seen that it was the route 83 he wanted out of Harstad and beyond. After that he had the route sheets on the seat beside him and his mobile phone to hand.

The houses gave way to landscapes of brilliant skies, sheets of water reflecting white clouds and snow-capped hillsides. Cannon found himself thinking this was not the country for crime. This was where he and Liz should be holiday-making, instead of which—

His mobile burbled, making him jump.

'Cannon?' Betterson's voice.

'Yes.'

'We've found the hire van and the walking sticks from Bliss's shop.'

'And?'

'The bludgeon that beat Riley's brains out, his DNA is splattered all over it.'

'Where?' Cannon asked.

'A tumble-down barn on a salt marsh, near a bus route to Skegness.'

'Spier?' Cannon said.

'Yes, but we haven't traced him yet. The press are having a field day at our expense,' he said with an ironic laugh, then he asked, 'Are you driving?'

'Bliss has jumped ship,' he said. 'Details later. I'm following him on a Norwegian road that's getting snowier by the minute. Liz is still aboard the *Nordsol* with Higham, notifying the police what's happening.'

'What *is* happening?'

'Bliss got himself in a cleft stick on board the ferry.' Cannon told him of the latest murder.

'The Norwegian police?' Betterson demanded urgently.

'At the other end of this road, waiting, I hope,' Cannon said, gritting his teeth as a large lorry came at speed towards him, hooter blaring. Cannon on the precipice side of the road fixed his eyes on his share of the road and gripped the steering wheel. 'I need to concentrate,' he said, his mouth dry.

'I'll speak to Oslo,' Betterson said briskly.

Cannon let out his breath as turning a corner the road sank softly down towards a wooded fjord, but that relief was short-lived as he heard an engine noise coming closer and louder overhead. The white underbody of a white, blue and red helicopter with the huge letters POLITI came low in front of the car, for seconds filled his windscreen. It flew alongside him for a bit as if certifying his identity, then swept up and away following the road to Tromsø.

He was reassured, it was a comfort to know the police knew exactly where he was. He was not alone.

But what happened if they buzzed the taxi? If Bliss became alarmed, he was now so steeped in innocent blood one more victim would be quite inconsequential to him.

Cannon had two courses of action. He was not armed but he could put his foot down and try to catch up with the taxi, and hope he could deal with Bliss—he was doing that anyway, he thought. The other thing was he could pass on his assessment of the situation to Liz, who could caution the police about the type of schizophrenic man they were dealing with.

He pressed contact 1 on his phone and Liz answered at once.

'What's happening your end?' he asked first.

'We've sailed for Tromsø, we've a forensic officer on board, and Oslo are sending helicopters.'

'One's just had a look at me. I'm afraid for the driver if they buzz the taxi Bliss is in.'

'Orders to…' Liz's voice broke up into crackly, unrecognizable static, coming back in with, 'So they've thought of that. Will you…' And she was gone; complete silence.

Did his phone need charging? Was he out of signal range? He glanced quickly at the valley he was driving down into. The great snow-covered hills were probably cutting off all signals. Then he saw ahead and to his left a black shape, stark among the shining whiteness, clinging to every slope and tree. A car? The taxi?

It was well down a kind of track, a footpath. Surely no one went down there intentionally in a vehicle? He braked and, in spite of the chains, slid on a layer of hard-packed snow into the side verge. He threw open the door, snatching the key from the ignition, and went running, slipping and sliding down the track.

It was certainly the taxi but he approached it much quicker than he intended. The slope increased and it was all he could do to stop himself crashing into tree stumps and stumbling over fallen branches. He began to feel the slope must be almost vertical, and he finally stopped himself with both hands hard on the side of the Toyota.

Anyone within a kilometre must have heard his approach, he thought, so there could not be anyone alive, or conscious, inside the vehicle, or anywhere near.

Pushing himself upright, he saw the far back door and the driver's door were both open—and there was blood on the driving seat. He prayed it was blood from an accidental crash.

He pawed his way round to that side of the car. Here there was a confusion of disturbed snow and vegetation, and blood spots in the snow stood out like beacons. These led away from the car, and he followed the lead as quickly as he could. Did he call out? Not yet, he decided, for the blood spots were getting much closer together, and it seemed whoever was bleeding must be the driver.

The side of this fjord looked precipitous right down to the water some hundred metres below, where there was a path or a road around the shoreline. If whoever was injured had gone down there, they were going to take some recovering.

But the trail of blood told its own story. The man had tried to keep on the same level line going away from the taxi, then the spots began to go upwards, from branch to stump, stump to trunk, upwards half, a quarter of a metre at a time.

Cannon was forced to pause and take breath, so how an injured man was faring he could not imagine. He looked around, listened. He had never seen such spectacular scenery in all his life—a manhunt in para-dise—and, as he was still, he heard something between a stifled sob and a groan.

'Hello,' he called softly. 'If you are the driver of the taxi I've come in your brother's car to look for you.'

The groan turned into a deep, heartfelt sob, sounding very close, intimate, in this dense patch of firs. Cannon moved cautiously across the slope from tree to tree. 'I've come from your brother's office in Harstad to help...' he ventured. 'Where are you? Speak to me.'

A hoarse whisper came. 'To your left, I can see you. I'm here, here. Please come...'

Hanging on to a low branch of one fir, Cannon half swung his way across to the next. Sitting with his back to the butt, he found a man whose dark distinct eyebrows and deep-set eyes echoed those of his elder brother.

Blood had soaked his blue shirt collar and dripped from the sleeve of his black leather jacket—and he looked terrified.

'OK, so my name's John Cannon and I'm going to look after you,' Cannon reassured him as he gingerly eased the slashed jacket collar from the young man's neck to begin to assess the wound. 'What's your name?'

'Name's Albin. I didn't think anyone would find me. I'm not bleeding to death, am I? My back feels…'

'Not going to let that happen, Albin,' Cannon stated. 'but we must ease you out of this jacket. I was taught first aid when I was a young policeman,' he said, very evenly, very calmly, 'and while we do that can you tell me where your passenger went? It's important.'

'He tried to murder me,' Albin began, and relief at being found released a flood of information. 'A helicopter came low over the car. I glanced up and caught a glimpse of a knife near the back of my neck. I swerved, came off the road, hit a kind of track, plunged down— but he still tried to stab me with the knife, I saw the blade flash. The second time I—' He broke off, swallowed hard before going on. 'When the car came to a stop, I'd undone my seatbelt and I fell out—I just lay still—I think he thought he'd done for me.'

Cannon, seeing the extent of bleeding and the depth of the slash down the boy's back, thought but for the crash, the leather jacket and the grace of God, Albin might well have done for. He gritted his teeth and summoned up the skills he had learned as a rookie cop for such emergencies. He peeled off Albin's shirt and made a pad, then his own, and tore that into strips to secure the pad.

'There's no arterial bleeding,' he reassured the young driver, but he reached for his mobile again. Still no signal.

'He intended to kill me, I saw it in his eyes.'

'So did you see where he went?'

'I've seen eyes like that before, a dog who turned killer...evil.'

'Did you see where he went?' Cannon repeated the question.

'We had to shoot it,' Albin said, then returning from that horror to the present he refocused on Cannon.

'Down,' he answered at last, 'down towards the roadway at the edge of the fjord. I heard the helicopter again, thought it was coming back, and I saw him looking up. That was when he plunged down towards the water. He's on the run, isn't he?'

'Yes,' Cannon answered unreservedly, draping Albin's jacket back around his shoulders. 'Do you think you could walk as far as your brother's car if I help you?'

Albin nodded, and as Cannon assisted him to his feet, he asked, 'So is this man a murderer?'

'A multi-murderer,' Cannon said.

'A serial killer,' Albin said.

Cannon opened his mouth to deny this—and yet this was just what Bliss, the mild professor who had been the star of his pub quiz team, was—and this young man would have been his latest victim but for the grace of God.

'You knew him?' Albin asked as they paused before beginning the climb.

'I'm beginning to,' Cannon replied, 'and I have to catch up with him before—'

'He murders someone else,' Albin supplied.

'Before he murders one man in particular,' he said, adding silently, One who's supposed to be in my charge, as he propped Albin on his uninjured side.

Albin was young and strong but the pad on his back

had not completely stopped the bleeding. He needed urgent medical attention. The bleeding was not improved when to get him to the roadway Cannon was forced to give him a fireman's lift for the last gruelling fifty metres. Draped over his shoulder, the blood began to drip again from Albin's fingertips.

They were in sight of the road and the hire car when a motorist drove by. Cannon raised a hand urgently but although he thought the driver glanced his way, he did not stop. Then a timber lorry thundered past—again he lifted a hand. It screeched to a halt.

'Going to put you down,' he told Albin.

The young man's knees gave way and as Cannon supported him in a sitting position, a short, burly man with powerful shoulders climbed down from his cab and ran towards them.

'What's happened?

'We need an ambulance. I've no signal on my phone,' Cannon said, 'his back's badly gashed.'

The driver noted the blood down Albin's arm. 'I'll call my base on my radio, I'll be able to get through to them—tell them to call the air ambulance.'

He ran back to his lorry. It seemed an age before he returned, though it was only minutes, and he brought a first aid box with him. His base had contacted the emergency services and confirmed that the ambulance was on its way.

'There's an area some two kilometres or so further on where there's a fork down to the fjord and also a big enough clearing for a helicopter to put down. I've told them we'll be there but I think we should perhaps try to stop the bleeding before we move him further.'

They mutually decided to apply another firmer pad

over the makeshift dressing. This done, Cannon asked for the use of the radio to contact the police.

'So this is not a road accident,' the lorry driver said when Cannon had finished giving details to the police, and Albin, very pale but calmer, had filled in a few details.

'No,' Cannon said, 'and if you'll help me get Albin into the car, as soon as I've seen him safely on his way to hospital I'm—' Cannon broke off to ask, 'You say where we're to wait, a side track goes down to the waterside?'

TWENTY-TWO

CANNON HAD REALIZED that instead of plunging immediately down to the fjord, the track marked 'Unsuitable
for vehicles in wintry weather' actually gained height
before descending the far side of the hill in a series of
hairpin bends.

He reached the summit in time to see the air ambulance disappear over the next peaks to the north. He
guessed he was not only above the tree line but almost
directly above the road where the timber lorry would be
again on its way. He had made a mental note of the lorry's number and the firm. He would ensure *that* driver
would receive proper thanks.

Cannon estimated that the road snaking down, disappearing into the trees then glimpsed only briefly as a
white straight line between the firs, must be ten, twelve
times the distance a funicular would have to travel.

He was still above the tree line when his mobile
came back to life. It startled him, and he fumbled and
dropped it into the floor of the passenger seat. He pulled
over with the rueful thought that, after the wait to see
Albin away, a few more minutes would hardly matter.
But as he scooped up the phone he acknowledged he
had known times when a few minutes, a few seconds
even, had made the difference between life and death.
Now it could mean the difference between catching or

losing Bliss—between life and death for Higham or some other poor innocent.

'Cannon,' he answered.

'It's Toby.' There was some excitement in his voice. 'I thought you should know straightaway I've seen Bliss's, or to be correct, Michael Evan's father.'

'And?' Cannon said, ready to put the car into gear and move off again.

'My old Professor Heaven is undoubtedly his son.'

'And Bliss is Heaven,' Cannon added.

'Yes, and I don't think there's anything random about Bliss being in Norway. It was the professor who pointed me in the direction of my first appointment in Oslo, but what I did not know was that his grandmother was Norwegian and she had family interests in a big fish-canning business years ago. She left her grandson her house there. He apparently spent many holidays there with her. The father said his other son needed too much care and nursing to allow anyone else to go. The interesting thing is this property is practically on the route of the Hurtigruten ferries. It's apparently near a place called Harstad. I've never heard of it but—'

'I have,' Cannon interrupted. 'Bliss jumped ship there, I'm driving near there now trying to find him.' He slipped the car into gear. 'Have you an address for this property?'

There was a moment's silence as Toby absorbed this information, then he went on, 'The old man thought it was called Villa Christofferson, or something like that, definitely had the name Christofferson in it, that's all he could remember. He said neither his wife, nor he, had ever done anything about it.'

'And his son Michael?' Cannon asked.

'He just said what *he* did was nothing to do with him. He could not even bring himself to speak his name. He talked of his younger son who died, and his wife. Eventually said the last time he had seen "the other one" was at his son's funeral, and he had told him never to bother to come back.'

'And it was coming back from his brother's funeral that Bliss had the disastrous road crash. Seems to me,' Cannon added as he negotiated the next hairpin bend, 'it's Bliss's father who…' He left the rest unsaid as he added, 'Bliss has tried to kill a local taxi driver. Can you…'

The bend negotiated in a one-handed, slithering, ungainly skid, Cannon thought he should ring off and concentrate. He didn't need to; it seemed the lower altitude had already cut out the signal.

He drove on as fast as he dare, shaking his head as he realized that *none* of this was haphazard, *nothing* was being left to chance. Bliss had planned all this— had planned to put the fear of God into Higham before jumping ship at Harstad, an area he had known since his childhood. He even had a ready-made bolt hole in the property his grandmother had left him.

Cannon's one break was that he now had a focus. To find this Christofferson villa had to be less of a shot in the dark than just driving around the side of the fjord in the hope of sighting Bliss, or of actually coming across another person he could ask. He'd seen no one since beginning this downward drive.

He reached the bottom road without mishap, but now had the choice of a right or left turn along the waterfront. He decided that as none of Bliss's previous actions had been random, it was possible the man had climbed down from the main road at a point which would bring him within reach of his inherited property.

Calculating more or less where Bliss's descent had been by the shape of the hilltop he had seen the air ambulance fly over, Cannon turned towards the open sea.

There were certainly no houses or buildings of any kind at first, but then he came to a stretch where there were small wooden houses that looked like holiday homes, or summer cottages. Was Villa Christofferson something like this? It sounded grander. There was a shallow bay where wooden quays had been built, one or two had boats moored alongside, with shacks, or boathouses, nearby—and from the back of one of these huts smoke curled up into the blue sky.

Cannon stopped and had just closed the car door when a tall grey-haired man in fishing smock and waterproof trousers came from behind the hut, wiping his hands on a cloth. He greeted Cannon in Norwegian, but quickly switched to the country's second language.

'You like a fish breakfast,' the man asked, 'caught this morning, just frying?'

'If only I had the time,' Cannon answered with a smile, 'but I am looking for the Villa Christofferson.'

'Christofferson Huset I know,' the man replied, 'but no one lives there.'

'That's the place,' Cannon said.

'You're going to buy it?'

'I am looking for the man who owns it, and who I believe is in the area today.'

'Ah!' The fisherman beamed as if he had been given an unexpected gift. 'That will be young Michael then— not so young now, of course—tell him Tomas, Tomas Midvinter, sends him greeting.'

'You know him?'

'As a boy, yes. We had many good adventures.' He laughed expansively and looked about to reminisce at length. 'We planned to sail around the world together.'

'I would love to hear but my time is very short,' Cannon said. 'If you could direct me…'

The directions given, Tomas Midvinter called after him, 'Tell Michael I am here in the cabin.'

Cannon raised a hand in acknowledgement of the message—a true answer would have taken some time.

EVEN WITH DIRECTIONS, Cannon found it difficult to locate what Tomas had described as the back entrance to the property, a mere half a kilometre away from his fishing hut.

It was only when he slowed to a walking pace that he finally spotted a break in the grass verge. He pulled in, got out, stooped beneath low growing trees and parted high dead grasses, finding stout wrought-iron gates between two green and moss-covered twisted brick pillars. 'They match the chimney pots and greater front gates,' Tomas had said. 'It used to be a grand old place.'

Cannon climbed over the immovable gates. The driveway was just as overgrown and he found he had strayed from the path on to what must originally have been lawns, but he could glimpse a building through the remaining copse of trees.

This was more like it, he thought as he drew nearer, noting that although the snow cover was not thick and the unkempt grass poked through the whiteness everywhere, he could see no signs of footmarks. Christofferson Huset loomed larger and larger, until it was like coming across a fairy-tale palace in a wilderness. It was huge, three storeys, four where there were turrets at either end, yet its second-storey and heavily decorative roof facia gave it a homely, almost Hansel and Gretel feel. Cannon had to stop himself just wandering up to it and staring. It invited attention; it cried out for renovation.

He kept to the trees and walked along the side of the house towards the front, all the time scanning windows and ground for signs that anyone else was there.

He was surprised to find the house was nearly as deep as it was long, a square perhaps with a central courtyard.

He moved in to the side of the house, and tried his mobile once more, but now it was perhaps the trees that blocked the signal. He could neither let anyone know where he was, nor summon assistance. He began to walk round to the front of the property. He turned the corner and drew in a quick gulp of frosty air as he saw another set of footprints coming from the opposite direction, straight towards the front door. He also noted the odd pieces of snow which had fallen from the shoes of the other caller as he crossed the tiled portico. One of the double doors stood ajar.

So Bliss *was* here in this house. Cannon had somehow to stop him leaving to kill again.

Cautiously he edged his way towards one of the tall, elegant windows flanking the front doors and peered directly into the hallway. Bliss had evidently inherited the house and the contents, for it looked as if nothing had been moved or cleaned since the owner had died. There was a large chandelier above a sweeping staircase, two walking-stick stands, one each side of the double doors, each with a good number of sticks in. Was this why Bliss liked buying and selling walking sticks? Then there was a heavily carved hall table, chairs— and in the bright triangle of light from the open door he could see wet marks where the other caller had gone straight towards the stairs.

Cannon paused, thinking the last time he was in this kind of situation he'd had to hand either the resources of the Met, Liz or Betterson, or Paul Jefferson, or even Hoskins nearby. Any of these would have been a comfort. He would have felt easier if someone knew where he was.

Then echoing like a thunder-clap through the silent house came the unmistakable sound of a shot.

TWENTY-THREE

CANNON WAS IN the hallway before the echoes of the shot had died away. Then he almost felt Liz's hand on his arm, heard her caution, hold on, take stock.

He stood until the silence became complete, stood looking at wet smudges of footprints that went straight across the hall and up the stairs. He raised his eyes to the landing, the smell of cordite stronger now as it drifted downstairs. There was little doubt where the shot had come from.

Bliss had, it seemed, known exactly where he was going. Had he also known what for? To find a gun secreted here to kill himself with? Had he come back to the place where his childhood had been happy, and unfettered by parents who seemed unable to take their eyes or attention from their disabled child? Did that man now lie dead upstairs? Were Liz and Higham going to be safe after all?

Cannon moved to the bottom of the stairs and put his weight on the first tread. It creaked like an un-oiled door to a dungeon. He stood for a moment, one foot poised, then moved it over and placed it carefully as near to the wall as he could, putting his weight down gently. The squeak was minimal but he paused again, holding his breath, as sounds came from above. It was as if someone had laid an object down, something metallic on to a hard surface. Then there were quieter sounds, perhaps of things being sorted, moved around.

Had Bliss shot himself and his body was sprawling and settling over a table or desk—or was there someone else in the house, someone who had entered by a different door?

Cannon took the rest of the stairs three at a time. If surprise had gone then speed might help. The landing went to the right across the gallery open to the hall and to the left down a corridor with many doors. The third one along was open and as Cannon turned his head in that direction, the smell of cordite was stronger. and there was a draught of icy air.

'John Cannon!' he called. 'Coming in. Can we talk?'

He went forward, wondering if these were his last few steps on this earth. He moved partially, then fully, into the doorway. He could see no one but noted that the glass doors were open on to a veranda. The smell of cordite lingered; there was no doubt this was the room in which a gun had only just been fired.

He moved fully into the room and seeing no one standing, or sitting, walked in so he could scan the whole of the floor space. No stains, no blood splatter on walls or ceiling. He went out on to the small veranda and looked into a central courtyard; it was completely deserted. There were no footprints and no signs of any violence on the veranda.

He noted a roll-top desk had been opened and on it lay an empty cartridge box. There was a large cupboard, which he saw with mounting interest had clips like those used for billiard cues but were instead holding a fine collection of yet more walking sticks. He wondered if Bliss had visited this place when he first came to Norway. He could have collected a sword-stick from here. Cannon had always had difficulty believing it was possible to smuggle one through customs.

Then he noticed there was a door in the panelling near the cupboard, which presumably led through to another room. It was closed, but must have been the way Bliss had gone. He moved towards it and had his hand on the handle when a voice behind him said, 'Stop where you are.'

He span round and faced a man he did not recognize—at first. The man he had known from The Trap quiz team, the mild academic, who had known the answers to the more obscure questions, was no more. This man's own grey hair grew thinly just on the area of his head not covered with scars, which was not large. He looked at Cannon as if he had never seen him before and his expression was hard, uncompromising. The walking stick he carried was aimed like a gun at Cannon's middle. Bliss flicked the gold ring at the top of the cane and a thin straight trigger sprang out. He hooked his finger around it.

'John Cannon,' Cannon heard himself saying as if he was introducing himself to a stranger. 'Liz and I were—'

'On the boat, interfering,' Bliss said, then accused, 'Now you have followed me here! I don't like people who interfere.' He raised the stick a little higher. Cannon had never seen such a weapon before but he had no doubt he was looking straight down the barrel of a weapon that could send a fatal spread of shot into and through his body at that range.

'Liz would only want to help,' Cannon said. 'She always wanted to help you.'

'Turn round. Don't look at me!' Bliss shouted.

'I was looking at your stick. I've seen sword-sticks but never seen a gun-stick before.'

'They're always here,' Bliss said.

'Did your grandmother collect walking sticks?' he asked, trying to buy time, trying to assess how much or how little pressure Bliss had to put on that trigger to fire.

'My grandfather. My grandmother just looked after them. I always helped her.'

'You did a good job,' Cannon commented.

'Oh yes, it still works well.' Bliss's words were matter-of-fact.

'It's a wonder you can get the cartridges,' Cannon replied as conversationally as he could, 'or do modern ones fit?'

'I have enough for my purpose,' Bliss replied shortly, 'and we need to go downstairs. I don't want you up here.'

With the gun aimed at his middle and Bliss's finger on the trigger of a gun that had to be over a hundred years old, Cannon turned and walked ahead of him. He wanted to tell him to hold the stick steady, watch it as they went downstairs. Instead he said, 'I met an old friend of yours…'

'No talking,' Bliss said as dispassionately and authoritatively as any headmaster.

'Tomas Midvinter,' Cannon added.

'To the left, the door in front of you,' Bliss ordered as they reached the hall.

Cannon turned towards the door and thought, Below stairs—he doesn't want a mess in the house proper.

'He wished to be remembered to you,' Cannon added.

'Stop talking!' The tone was impatient now.

Cannon half-turned to glance back at him. An icy chill thrilled up his spine. Bliss was now looking at him with dark, concentrated intent: his eyes held the look of a predator before the fatal pounce, the contained, pent-up energy before the kill, the intended action wiping out all other thoughts or emotion.

Cannon used the only weapon he had. 'Liz...' He paused to try to swallow. 'Liz,' he repeated.

'Open the door,' Bliss ordered.

Cannon opened the door, wondering if he could throw himself inside out of range, make Bliss shot at an angle, so he did not take the full force of the spreading shot. He glanced behind himself to assess the prospects, and saw only a steep flight of wooden steps, no more than a broad ladder down to a cellar.

'Liz...' He began talking again for his life. 'Liz wants to thank you for the easel you sold her, and you remember she did not tell when you hid your swimming trophies...'

Cannon saw the click, the off-switch thrown, the electricity cut off as if by a lightning strike, the murderous intention thwarted by a memory—to be replaced by a look in Bliss's eyes of incandescent fury.

Without warning the man lunged at Cannon with all his force. The end of the gun barrel caught Cannon in the ribs—the pain was excruciating—then again, winding him, and again pushing him off balance. Cannon tried to grab the stick but it was too slender, too smooth and it slipped through his fingers as he fell.

TWENTY-FOUR

HE MUST HAVE lost consciousness for a time, came to in complete darkness, disorientated, caught somehow, hanging, head down, but what he could still picture was the vehement hatred in Bliss's eyes, and the smell in his nostrils was blood and dust.

Cannon knew he had distracted the man, thwarted his capacity to assassinate—for that moment. The story of the shared moment of secrecy when Bliss and Liz had been children had saved his life.

He half lifted his head. Everywhere hurt. Gingerly he lifted his arms, felt his head, wondered how long he had been out. There was a sticky patch of blood where the back of his head must have struck the floor; only he had not quite finished falling. His right foreleg had gone through the rungs of the ladder and he was hanging from it. Surely it must be broken, he thought, with a groan.

It was the sound that broke from his own lips that startled him back to reality, so loud in the silence. Bliss could still be above, could have recovered his will to kill. Cannon at that moment was unable to help himself, or anyone else, let alone do anything to thwart Bliss from going on to kill his long-tormented victim, Higham.

He flexed his stomach muscles, catching his breath as the effort pinpointed *exactly* where the gun-stick had been pushed at him with full force, but thoughts of Bliss catching up with the *Nordsol*, getting back on board in some disguise or other, made him draw himself up, but not far enough. The steps were broad and to free his leg he must grasp the rear of a tread. He lay back, rested, waited for the screaming muscles to recover and wondered if Bliss might not go straight on to Kirkenes and wait for Higham and Liz and Cathy there.

Once more he clamped his teeth and forced his stomach muscles to contract, curl up, lift him. He grasped the back of a step with one hand, and knowing he probably would not be able to do this again he desperately made a final muscle-jerking, pain-searing grab and caught it with his other hand. Balled up, he knew he was grasping the step below his leg. To free himself he must get his hands on the same level as the leg which was trapped, the wooden tread of the step above, straight across the middle of his shinbone.

His arms were trembling now and silently he mouthed, 'This is for Liz.' He released his right hand and, thrusting it alongside his trapped leg, grasped the back of that step. The other hand was a fraction easier. He angled himself sideways until he could feel his shoe was touching the back of the step. A final pull upwards and, as he turned his foot sideways with his shin no longer pressed against the step anchoring him there, he fell, this time in a heap on the concrete floor.

Gingerly he gathered himself together and finally made it to his feet. His leg felt as if every muscle and tendon had been torn, but he could feel no shattered bones. Supporting himself on the side of the ladder, he could just bear to put his weight on it. Slowly he made his way back up to the door, lifted the old-fashioned latch very slowly, but the bolts on the other side had been shot into place.

Now what? He thought of the *Nordsol* sailing for Tromsø, of Bliss turned predator, and felt his way back to the bottom of the steps and held on to them while reaching out his left hand for a wall he could follow. There might be another way out of this basement cellar. He released the steps and took a step to his left. Nothing. Another step and his fingers touched brickwork.

He immediately began to feel his way along the wall, pushing his feet out carefully to ensure there was neither obstacle nor pit, and thinking, ironically, he could do with a walking stick. Just as he felt the wall was endless, his hand moved into space. He turned left and went on, reassuring himself that at least if he followed it all the way the worst that could happen would be that he was just back at the steps.

As he went in this new direction he began to wonder if the darkness was less intense. He tried to assess what part of the Christofferson Huset he might be under, whether there was a chance of a light source and the possibility of another way out.

He moved quicker as he realized he really could see more. The darkness was fading to a gloom. He could see that the basement he was in was vast and empty, and that the light was filtering down from a series of square skylights made of thick glass bricks interspersed with gratings, and all between great girders some three metres above his head. There was no possible way he could get up there, and not much he could do if he did. He calculated from the little he had seen from the upstairs veranda that he could be under the central courtyard.

Then staring upwards he started violently, raised an

arm as if to protect himself, as the sole of a man's shoe landed on and moved across one of the glass panels and on to the next.

'Hi!' Cannon yelled. If it was Bliss—and who else could it be?—he might delay him, might divert him again. 'Hi! Stop! Stop!'

The feet stopped, both together on the next glass section, then they disappeared, but Bliss's answer came startlingly loud. Cannon realized he must be stooping down to the grating almost immediately above his head.

'You intrude and interfere too much.' The voice if not the words sounded calm, much like the man Cannon had known in his public house.

'So perhaps Liz next then…' Bliss's voice fell to a level of quiet satisfaction. 'And then, oh, then *Mr* Higham.'

'Listen to me,' Cannon begged. 'Why Liz?'

There was no answer.

'Listen! Listen!' Cannon demanded. 'I understand Higham but why Liz? She was always on your side. That's not fair, not justice!'

'She told my secret—and—and you're dealt with, dead really, so…she'll come to *you*.'

There was bitterness in those last words, 'she'll come to *you*', and even as he spoke Cannon could hear he was moving away; he yelled again and again, then had to resist the urge to punch anything in range—wall, floor. But he had been brought up in a school that did not lose control easily. He had been taught by the hard knocks his family had gone through that, as his father had said, there was only one way for everyone, and that was forward, however hard it was. He remembered when things changed dramatically in the London fruit and veg trade and his father's health had begun to fail, the old man had sung the Scottish ballad, 'Keep Right On To The End Of The Road', and had added, 'And I'll make it as good an end as I bloody can.' And he had.

'And I'm not there yet,' Cannon muttered, 'not by a long bloody way.'

With a new reckless determination, he limped rapidly on his journey around the walls, realizing as he went he must be describing a large L-shaped basement—but there was no sign of another way out.

Back at the steps he knew his only escape was through this door somehow. Could he work at the hinges? What had he in his pockets? Years ago men would have had useful things like penknives with gadgets, but now he had money, cards, a mobile phone, which he tried automatically once more—it did not even light up. His cards seemed the best bet—he had seen a Yale lock opened in seconds with a bank card but bolts and hinges were a different matter. Beggars could not be choosers, however; desperate beggars at that.

He was carefully fingering through the plastic cards in his case, trying to find which felt the strongest without dropping any of them, when he thought he heard something from the other side of the door. Was Bliss still in the house?

Surely what he could hear was someone calling, shouting a name. He pressed his ear to the door, held his breath and listened intently. Faintly and moving away, he heard, 'Michael! Michael Evan! Are you here?' A silence then a little more uncertainly the voice called, 'It's Tomas, Tomas Midvinter.'

'The fisherman!' Cannon exclaimed and began hammering on the door with all his strength and shouting his own message. 'Tomas! Let me out! The door in the hall, the cellar. Tomas! Tomas Midvinter!'

He could have sobbed with relief as he heard the noise of the bolts being pulled back and, hardly waiting for the second one to be fully drawn, he burst out.

'What is this?' Tomas Midvinter stepped back defensively, pulling a walking stick from the stand next to him, raising it to fend off this dust-covered dishevelled man leaping out at him. Then he recognized the man he had met earlier, lowered the stick and stood back to view Cannon more closely.

'What's happened? Why are you locked in the cellars? Have you seen my friend, Michael? It smells as if someone has let a gun off in the house.'

'Yes,' Cannon agreed, then asked, 'Is my car still on the bottom road?'

'Yes, I parked my Land Rover next to it,' Midvinter said, then asked quite as sharply, 'Is Michael safe?'

'He's left,' Cannon said brusquely. 'I must get to my car. I'll tell you as we go. This is a matter of life and death.' He took a step forward and his leg gave way.

'You'd better have this.' Tomas handed him the brass-handled walking stick.

'Thanks,' Cannon said, headed for the front door, then asked, 'Do you have a mobile phone?'

Tomas produced it. Cannon glanced at the model he had not seen before and asked him to ring Liz's number. He had faith in her understanding the situation quicker than anyone else, and doing the right thing. 'She was my partner in the London Metropolitan Police,' he told Tomas as the Norwegian ensured the phone was ringing out then handed it to Cannon.

He ascertained Liz and all aboard were OK, told her

what had happened and of the particular threat to her first and then to Higham. 'You'll let all the authorities know, ashore and aboard?'

In answer to her question he told her he intended to try to follow Bliss in his car.

Handing the phone back to Thomas, he saw the man was completely baffled. 'Who is Bliss?' he asked.

'Your friend has had several names. Michael Bliss was the latest.'

'His real name is Evan,' Tomas Midvinter said, his pace slowing as he added, 'I find this all difficult to believe.'

'So do I,' Cannon said. 'I knew the man well before any of this came to light. I'm no expert but I believe there are reasons linked to his home life why, after a serious road traffic accident, the injury to his brain has turned him into a ruthless killer.'

Now Tomas stopped altogether, shaking his head. 'Michael? You make him sound like a mad dog!'

'Part of him is. That part is not the Michael Evan you knew,' Cannon said, adding, 'I must get to my car.'

Tomas led him to a more direct path towards the back of the house and the bottom road.

Cannon's hire car was there but Tomas's Land Rover was not.

'Looks like he preferred your vehicle,' Cannon said.

'I left the keys in the ignition,' Tomas admitted, 'and I was packing up my fishing shack for the winter. I had all my bedding and camping gear in the back.'

'Could you ring my partner again and give her your vehicle details,' Cannon asked, 'then I'll give you a lift back to…'

'I live in Tromsø,' Midvinter said. 'I have an accountancy business there, if you're...'

'Yes, it's the ferry's next call,' Cannon told him, opening the car and starting the engine as Tomas spoke to Liz, told her the details of his stolen car, and then held it for Cannon to confirm what he was doing.

'We sail from Tromsø at half past six,' she reminded him.

Midvinter heard and shook his head. 'It will take us four hours, perhaps more.'

'Did you hear?' Cannon asked Liz. 'I'll try but...'

'Perhaps,' Midvinter suggested, 'you should think of flying from Tromsø up to Kirkenes and be there to meet the boat when it arrives.'

'That sounds like a good idea, John,' Liz put in. 'You can't imagine how strict Captain Anders has security aboard now. I doubt if Bliss would manage to get back aboard.'

'OK,' Cannon said. '*If* I miss you at Tromsø I'll look into that.'

'Take care,' she said, 'don't drive too fast.'

It was a message he saw rewritten on Midvinter's face several times as he put his foot down to the floor.

'We have to drive south for a time before we can go north to Tromsø,' he told Cannon. 'Our roads are not... well...certainly not direct.'

They were soon driving with headlights on and a light snowfall whirling in mesmeric patterns beyond the windscreen wipers. 'We're not going to make it,' Tomas said, but Cannon drove grimly on, feeling Captain Anders would delay—for a time.

When they reached the road overlooking the fjord, Tomas said, 'There's your ship,' and pointed out into mid-channel where the lights of the *Nordsol* were bright in the evening light as it headed out on the next leg of its journey.

Cannon pulled into the car parking area near the Hurtigruten terminal. 'Now what?' he wondered aloud.

'Well…' Tomas began, then exclaimed, 'Hey, wait a minute! There's my Land Rover!'

Cannon came to a quick halt, was out of the car looking after the fast-disappearing ship and asking, 'So is he on board?'

Midvinter was examining his vehicle and shouted that the keys were in the ignition still but everything else had gone: sleeping bags, blankets, camping gear. 'He's got enough equipment to be self-sufficient,' he added, shaking his head.

'So does that suggest he's taken another vehicle, one we have no details of, and is *driving* up to Kirkenes?' Cannon asked. 'In that case, why come here to park?'

'Michael often flew to the airport here when he came on holiday,' Tomas said, locking his vehicle and pocketing the keys. 'He'd know exactly where he could park and pick up another vehicle without much fear of being seen.' Cannon glanced at the blank warehouse walls round about. 'But should you be thinking of driving after him? The shortest route from Tromsø to Kirkenes is some eight hundred kilometres and you have to enter and leave Finland twice. You could try to follow him and miss him in many, many places. You don't know what vehicle he's in.' Midvinter threw out his hands in concern. 'Surely it must be better to fly to Kirkenes where your partner will arrive in, what, a day and a half's time.'

Cannon considered for a second or two; he could update Liz on the situation and she would do the rest.

'If we go straight to the airport,' Tomas said, 'you should get on the late-night flight. Public transport in this area is flying.'

'Thanks.' Cannon was touched by the man's unquestioning help. 'You do understand about your old friend? You trust me?'

'I've put my life in your hands for the last few hours so...' Midvinter said.

'Whatever happens I'll let you know the outcome,' Cannon said. 'A letter to your business address, perhaps.'

'Come,' Midvinter said. He opened the car door, at the same time diving deep into an inside pocket under his fishing smock and pulling out a business card. 'I would like to know.'

'Sure,' Cannon acknowledged, taking the card.

'I presume you have your travel documents with you?'

'Yes, I made sure they were in my wallet when I thought I might leave the ship at some point,' Cannon said, 'but I wouldn't mind buying a bag and a few essentials. I'm going to be at least one night without anything.'

'There's a department store on the way, we could call there. The airport has only the usual duty free goods,' Tomas said.

Shopping was never done so quickly, and with a new haversack containing a change of underclothes, a thick jumper and a waterproof anorak, they drove to the airport, which was on the far side of the island the city was built on. By UK standards it was small. Cannon noted there were international flights just to Murmansk and London, otherwise most flights went in and out to Oslo, with fewer marked up to and from Kirkenes.

At the ticket desk Cannon got a seat on a plane leaving at ten minutes past ten that evening. The two of them went to the waiting area and Tomas suggested they both have something to eat and drink. 'My wife is away to her sister's this evening; it will save me having to get something when I reached home.'

'That would be good,' Cannon said, 'and this is on me.'

Cannon was a bit hampered with the walking stick and when he put it under his arm as they queued with their trays, Tomas said, 'Ah, yes, the stick,' as if he thought he ought to return it to Christofferson Huset.

When they had eaten their meal of ribs and chips and drunk a couple of cups of coffee, Cannon said he thought Tomas had done enough and should not wait any longer with him.

'There is just one thing,' the Norwegian said quietly. 'I must take the walking stick with me when I go.'

Cannon had found it a help and would have liked to have kept it. He was about to say so when Tomas added, 'If you pass it to me this side of the table where no one can see I will show you why.'

Cannon frowned but did as he was asked. Tomas took the head of the stick into his open palm and traced the outline of the brass beak of the bird of prey, which Cannon saw now was made in two halves, the bottom slotted into the top where the user's hand rested.

Tomas curled his hand around it as any user might, but then he squeezed the bottom part of the beak until it disappeared under the top curve with a distinctive click.

Cannon's mouth dropped open. This was yet another gun-stick.

'There were several, and sword-sticks, in the house,' Tomas said quietly. 'We used to look at them when we were boys and no one was around. I remember we even loaded one once. Wonder we didn't kill someone then.'

'I could have been arrested,' Cannon said, leaving the stick in Tomas's hand.

'Thanks for all your help.' Cannon stood up to shake his hand as Tomas prepared to leave. 'You're a good man.'

'So was Michael Evan when I knew him,' Tomas said, holding on to Cannon's hand to add, 'You will remember that.'

Cannon nodded.

TWENTY-FIVE

CANNON HAD WELCOMED the speed and seeming urgency which all planes have to achieve to take off, but once above the snow clouds the sense of speed was lost, and he began to worry.

If anything happened to Liz it would certainly be his fault for hurling himself off the boat, leaving her behind. Reckless, he judged himself, irresponsible— and what had he achieved? Then he was disconcerted by a break in the clouds and the lights of Tromsø clustered around the waterfront: the coloured brilliance of advertisements; shops, cafes, and the illuminated multi-pointed arches of the cathedral, reminding him of Sydney Opera House, all reflected in the water. He saw the lights of the bridge across a fjord. Then the clouds closed like a dense curtain.

The flight was about an hour and Cannon decided he should use his time to more advantage and caught the stewardess's eye. 'I've never been to Kirkenes before and have to find a place to stay tonight. Is there a hotel near the airport?'

'No, sir.' The stewardess bent over him to whisper as others nearby had their eyes closed. 'You will have to take a taxi but once you are in the town I don't think you will have any difficulty finding a room. If there's not a taxi outside go straight to the office near the exit and they will call one for you.'

'Not walking distance then?' he asked.

She shook her head. 'Nothing is exactly near the airport,' she said, 'and you'll need all your warm clothing on when you leave the plane. It is night and there's already a lot of snow in Kirkenes.'

From what he saw from the window as they came down it was a white-out; only as they were really low could he make out buildings and the lights of a small airport. Any town lights were not visible from where he sat, and the stewardess was right: he was glad he had pulled on his new jumper and anorak over his other clothes, and he promised himself a good woollen hat, scarf and gloves the next day.

He was surprised to find his name on a placard held by a man just inside the exit doors, then his hand shook and his bag taken.

'Forstmann. Kripos,' the man, of almost the same tall and athletic build as Cannon, announced, looking him straight in the eye as if to make sure he knew that Kripos was the special agency of the Norwegian Police Service who dealt with serious crime.

'I'm *very* pleased to meet you, *very*,' Cannon said.

Forstmann gave a tight-lipped smile and nodded. 'A room has been arranged for you at a hotel as near as possible to the Hurtigruten terminal, and I've a car to take you there.'

As they walked to the car Cannon asked if there had been any sightings of Bliss. 'Though I suppose you will be looking for him as Michael Evan.'

'Both,' Forstmann said, 'and Heaven, but the only sign so far is that we've had a couple of cars go missing on the route from Tromsø to here. He could be swapping cars, and if the second vehicle stolen was also him, he must be here, or nearly here by now.'

'I thought road blocks—' Cannon began.

'Oh! They were, but this man knows this part of the world pretty thoroughly, I would say.'

'He spent many holidays here as a child; his maternal grandmother left him her house in Harstad.'

'Ah, that explains a lot,' Forstmann said. 'We felt at one point that he must have walked over a few hills to miss one of our road blocks, then picked up a car on the other side—and he may have done that more than once.'

'He took quite a lot of camping gear out of the Land Rover in Harstad, left the Land Rover but still took the gear,' Cannon said. 'It surely must be cumbersome. Has any of that been found abandoned?'

'These things are usually well packed in portable haversacks,' Forstmann commented, 'but why would he burden himself?'

Cannon shook his head. 'The only thing I would say about this man is that he seems to plan his movements in great detail, with deadly zeal you could say. Up to now there's been nothing haphazard or, it seems to me, unplanned in what he's done. What might seem spur-of-the-moment actions later turn out to be preconceived.'

'A mad murderer to be reckoned with, then,' Forstmann said as he drew up before the glass doors of a very modern-looking hotel. 'Before you go in I have to supply you with this.' He pulled out a mobile phone. 'You will find my name and the names of various police officers and their duties and ranks in the contacts. Run through them as soon as you get in.'

'You might learn more about how well Bliss knows

the area from this man.' Cannon produced the business card Midvinter had given him.

'Yes,' Forstmann said, 'we already have his details from your…partner? Liz?'

Cannon nodded.

'I'll see you in,' Forstmann said and once inside shook his hand in what Cannon felt was a very meaningful way. 'We'll be around when the *Nordsol* docks,' he said.

At reception Cannon asked if he might have something to eat sent up to his room. He was given a twenty-four-hour menu and chose a pasta salad. He found his room, put on the kettle, explored the mobile phone, then sent all his important contacts his new phone details. He opened up the mini-bar and was alternately sipping tea and whisky when his door was tapped.

A very young-looking waiter, his ears his most prominent feature, carrying a tray, hovered in the doorway.

'That all right, sir?' he asked, as Cannon took the tray.

Cannon looked down at the film-covered salad, which was colourful and elaborate, and wished he had ordered a sandwich. He nodded. 'Fine,' he said, then nodded down at a brown-wrapped parcel on the tray and asked, 'What's that?'

'It was delivered for you as I came through from the kitchen, so I put it on the tray and brought it straight up.'

'Who delivered it?' Cannon asked sharply.

'Just a man, sir,' the youth replied. 'I only saw his back as he left; he had given it to the night porter.'

'OK, thanks,' Cannon said.

'Good night, sir.'

'Good night,' he replied absentmindedly as the door was closed. A surprise present? An unwanted 'present'?

He put the pasta on the side and laid the tray and the parcel in the middle of the small table by the armchair, tipped his whisky into his tea and sipped. Half the size of a small shoebox and wrapped in dull brown paper, neatly stuck all around with parcel tape, it could have come straight from a shop, or dealer of some kind. But what kind of dealer? The parcel was not quite pristine enough for a shop. It looked as if it had come out of a warehouse, off a storehouse shelf. Reassuring himself that surely the only people who knew where he was at that moment were the police, he picked it up and made a start on the tape.

It was quite a task to find a corner. He resolved in future to carry a good penknife in his pocket as again he used a bank card to dig below the tape and strip it away.

He upended the whole contents of the box on to the table: a smaller box and a bubble-wrapped item, both with yet more tape around them. He picked up the parcel—and knew immediately what this 'present' was. He sat with the squat but business-like-feeling revolver in his hand, still in its bubble wrap, and knew the smaller box would be bullets for this small-calibre gun. He wondered if this was not a present after all, an 'unofficial' present? From Forstmann, or Kripos?

He did not speculate further; the gun was in his possession and he was glad of it, though it underlined that his position could be perilous. He pulled the wrapping from the revolver, an automatic with a flat profile, suitable for concealed carry. He felt this gun had been carefully chosen for him. There was nothing unplanned in this whole affair. He was being armed and Bliss was carrying the camping gear for definite reasons. But what? What did Bliss intend?

Cannon cast his eyes in the direction of the pasta salad, decided he definitely was not hungry enough for that, had a long hot bath to ease his aches and bring out the bruises, ate the biscuits provided on the tray with another whisky and went to bed to consider the next day—a whole day before the *Nordsol* docked— and Bliss's need for Midvinter's gear.

He slept solidly and forced himself up and under the shower to bring his aching, complaining body into some sort of action. Going down to the restaurant for breakfast, he found the hotel had a good number of guests. One group of twenty or so were already in the foyer, and as he passed he heard talk of a trip they were making to the Russian border. 'Here's the bus,' someone called, and all streamed happily out of the front doors.

At the breakfast bar he realized just how hungry he was, and while piling his plate heard talk of a snow-mobile safari and a visit to see new puppies at nearby husky kennels.

Walking back to his allocated table near the window, he found the party of four at the next table equally involved in what they would be doing that day. The older couple had obviously been before and were advising the young couple what they 'really must' do and see.

'The Ice Hotel is a must,' the older woman said, 'well, from Christmas to April it is…'

'We were more interested in the trips with the husky-drawn sledges,' the younger man said.

'Ah!' Now the older man took over. 'Now you're talking—that's where you get a feel of the real Arctic wilderness. We should do it again!' He looked at his partner, who shrugged and gave a pretend shiver.

'You need the right clothing,' she said. 'Some youngsters were actually proposing to sleep out there.'

'Well, they had all the right gear...'

Cannon thought he might have a look at this wilderness where you needed 'the right gear'.

Finishing his breakfast, Cannon began to have the feeling that all the actors in this drama were assembling at this northern city to play out the final act. Bliss was most likely already here, waiting in the wings—and the rest of the cast?

He knew Liz, Cathy and Higham were sailing towards Kirkenes, but when would Toby arrive? Was the exhibition bus already here or not? Was their original plan ever going to work? Cathy was supposed to transfer to the bus and return to Bergen with her brother; he, Liz and Higham were to stay on the *Nordsol* and cruise back to Bergen, where they were all to meet up to fly home. Cannon felt Higham had agreed in the first place just to get out of Oslo quickly—parting with Cathy when the time came might be quite a different matter.

He had some phoning to do. He glanced out of the window at a land of snow, sea and sunshine, and saw a waiter carrying blankets and cushions to several long seats outside on a veranda overlooking the bay.

He took his mobile phone and a third cup of coffee outside, wrapped himself in blankets and could not believe how warm and invigorated he felt by the view, the air, the warmth and comfort of his seat. He was quite prepared to do a lot of phoning from here.

He called Liz first. 'Where are you?' he asked.

'Me, or the ship?' she asked.

'Both.'

'And where are you?'

He told her in detail.

'That sounds OK,' she said, then told him she was with Cathy and Higham at breakfast and the *Nordsol* was just leaving Haveysund. 'I think we have several short stops during the day and night before we reach you.'

'The police have reason to believe Bliss is already here. I'm going to contact Toby and we should both be on the quay when you dock.' He dropped his official manner to ask, 'Sure you're OK?'

'Sure...' Her tone was not convincing. 'Wish you were here.'

'Love you,' he said.

'Love you,' she said and her voice was less than steady.

'See you tomorrow...'

He had just rung off when the phone bleeped the signal for an incoming text message. From Toby, it read: 'Air crew strike—not sure when arrive. Bus also late.'

Cannon felt doubly glad for the phone and the revolver.

LATER THAT MORNING Cannon joined several others from the hotel who wished to have a look around at the huskies and perhaps make up their mind about joining a wilderness safari later.

They were driven by the hotel minibus to what was the site of the Ice Hotel, which was rebuilt from ice blocks each year well before Christmas and was open for guests to stay until the following April.

Cannon was intrigued to find that the timber build-

ings associated with the Ice Hotel consisted of a shop
and reception area, then there was a short distance to
walk to the mountain of snow and ice remaining from
the previous year's tourist attraction. Beyond this were
similar timber buildings which the bus driver explained
were toilets, showers, rooms where special sleeping
suits were kept, all associated with the Ice Hotel. There
was also a restaurant, which was open and where they
could eat if they wished.

Now, with the previous year's hotel no more than a
series of fantastic photographs showing ice sculptures
along the ice corridors and happy smiling faces of visitors in ice-block beds cocooned in thermal sleeping
bags and furs, the small party was directed to where
they might see the huskies. The driver was happy to
wait in the restaurant until they were all ready to go
back to Kirkenes.

Free to wander, Cannon left the others as they went
straight for the dogs, some already harnessed to sleighs.
Cannon headed for a rise below a clump of birches and
firs from which he could view the whole area in more
detail.

It was clear where the sleigh rides went—the tracks
going off into the distance showed as lines of deep
shadow, the sun was so low in the Arctic sky. The
landscape was beautiful and from just below he heard
squeals of delight as the younger members of the party
were introduced to the huskies and one of the dog han-
dlers produced a husky puppy from beneath his coat.

Cannon wondered if Bliss intended to stay up here,
out of the town, out of sight, and wait for his opportunity to finally finish his vendetta against Higham? Was
this the place where the drama must end? The police

alerted, following to this northern extremity, closing in? Cannon shivered as the sun finally dipped below the horizon. Where could Bliss go from here?

TWENTY-SIX

THE FIRST CALL to Cannon's room came before his early alarm call. It was Forstmann.

Without preamble the Kripos man said, 'A section of the ice blocks on the site of the Ice Hotel have been made into a kind of rough igloo. Bliss apparently spent last night there. He left some of Midvinter's gear: a sleeping bag and a camping stove. But we've not found the man—so far,' Forstmann added, his voice steely, going quickly on: 'I've spoken to your partner, Liz Makepeace, and told her that we want the party to behave perfectly normally. I believe the daughter wishes to go to see the huskies near that site. We want her to do that—'

'Wait a minute,' Cannon interrupted, 'you're saying you want to use the daughter...'

'And her father, who your partner assures us will insist on going with his daughter.'

'As bait,' Cannon put in. 'Using live bait is always risky, too risky in my opinion.'

'No, not in this trap, I assure you,' Forstmann said. 'Your people will be perfectly safe.'

It was almost the same words used to Cannon when Liz had been part of an undercover operation with the Met that had nearly cost her life. 'Perfectly safe...complete cover.'

'This man is clever, devious, has more than likely got a gun, plans every move,' Cannon re-emphasized.

'So do we,' Forstmann said, going on, 'What we need you to do is meet the *Nordsol* as arranged with the brother, and both go aboard—that's been arranged...'

'Toby Higham?' Cannon queried.

'He's landing as we speak,' Forstmann said, 'and will be on the quayside waiting for you. Captain Anders has been informed. OK?'

It was not so much a question as an end to the conversation.

Cannon breakfasted almost alone in the dining room, plagued by the last words he had heard Bliss say: 'Perhaps Liz next then—and then, oh! then *Mr* Higham.'

Over my dead body, he thought, sobered then by the realization that had it not been for Midvinter it might well have been just that.

He checked out of the hotel and walked to the docks in time to see the *Nordsol* approaching her berth. With an arrival time of nine and departure three and a half hours later, there were no new boarding passengers around as yet, but the dock was ready for this regular arrival: warehouses' doors were open and the ubiquitous forklift trucks were trundling busily around, like ants foraging among and rearranging piles of goods.

Cannon kept a lookout for Forstmann, Toby, or anyone who looked as if they might be loitering. He waited opposite the area where the *Nordsol* was now looming over its allocated bay. Water boiled as the gap lessened between ship and shore, though it finally came to a stop, and the engines were cut off, without so much as a bump on the fenders. The mooring ropes were being hauled into place as he heard someone call his name.

Toby Higham came from one of the terminal offices. He looked tired, drained and as if he had slept in the same clothes for days. He had certainly not shaved for quite a time and looked rough, older—and even more like his father.

'What happened?' Cannon asked as they gripped hands.

'Every kind of delay,' Toby said, shaking his head. 'If it wasn't for Olav Forstmann's help I wouldn't be here now. I could do with a shower and change of clothes.'

'You can come to our cabin when we get aboard, I'd be glad of a chance to talk to you without the family around,' Cannon said as the ship's crew began the procedure of putting its passenger gangway in place. He looked up and could see Liz standing at the rail.

As they walked aboard, Toby said, 'Olav has put it to my father that there is a real chance to catch Bliss and to finish the whole cat-and-mouse affair once for all.' He paused. 'And to my surprise he says he's agreed to...'

'Play bait,' Cannon supplied. 'Forstmann told me.'

'Yes.' Toby stopped walking and shook his head. 'I think my dad has just reached the end of his tether. He feels his nerve will completely desert him if he doesn't do this now. He just wants to be free of "this long, long curse", and Olav has convinced him that this is a chance not to be missed and he's so keen for it to be all over and done with before he joins up with Mother again at Bergen.' He began walking again. 'I think we have to go along with it.'

As they reached the top of the gangway, Liz came forward to greet them. 'Good to see you *both*,' she said but the tears blurring her eyes were for Cannon. She frowned them away, adding sternly, 'You're limping.'

'I'm fine,' he said as Captain Anders and his older second officer joined them.

The captain nodded to Cannon. 'Please to see you safely back,' he said, then looking at Toby added, 'And this will be...'

'Mr Toby Higham,' Cannon said.

'Welcome aboard, Mr Higham,' Anders said. 'I understand your stay is only while we are in port.'

Toby nodded. 'That's correct. I leave Kirkenes by bus tomorrow.'

'And I am taking Toby to our cabin so he can get cleaned up,' Cannon added.

'Please keep me informed of your movements until you leave my ship, and there will always be an officer at hand,' Anders said, turning to nod to the serious older officer who he obviously completely relied on. The officer inclined his head to them, did not speak, but dutifully followed them to station himself at the end of the corridor leading to their cabin.

'The captain runs a tight ship,' Cannon commented as they let themselves in.

'Tea, coffee, or something stronger?' Liz asked.

'Tea would be good,' Toby said, then glanced at the shower. 'But first I'd...'

'Help yourself,' Liz told him.

'If you need anything, sing out,' Cannon added.

In a very short time they heard the water begin to run. He turned quickly and pulled Liz into his arms. 'I've been wanting to do that for long enough.' Then he added, his voice falling even lower, 'Been moments when I thought I never would again.'

'John?' she questioned, but he shook his head.

'Not now,' he whispered. 'Just let me hold you. In fact,' he added, 'I think you'd better marry me.'

She was perfectly still in his arms, and for long seconds the only noise was the sound of the water running and Toby moving about under it.

'I mean it,' he said.

'You've been through quite a trauma,' she said, 'but when we get home and it's still what you want... OK.'

He lifted her bodily from the ground, looked up at her and said, 'Rapunzel, Rapunzel, let down your hair.'

She looked at him with mischief in her eyes, lifted her hands to the clip that held her hair back and shook her head so the long blonde hair fell forward, then she lowered her head so it fell over his face.

'My grandmother would have called you a brazen hussy,' he whispered as the water in the shower ceased.

'You'll just have to make me into what your granny would have called an honest women then,' she said, kissing him on the nose.

'I can't wait,' he answered huskily.

By the time Toby emerged they were both busy making tea and Cannon was pouring Toby something a little stronger to go with it.

Cannon was to learn that Liz too knew of Forstmann's plans, and also felt there was a good chance of catching Bliss. And they should take it. 'Forstmann and his men know exactly what they are doing,' she said. 'However well Bliss knows the area, the police have local men who know it better.'

'We've been here before,' Cannon said, staring meaningfully at her. There was a pause when she seemed to stare into space, then he saw her relive the moments when she had been hit across the jaw with an uppercut that would have floored a heavyweight boxer, then been thrown into the path of a speeding 4x4 in a sordid multi-storey metropolitan car park.

'This I think is different,' she said, but her voice shook and she turned away to the window.

'There is no need for you two to be involved if you do not wish to be,' Toby said gently. 'You have, after all, done so much already. If it wasn't for you this chance would not have arisen. I understand far more than I did since I saw Bliss's father, real name Norman Nigel Evan. I realize how I made the situation worse, blethering on about my father and his devotion to my sister. In fact, probably caused the whole situation—'

'No,' Liz interrupted, 'no, no! You told us that after the disabled brother's funeral, his father told him never to bother to come back again. He drove away from that funeral with those words ringing in his ears.'

'No wonder he crashed,' Cannon said.

'And no one went near him all the months it took him to recover,' Toby said.

'He never has recovered, has he?' Liz said quietly. 'His brain, part of his brain, was mortally hurt, wounded, his thinking twisted.'

Cannon recalled what Midvinter had asked him to remember—that Michael Evan had been a good man. In his mind he saw white-clad sharp-shooters ready to take the professor out at the first opportunity. Perhaps they might at least save his life by being there, and shouldn't an academic, a professor, find some outlet for his thoughts and ideas, even in protective custody for the rest of his life?

'John?' Liz prompted, as Toby waited for a decision.

Cannon searched her face. She did not let him down, gave a tiny but positive nod.

'Yes,' he said, 'so many innocent lives have been lost already. We have to help, of course.'

TWENTY-SEVEN

THE MERE SCATTERING of people Cannon had seen on his first visit to the site of the Ice Hotel was not repeated on this second visit.

This time when their party arrived there was a group of skiers, come to take advantage of the early good snow conditions. Cannon was sceptical about the truth of that and about the party of dog lovers they joined in the restaurant who were all going on sleigh rides. He and Liz exchanged knowing glances. While the quilted clothing might have hidden any underarm or waist gun-holsters, they were both pretty sure they were there.

Before setting off it had been decided that Cannon should be free to either join the party going on the ride, or not. He felt Forstmann was not sorry to have a free agent who could observe outside the box of the official operation—but knew enough to keep out of the way.

Liz would at all times stay with Cathy, and Higham would be shadowed by Toby and a friend—Forstmann. Then, if all went well, Higham, Liz and Cannon would return to the *Nordsol*, Cathy and Toby would board the museum bus to travel south, and Bliss—well, Bliss, Cannon hoped, would be in custody in preference to lying in a pool of blood-soaked snow, but one or the other.

There was not a lot of time for dallying, with the *Nordsol*'s sailing time now less than two hours away.

Cannon, seeing no one in the least resembling Bliss at the base, opted to go with the sleighs, choosing the one Cathy and Liz were in, which would travel behind the one carrying Higham with Toby and Forstmann. They were also accompanied by the skiers at a respectful distance, but Cannon was sure they were shadowing the party.

The dogs were eager, barking, wanting to run, impatient when the sleighs stopped to let the fittest visitors take turns in charge of the sleighs, gripping the handles and standing on the runners when on the flat or downhill, but running up the hills to help the dogs.

After about half an hour they were all brought to a halt to allow everyone to get out of the sleighs and take in the scenery and the peace, the false sense of peace. It would, Cannon thought, be easy to forget that anything out of the ordinary was looming.

The skiers were now nowhere in sight. He supposed they were circling the bigger clumps of firs that spaced the snowy slopes. Even behind the shelter of these firs Cannon felt anyone not in a white suit would soon be seen. Any movement in the still landscape would stand out a mile—and then he saw that minimal movement.

No more than a small brown smudge, but that blur had come from behind a tree and gone back again, and though it was difficult to judge distance as snowy slope succeeded snowy slope and the trees varied in height, it could have been a man, certainly in a white suit, but with the upper half of his face showing, probably with snow goggles over his eyes. Cannon glanced at Forstmann, who appeared to have seen nothing—or of course it could be one of his own men. Cannon walked to the policeman's side and explained what he had seen.

'No,' Forstmann said at once, 'no one beyond the line of trees that lie immediately to our left. You're sure?' he asked.

'Yes,' Cannon said briefly, 'I'll move casually out that way. I know this man. I should be able to tell before I get close, and I'm prepared.'

Forstmann acknowledged his possession of the gun with a nod.

'If I raise my right arm high in the air as if I'm greeting the man, you'll know it's Bliss. OK?' He took a little satisfaction in being the one who this time cut short any other ideas Forstmann might have as he moved quickly away.

Within the first few strides Cannon had transferred the gifted revolver from his waistband to inside his mitten. Behind he could hear Forstmann talking on his radio in low monotones.

Cannon kept his eyes on the small coppice of firs which grew on the brow of the hill, alert for another movement. He remembered the gun-sticks and practice shot at Christofferson Huset and slipped a finger nearer the trigger.

Then it looked as if a large section of snow moved, but this much nearer he could now see the man's clothes were not quite as white as snow. Cannon moved on at the same pace but slightly altering his line as the figure moved away and upwards at an angle, taking advantage of every tree as cover. Cannon frowned as the man was forced to move into the open for two, three seconds, and he saw how very much of the trunk and branches he masked. He looked a big man, but distance made size difficult to judge in this landscape—and who else could it be? And if it was not Bliss, why was he running?

'Stand still if you've done nothing; they chases runners': a phrase from his old dad's philosophy.

'Indeed they do,' he added aloud as he became aware that there were figures—skiers—coming rapidly into view to the left and to the right. The man Cannon followed topped the hill and stood momentarily exposed—great snowman against blue sky—then, as he saw his pursuers, he threw himself forward and down, out of sight.

Things happened quickly now; the skiers swooped in, converging on the spot where the man had disappeared from the skyline.

There would be no escape—then there was a shot, echoing loud across the snowy wasteland. Heart pounding as he raced to top the rise, Cannon found it difficult to know where the shot had come from. Had one of the skiers shot Bliss? Had the end already come? Perhaps, though, Bliss was only injured, shot maybe in a leg to stop him running?

Many ifs and buts crowded his mind as he took great strides, half running, half glissading, down towards a great disturbed area of snow where the man—or his body—had fallen and rolled.

Liz, like everyone else, had her eyes fixed on all that was happening ahead, until the shot rang out, and Higham shouted, groaned, clutched his chest and slewed sideways against his son.

She was at Higham's side almost as soon as Forstmann. Toby had his arm around his father, taking his weight, lowering him as gently as he could down to the ground.

'Dadda?' Cathy gave an agonized shout and ran towards them.

'Stand back!' Forstmann ordered and gestured to Liz to stop Cathy hampering what needed to be done, while at the same time telling all of them, 'He has body armour so…'

Higham took a great staggered gasp of air as he lay with Toby's arm under his head, but his hands fell from where he had clutched his chest as he lost consciousness.

'Undo his anorak,' Forstmann said, which Liz did as he felt in Higham's neck for a pulse. Immediately under the anorak was the bulletproof vest. There was a deep, puckered depression exactly over the heart. 'Such an impact could—' Forstmann began and was immediately on his radio requesting an air ambulance. Liz carefully pulled apart the Velcro straps and opening the vest revealed where the tip of the embedded bullet made a sharp point at heart level.

There was no blood but Liz frowned as she imagined the trauma and extent of internal bleeding that could have caused. She organized Toby and Cathy to bring all the furs from the sleighs and swathed the unconscious man in them.

A message on the radio told them that an air ambulance was diverting from another incident. 'Fifteen minutes,' Forstmann informed them.

'Thanks,' Toby said.

'Watch his breathing,' Forstmann told him, 'if it changes call out.'

'Come on… Dadda,' Cathy pleaded, 'help is…coming.'

Forstmann received two more messages in quick succession, and walked away from the group to take them, but his gaze was on his men grouped on the skyline. He gave rapid orders in Norwegian.

Liz was concerned about Cannon, but was convinced of one thing and followed Forstmann to give her opinion. 'The bullet that struck Higham didn't come from the man they're chasing over there—if there was a man. I would have said it came from our left.'

'They've caught someone,' he answered shortly.

CANNON WAS ON the spot as the man in the off-white suit was pulled from the miniature avalanche he had caused as he fell and rolled. That it was not Bliss was immediately apparent; he was far too tall, too hefty. Cannon wondered if he was a hunter, though he had no idea whether hunting was allowed or done anywhere in the area. He dismissed the idea that he was either an *innocent* visitor or resident. Why should he hide behind trees or run when challenged?

It was taking several men to overpower him and in the end Cannon saw one of them point his automatic rifle and order him in several languages to put his hands in the air. At last, with several more weapons threatening, he did as he was told. Handcuffs were quickly snapped on and he was encouraged to begin the walk back.

Cannon went nearer as the hood was pulled down from the man's head and his goggles removed. He stopped in his tracks. It was not Bliss, but he recognized the man well enough. It was the joker who had disrupted the quiz evening at The Trap, the man who had somehow helped trigger a series of events and murders—and had now turned up in the northernmost tip of a foreign country. Cannon would have judged him hardly capable of undertaking such a journey, at least not without considerable help. Perhaps that was the clue, and that help could surely only have come from Bliss. The stay in Bliss's apartment, the van hire and visit to the antique shop, the keys to the jewellery cabinets— it added up.

'Spier!' Cannon exclaimed. 'Why?' Then he shook his head. Perhaps he knew why; it was more the 'how' that puzzled Cannon.

'You know this man?' one of the skiers asked.

'I do,' he said and both men looked round as Forstmann arrived.

'What's this?' he asked.

'This man, I think it would be correct to say, is Bliss's paid accomplice,' Cannon said.

'So where is the boss man?' Forstmann demanded of Spier. 'Where is Bliss?'

Spier shrugged, shook his head, glared at Cannon. 'What're you doing 'ere, Mr Landlord?' he asked.

'Is he armed?' Forstmann asked.

'Not so far as we can see or feel,' one of his men answered, indicating the spot where they had dug Spier out. 'We're looking around to make sure he's thrown nothing away.'

'Take him back to the restaurant,' Forstmann ordered. 'The rest of you spread out and work your way back down. This is not the man we're looking for, so keep a sharp eye out for anyone or anything else. The shot could have been fired from…' He indicated a spread of snow over beyond where the sleighs and Higham waited. 'But keep the flat ground the other side clear for the air ambulance to land. It should be here in about ten minutes. Also see no one leaves the whole area—no one!'

A skier pointed southwards: the helicopter was already a growing dot on the horizon.

'Right,' Forstmann said, turning to Cannon, 'I think
you and I better have a chat as soon as we've seen
Higham away.'

They hurried back to the fur-wrapped figure.
Higham was still unconscious and his breathing ragged.
Toby looked anxious. 'Will I be able to go with him?'
he asked.

'And…me,' Cathy begged.

'That is the pilot's decision,' Forstmann said briskly.
'Does anyone else in your party know the man we've
arrested?'

'My partner,' Cannon said.

Liz glanced swiftly and questioningly at him and
then towards the group of men surrounding their prisoner.

'It's Spier,' Cannon told her.

'Spier!' Her incredulity could not have been greater.
'Spier? The man who…at home…caused…'

'Yes,' Cannon confirmed.

Liz glanced at the concerned son and daughter
crouched over their father, and but for them Cannon
was sure she would have laughed aloud in disbelief, as
she repeated again, 'Spier, from…'

He nodded towards the group as they drew nearer.
She could see for herself.

There was no more talk as the helicopter now hovered above the landing spot and all crouched or turned
their backs as the rotors stirred up a miniature blizzard.

It was quickly apparent that no one other than the
patient could be taken; they already had a road accident
casualty aboard. Higham was carefully strapped to a

stretcher and within minutes was away, leaving a frustrated Toby and a devastated Cathy behind.

Then Forstmann came striding back, radio in hand, to say that he had a police vehicle waiting for them to follow their father to Kirkenes Hospital. They could leave immediately but he wished to talk to Cannon and Liz in the restaurant he had commandeered.

Cannon was wondering where they might all catch up with each other again—and whether they were going to be on the *Nordsol* when it sailed—when one of Forstmann's officers brought in another man Cannon recognized. It was the driver of the hotel minibus he had used the previous day.

'Sir,' the man reported, 'this driver says he took a man from the area, and has just come back to pick up the hotel guests he brought earlier.'

'So what is the problem?' the driver asked, throwing out his hands in bewilderment.

'Can you describe this man?' Forstmann asked.

'He was just an old man in trouble.' The driver was impatient. 'An old man with a walking stick and a bad back.'

'Was he grey, dark, bearded?' Forstmann persisted.

'He was grey, what hair I could see under his hat and hood. He was well bent over his stick, middle sixties perhaps, and was, as I say, in trouble, could hardly get along because of his back.'

'You didn't glimpse his face?'

'He was clean shaven, freshish complexion, and I would say he was English,' the driver said.

'Where did you take him?' Cannon asked.

'He said he needed to get his back sorted before it got worse.' The driver looked to Cannon for understanding. 'That's why I left my hotel people here while I took him to the hospital.'

Bliss taken to the hospital where Higham was probably even now being offloaded. He met Forstmann's eyes and read the same thoughts.

'I'll have to leave you in the hands of another officer,' Forstmann told the driver, 'and we'll need forensics to look at your vehicle.'

'But for God's sake, the man will still be at the hospital!' The driver was irate. 'I wish I'd just left the old man here suffering, just left him to his fate!'

No one answered him.

'You and your partner come with me to the hospital,' Forstmann said to Cannon.

Whether it was an order or a request, Cannon was not sure, but he answered 'Yes' with alacrity.

There was no time wasted and as the police car raced, siren blaring, to the hospital, Forstmann radioed ahead. He said it was most urgent that the hospital detain an elderly man about sixty years of age, with a walking stick and possibly complaining of back trouble, until they got there. There were clearly questions at the other end and he added, 'Discretion, if possible, of course, but otherwise…' His voice changed. 'Anyway at all—*just keep him there* until we arrive. OK.' He cut the high-pitched questioning voice off.

The hospital was on one of the peninsulas that surrounded Norway's deeply serrated coastline and seemed to be near the ferry terminal. The deep, long blast from a boat's horn echoed across the water. Forstmann saw Cannon straining to look out to the sea and shook his head. 'I'm afraid the *Nordsol* has sailed,' he said. 'We'll try and reunite you, all of you, hopefully, later.'

Their entry into the reception area was hardly unnoticed. Forstmann's car had been followed by two others, and these men had been detailed to watch all exits. Forstmann led the way to the main reception counter where the girl had obviously already alerted her superiors.

'We have no man here with a back problem,' she said defensively, looking to an older senior nurse to support her.

'That is true, Officer, we have in fact had no "walk in off the street patient" as yet day. Could your man still be on his way here?'

Forstmann was explaining that the man had been brought in by a minibus, while Cannon was walking slowly around the reception area and saw Cathy and Toby sitting in another area of chairs along a corridor. He touched Liz's arm, indicating he was going to them.

'Is there any news of your father?' he asked.

'He has not regained consciousness, the doctors are still with him,' Toby said, 'but why have all the police come?'

Cannon explained. 'We think Bliss may have fired the shot and escaped the scene by persuading a hotel minibus driver to bring him to hospital.'

'If he was my old professor...' Toby began.

Cannon shook his head. 'I doubt you would have recognized him. He was walking very bent over, supposedly coming to the hospital with severe back trouble.'

Cathy gasped and nodded. 'There...was a man...he kept looking our way. He was...sitting...almost...opposite me...then...'

Cathy was becoming breathless with the story.

'Take your time,' Cannon said, sitting down beside her.

'Toby was still…talking with the doctor,' she said, 'but there was another…call and I heard the receptionist repeat…something about a patient with a…bad… back…and the man got up and left.'

Cathy paused, but when Cannon would have spoken she lifted a hand. 'But…' she went on, 'nothing was wrong…with his…back… I think. He…walked out… quickly.'

'Did you talk about your father while he was here?' Cannon asked.

'A doctor just came to say to move to these chairs, so we would be nearer to him,' Toby said.

The door at the far end of the corridor opened and a nurse came to them. 'Mr Higham, Miss Higham,' she said quietly, 'the doctor would like to see you both.'

TWENTY-EIGHT

SHOCK, TRAUMA, TIME were the words coming from the intensive care unit. Meanwhile, the police threw a cordon around the town. Liz said she felt a mouse would have problems escaping.

Toby and Cathy were at their father's bedside. Forstmann, having heard all Cannon and Liz could tell him, and spoken to Betterson, was at police headquarters directing operations. Liz and Cannon had been directed back to the hotel where Cannon had spent the previous night.

At the hotel they found the room Cannon had vacated was free. As they stood at the desk, a well-dressed man strode out of the rear office, fury written on his face. He nodded perfunctorily to them and stood back as they signed in. Once they turned away, Cannon heard him ask the receptionist if the minibus hire had been arranged.

'I do not want my guests waiting around for their trip to the Russian border tomorrow morning. You did tell them we had a driver?' His tone suggested that even so, the man left a lot to be desired.

Liz grimaced at Cannon but said, 'Know what, I'm really hungry.'

Cannon remembered the highly coloured pasta from the day before, and then the American fast-food restaurant almost next door to the hotel.

'Yes, come on.' He changed direction. 'We'll eat now, you never know what might happen later.'

The restaurant was bright and glitzy with pictures of mountain scenes on the walls. Cannon was sure that these were not local photos but the American Rockies. A demonstrative dark-haired waiter was seeing a large group of satisfied customers away with enthusiastic goodbyes—'*Ha det! Tilbake!*'—then turned with ease to Cannon and Liz and wished them welcome in English.

'You like here?' he asked as he showed them to a table on a raised section of the restaurant. They both automatically chose the long bench seats against the wall so they could see the whole of the dining area.

Cannon had seen the minibus driver as soon as he sat down. When the waiter had taken their order and moved away, Cannon nodded to him. Mentioning him to Liz, she looked casually that way and reported not only did he look uneasy but that he was leaving his table.

'Going,' Cannon guessed.

'No, coming over,' she whispered.

'Could I just speak with you for a moment?' he said as he reached Cannon's side.

Cannon moved along the bench for him to sit down.

'There was something I did not say.' The man's tone was repentant. 'But I shall lose my job I think if the hotel manager gets to know.'

'What is that?' Cannon asked.

'The man I took to the hospital gave me money, quite a bit of money really. He had it all ready in an envelope.'

'He had it ready?' Cannon's voice was low and urgent.

The driver put his hand into his pocket. 'I've taken the money, I needed to settle a debt, but it was in this.'

The envelope was well crumpled but as it was put on the table they could both see that written on it was 'the driver'.

Cannon pulled a plastic bag from his pocket and turning it inside out carefully pulled the envelope into the packet.

'So it is that serious,' the driver stated soberly.

'Yes, and if I were you I'd get back to the hotel. They're hiring another minibus for you to drive.'

The man looked at him in astonishment.

'We've just rebooked in there for the night and overheard the manager saying so,' Cannon told him. 'He's not a happy man but he did say that it was only the bus, as they had a driver.'

'Oh.' The man swallowed hard. 'I didn't know. I'll get back. Thanks,' he said.

'Not sure he'll get away with it,' Liz said, as they watched him go, 'but hope he does. On the scale of things he's done very little wrong.'

'He's withheld important evidence,' Cannon condemned, putting the plastic bag back in his pocket. 'This tells us that once more Bliss has outwitted everyone. It proves he planned *even this*, a bribe to secure a lift away from the scene of what he hoped would be, and yet may be, his final act of revenge against Higham.'

'And if it's not he'll probably come back and have another go,' Liz said. 'That seems his usual style too.'

'Not here, I wouldn't have thought,' Cannon said, 'he's too canny for that.'

'Cathy's promised to phone me with any kind of news of her father,' Liz said.

'And I must phone Forstmann,' Cannon was saying just as two large succulent slabs of ribs in their spicy aromatic sauce arrived, with bowls of fries, salads and breads. He swallowed. 'You start,' he said, rising to go outside to use his mobile. 'I'll be back.'

The restaurant and hotel were near to the docks and the nearby streets were busy. He walked to a quieter corner and as he waited for an answer watched the many fishing vessels moored up, their crews busy offloading their catches of king crab and cod, or cleaning the decks, while smaller craft were coming and going all the time. A real maritime community, sea in their blood. Cannon was thinking of the accountant, Midvinter, and his beloved boat, of the Viking panels in Christofferson Huset, as Forstmann answered.

'And we've got a positive lead,' Forstmann said after hearing what Cannon had to say. 'A nurse saw Bliss leaving the hospital, noticed him because she thought he was awaiting attention, but then was sure he left without seeing anyone. He took a taxi. We've just traced this driver and he's reported taking a passenger to Hammerfest, that's a six-hour ride.'

'So he can only just have reached…' Cannon began. 'But why Hammerfest?'

'It has one of Norway's largest airports,' Forstmann said, 'but we've had all airports on alert since the beginning so—' He was interrupted urgently at his end. 'I'll be in touch,' he said.

Cannon went back to join Liz, who signalled to the waiter as he returned. His meal had been taken away to be kept hot.

'So what did he say?' she asked.

'He's following a lead; he believes Bliss took a taxi to Hammerfest.'

'So he really did get out of the immediate area.'

'Looks like it,' Cannon said as he sliced meat from the end of his ribs, ate that, then dissected the first rib and picked it up with his fingers.

'There's an airport there but…' Cannon wondered if Bliss could have hoped to leave the country that way. It seemed a risk kind of not quite up to Bliss's standards—with everywhere being watched it was hardly clever.

Methodically he ate his way through his meal, though with this one thing niggling at his mind he hardly seemed to notice now what he put into his mouth.

'That was different,' Liz said as he reached for the glass of wine he had ordered.

'What was?' he asked.

'Well, I've known you have your epiphany moments in the middle of a crowded office at the Met, behind the bar at The Trap with customers waiting, but never while eating a meal before.'

If it was an attempt at light-heartedness it did not work. He stared hard at her, or through her, she was not sure which. 'Well, I've had no ideas,' he said flatly. 'I'll get the bill.'

As they went back to the hotel, the lights had gone on all around the shore and hills. Cannon walked past the entrance and Liz followed as he strode along the walkway, where the sofas were, to the end. Liz moved to the rail and looked at the upside-down mirror images of tiered lights in the water. Cannon stood back, motionless, very straight, hands by his sides—and, she guessed, seeing nothing at all. She shook her head, waited, and hoped this withdrawal would result in a sudden leap of understanding, as it had so often in the past.

'Bloodaxe and Odin,' he murmured, then repeated louder, 'Bloodaxe and Odin. What a fool!'

'You mean me, you or Forstmann?' she asked.

'Yes,' he replied, coming back to the now, where and who he was with. 'Yes, me mostly. Look,' he demanded of her, 'accept that every move Bliss has made has been planned. Right! His escape from the *Nordsol* to go to his house.' Cannon's voice was urgent, full of conviction now. 'Hammerfest must be halfway to Harstad and Christofferson Huset, yes, that's right.' His thoughts were developing as he talked. 'Yes, yes, of course. I meet Bliss's old friend who tells me of the exciting times they had sailing. Then in the house I see the whole hallway painted with panels of Viking invaders and Norse gods.' He put his hands to his head. 'And it takes me all this time to realize that Bliss has arranged a passage by sea from Hammerfest. The roads and the airport, forget those, he'll have hired a boat, probably belonging to some seafaring family he knew years ago. I bet even now they're heading across the North Sea towards…well, home!'

'Thinking Higham is dead?' Liz queried.

'Well, knowing he's in intensive care, and Bliss would know if he was going to stay free he had to move on quickly—he had to stick to his escape plan. The one thing he had not reckoned on was Forstmann giving Higham his own highly efficient police body armour.'

'With an idea like this I think you need to see Forstmann face to face,' Liz said.

He turned to look at her, as if seeing her properly for the first time since the driver had come to their table. She felt he weighed both her value and that of her suggestion.

'You're right,' he said and led the way back to the entrance doors of the hotel in time to see the minibus driver receiving delivery of the hired vehicle. The manager also stood there.

'I need urgently to go to police headquarters,' he said to both men. 'Will you give permission for your driver to take me?'

'There's no time to lose,' Liz added, feeling Cannon's eyes on her as she made the clichéd remark.

The manager's mouth opened and closed, then he flung up his hands, exclaiming, 'Feel free, as they say!' Shaking his head, muttering something in Norwegian, he strode back into his hotel.

'I think that means yes,' Cannon said.

Liz was pleased to see the driver grin.

CANNON WAS NOT grinning when he came back from seeing Forstmann. 'He's very sceptical about the idea,' he told Liz. 'He said all coastlines and shipping were too heavily supervised these days for it to be possible. I pointed out a few incidents I knew off the top of my head—illegal immigrants, smuggling, illegal fish catches being landed.

'He said it would have to be a small vessel to escape detection and wondered why anyone would try such a thing. I said he was obviously not a sailor himself, and the Vikings did it with oars and sails, which was probably a mistake and confirmed me as a nutcase.'

'So…'

'Oh, I still think he'll do a spot of checking, but I'm going to ring Betterson.'

Betterson, who at one time had been up to his shoulders in surf to catch illegal immigrants and very seasick to apprehend smugglers, was not at all sceptical.

'Look,' he said, 'whatever the outcome with Higham,

he has his son and daughter with him, and I could do with you two back here. You both know Bliss better than anyone *and* more importantly you have the ear of the locals. If Bliss does make landfall anywhere in this area, that's what I shall need. What do you say?'

'I think it will be more what Forstmann says, and also how comfortable Toby Higham and his sister are with the idea,' Cannon said soberly.

TWENTY-NINE

THEY CAUGHT A plane from Hammerfest to Oslo the next morning and from there a midday flight back to the UK. They were both weary, emotionally drained, and crowded airports and planes did not encourage anything much other than necessary mundane remarks. Half between waking and dozing on the second flight, Cannon, unable to leave the problem alone, muttered, 'Back on his own territory.'

'Why Betterson wants you there,' Liz had whispered in reply. Her exhaustion had more to do with the memory of parting from Cathy. The aching strength of the girl clinging desperately to her, Toby eventually pulling her gently away. A tender, concerned brother taking her into his own arms, reassuring her that their mother was on her way from Finland and would soon be with them. Liz had at last parted with the young woman with the promise that when she was back home they would both go to her friend and painting mentor, Paul Jefferson, for lessons. 'He's very good,' Toby had confirmed. Liz had truthfully added that she had meant to do this for a long time; the two of them would do it together.

She moved restlessly, looked beyond Cannon out of the plane window; it had seemed very little to offer when the girl's father lay so desperately ill. It had been all she could think of—but she would not forget.

If the journey up to that point had been tiring it was

nothing to the frustrations that built up after they had picked up Liz's car and begun their motorway journey back from Gatwick. After four hours of intermittent moving, crawling, coming to a stop at incoming traffic junctions, they pulled into a service station and Liz insisted on taking over the driving.

'I've rested up to now, now you must. Once we get home, you know there'll be so much to do taking up the reins again.'

'Taken us longer than the two flights put together already,' Cannon said and climbed gratefully into the passenger's seat for the rest of the journey.

Evening opening time was drawing to a close when they drove into the car park, and as their lights swung in across the front of the public house they both noted the neatness of the flower tubs, and that the one demolished by Spier's mother had been replaced and reset.

'Back or front?' Cannon asked.

'Front, let's do it properly,' Liz said, adding, 'The back's probably securely bolted if I know anything about Alamat's sense of duty.'

It was strange walking in through the front doors like two ordinary customers, and for several seconds they stared at the woman behind the counter as she greeted them with a smile and in stilted English asked, 'What may I serve you with?' Then her mouth and eyes opened wide. She looked from one to the other, threw up her arms and ran immediately to the far end of the counter and called through to the kitchen. 'Alamat! Come quickly!'

Their Croatian assistant came hurrying through in his cooking whites, his face alarmed by the urgency of

Bozena's call, then his face changed, beaming like that of his girlfriend.

He raised both arms and exclaimed, 'Mr Cannon, Misses Liz, welcome, welcome home.'

After the handshakes and the welcome, Cannon looked around his bar and asked, 'Where is everyone? Hoskins?'

'We have good few eating earlier, but I think...' Alamat cocked a rueful head, 'we are not so popular with the locals, we do not have the same small talk, I think, they come but go home early. You will find bar takings down, but meals up, up!' He grinned, putting his arm around Bozena. 'We are a good team.'

Cannon nodded but Bozena cut in before he could say more.

'You have had long journey. Alamat will bring meal upstairs to you, then you go to your bed. We sort everything out tomorrow—yes?'

'That sounds good,' Cannon said, 'but what about Hoskins? The bar doesn't look right without him.'

'He is very busy gamekeeping for Mr Higham's estate, you understand,' Alamat said.

'He says it is the time of the ducks,' Bozena said, 'and he will bring some.'

Cannon opened his mouth to disapprove of the very idea, but that too could wait until the morning.

LIZ, REVIVED BY a good night's sleep in her own bed, was downstairs first the next morning, intending to cook John a good breakfast before any business talk began. She could be sure Alamat would have her fridge and freezers well stocked. Instead, once she reached the bar she found herself looking around, first at her copperware and brasses. They shone and glowed as if burnished only a minute earlier, and tables and chairs had acquired a new gloss that she knew had only been achieved by hard vigorous polishing. She was momentarily not quite sure how she felt, and was even guilty of reaching up to the highest shelf above the bar and running her finger along it. Now she did tut at herself—how petty was that! Bozena was obviously a treasure—a divine gift, Alamat said her name meant—and he should hang on to her.

Her kitchen was just as neat, everything meticulously put in its usual place. Her mind was beginning to move to the idea that if they could increase their takings on the meals side, they could keep Bozena as well as Alamat, then she heard the sound of a car sweeping into the car park followed by a car door being slammed and the scrunch of gravel as someone strode towards the door. Cannon walked into the kitchen as the outer porch door was tried then knocked on.

'You're having breakfast before you do *anything*,' she told Cannon as he went to the door.

'Welcome home,' she heard Regional Detective Edgar Betterson say, 'Came the slow way, did you?'

'Well, the motorway…' Cannon began.

'We've found a seagoing yacht beached not far from here,' he said. 'You might have been quicker on that.'

'You think Bliss is—'

'*Know*,' Betterson interrupted. 'Forensics just confirmed his DNA but any trace once he left the yacht—' he spread his hands as if displaying emptiness '—what the tide didn't wash away, the wind wiped out.'

Cannon pulled out a chair for him and he sat down

gratefully, pushing his long legs wearily out under the table. 'We're searching, fingertip in the immediate area.'

Liz began making coffee, declaring Betterson looked as if he had not slept for days, and repeating her order that Cannon went nowhere until he had eaten.

'We're allowed to talk?' Betterson asked drily.

'We'll all eat and talk at the same time,' she answered. 'OK?'

The banter was clearly over as Betterson leaned across the table, hands clasped and shaking, towards Cannon, as he described in detail the place where a Norwegian yacht had been found. 'Owner a man who lives near Harstad, who did not know his boat was missing.'

'Harstad, where Bliss's house is,' Cannon contributed, 'and where the boat was found. That sounds like the place where we found Timmy Riley's dog.'

'That's what I was thinking,' Liz confirmed, 'and at high tide that's quite a channel.'

'He had some luck in that it was a high tide and there was a following gale force wind,' Betterson added.

'Luck would not have had anything much to do with it,' Cannon said. 'The wind was perhaps providential but the high tide—I can't believe Bliss didn't take that into account.'

'But if he deliberately sailed to arrive this near his home, where is he? We've found no trace, no witnesses, nothing. That's why I'm so pleased to have you back. I need people the locals talk to without reservations, with local knowledge, ears to the ground. Most of all, of course—' he leaned back and sighed '—I need to get this maniac banged up before he does more harm.'

'Yes,' Cannon agreed quietly, 'it needs finishing.'

There was a pause as all three dwelled on the truth

of that statement, then Betterson reflected, 'Spier being in Norway was a bombshell. None of us expected that!'

'Bliss has used Spier all the way along,' Cannon said. 'It seems to me from the first night here in the pub after Spier created a scene, even then I think Bliss saw him as a useful decoy.'

'Once the newspapers got on to Spier, it certainly made us waste time, money and resources trying to find him,' Betterson agreed. 'It became police trial by public opinion stirred up by the media.'

'Then he sets up a "burglary",' Cannon went on, 'using Spier to get rid of the tell-tale walking sticks. After that he shelters Spier in his flat in Skegness, keeps him indebted, then uses him as a red herring to get away from Kirkenes, but leaves him to his fate.'

'Bliss must have promised a great deal for him to undertake a journey to Norway,' Liz said.

'Probably told him he needed to get out of the country to keep out of our hands,' Betterson said. 'The one thing that man does *not* want is to go inside.'

'But Spier's usefulness is at an end now,' Cannon said.

'Unless…' Liz began, and immediately had their full attention. 'Unless Bliss is manipulating Spier's mother. He might say he could exonerate her son from being charged if she co-operated with him—hid him, say.'

'Wouldn't have thought she'd have tried that again, she's been under observation for weeks,' Betterson said, 'but I could arrange a search warrant, make sure, look in Spier's hidey-hole.'

'Hardly seems sophisticated enough for Bliss,' Cannon said, 'but I'll talk to the locals, see what they think.

I could drop in on Mavis Moyle. I presume she's in the picture?'

'Enough to make her very wary,' Betterson confirmed.

'Right, and I'll see Hoskins, of course. You know he's gamekeeping?'

Betterson pulled a face. 'Well, he should be good at it.' He rose from the table.

'I've got sausages and bacon ready,' Liz said.

'I'd better not stay...'

'Make them into a sandwich,' she offered.

As she was doing so, Cannon's mobile burbled.

'Toby Higham,' he mouthed to the other two, and both now waited to hear. 'Good, good,' Cannon said, then shook his head. Call over, he explained, 'Alexander Higham has regained consciousness. Apparently his first words were "let's go home".'

'Another reason we must catch up with Bliss,' Betterson said grimly. 'Can you imagine what the newspapers would do to us—me—if Higham comes home and Bliss still manages to get at him?' He shuddered. 'Doesn't bear thinking about.'

'He will kill anyone who gets in his way now,' Cannon said quietly, 'anyone.'

THIRTY

AT MAVIS MOYLE'S COTTAGE, Cannon found everything locked up: her home, Bliss Antiques, not even a bedroom window ajar. Mavis must now feel she had no obligation to open the shop, for there was little likelihood of her being paid any more, and any takings would, he imagined, be an embarrassment to someone like Mavis.

While he still stood looking up at the cottage, a car drew up beside his jeep and Sergeant Maddern joined him at the gate. 'Mavis all right?' he asked.

'No one at home,' Cannon answered. 'Knocked but everything's locked up.'

'I know she's been getting out somewhere every day now she's not opening the shop or, as she says, she can see no one. I'll just have a look round myself.'

Cannon waited while the sergeant went through the same routine he had just finished, knocking at the doors, looking around generally—and finding nothing untoward.

'I'll drop by again,' Cannon told him. 'I'm off to see Hoskins now.' He gave a laugh. 'I probably won't be able to find him either.'

'If all the rogues were as good-hearted as he is we wouldn't have much to worry about,' Maddern said, adding, 'but don't quote me.'

WHEN CANNON PULLED up into Hoskins' lane it was early evening. Low rain clouds were under-lit by a sunset of deep dramatic golds and reds, but again there was no sign of life.

Even so he strode up the central front path, ducked beneath the browning clematis on the trellis arch and knocked loudly at the front door. It was not unknown for Hoskins to fall asleep in his chair after his tea.

He knocked again, twice, then made his way round to the back of the cottage, in through the back porch where Hoskins' old bike habitually stood when he was at home. It was not there but there was an envelope drawing-pinned to the kitchen door. He found it was addressed to 'Mr John Cannon'. Very formal, he thought, though obviously Hoskins not only knew he was back home but had assumed—quite rightly—that Cannon would come looking for him.

The note inside read. 'Gone back Higham's place—drive up to Ford's cottage—meet you there.'

He phoned Liz.

'You'd better do as he says,' Liz said. 'Do you want me to let Betterson know?'

'Not at this point,' he said, 'I'll just go and see what the old boy is up to and get back to you.'

The grassy, rutted way up to the thatched cottage had already become more overgrown since Ford's 4x4 was no longer in use. Cannon pulled into a gateway and walked the last fifty metres, going past the for once empty gibbet-line.

'About time you came back,' a voice said behind him.

He started, swung round to see Hoskins leaning on a tree at the edge of the path he had just walked along.

'Damn it!' he exclaimed. 'How do you do that?'

'Keep still and think yourself part of the background, works every time,' Hoskins replied, pushing himself upright. 'I was just watching the sunset through the trees.'

As he came to Cannon's side, they both stood for a second or two longer, watching Disney being upstaged.

Then Hoskins' voice took on a serious note. 'Missed you both. Pub like a new pin, mind, but getting like a house where you daren't sit down in case you crease the cushions. Glad you saw the note—went back specially to put it there.'

'So what's happened?'

'Sergeant Maddern's kept me up to date,' he said, 'though reckon I saw that boat afore he did.'

'So you know?'

'Aye, I know that, but little more.'

'So you've seen no sign of the prof? Bliss?' Cannon asked.

Hoskins shook his head. 'Not…no.' He stopped then began again. 'And neither has anyone else, if he did sail that boat over.'

'Oh, he did,' Cannon told him. 'The forensic boys have confirmed that.'

'And is it true he's murdered a sailor on board the boat you were all on, and had a go at Higham?'

Cannon nodded—the old boy had been kept well informed, and very wisely. To have Hoskins on your side in these circumstances was like having a good bloodhound when there was a scent to follow.

'Have you been up to Higham's house?' he asked.

'Round there every day. Don't go too near the house, the extra security lights and cameras have that place well covered. You know it's empty?'

'Well, I…'

'I mean the housekeeper and her husband,' he said as they turned to walk on. 'They've gone to visit their daughter in Australia while the family are away.

Higham's other son is in charge of the business and the property, though as far as I can gather he never sets foot outside London. The security firm send him pictures from their cameras "on-line", whatever that means. Give me a couple of men with dogs any time.'

Cannon made a sympathetic grimace.

'Before they left, the housekeeper asked me if I'd keep an eye on their cottage *and* the big house, wanted me to have keys to both places.'

Cannon looked over at him but he shook his head. 'No fear,' he said, 'I didn't want that responsibility. I don't do houses, told 'em as much but—' he blew out his lips in resignation '—doesn't mean I haven't been keeping an eye on the place.'

Cannon was silent, waited. Hoskins like many others was liable to go off at a tangent if his line of thought was interrupted.

'I've been all over the gardens round the big house and the cottage; no one has been there since that boat arrived.'

'Which,' Cannon said quietly, 'as Higham is making a recovery and talking of coming home is good but...'

'Bloody worrying, I'd say,' Hoskins concluded. 'Where's Bliss gone?'

They both shook their heads.

'The man has to eat and sleep,' Cannon said. 'DI Betterson is off to search Spier's mother's premises.'

'Long shot,' Hoskins judged. 'The prof's cleverer than that.'

Cannon nodded, Hoskins' judgement so often the same as his own.

'So you don't think Bliss is anywhere near—or even in—Higham's house?'

'No, thought he was more likely to be here,' Hoskins said as they arrived at the cottage. 'No security here, but with all this—' he indicated the police tape surrounding the property '—well, you'll know how far to go, looking round, I mean.'

'What've you done up to now?' Cannon asked.

'No, nothing, not crossed the line,' Hoskins said and shuddered at the memory of what they had found before.

By the time they had satisfied themselves that no one had broken into the cottage since the police had secured the crime scene, and cautiously searched the outbuildings, it was dark.

Hoskins, satisfied that Bliss was not holed up anywhere there, announced, 'Reckon it's time we were both at the pub. Your good lady will find me some supper, save me going home first. We can put my bike in the back of your jeep.'

'Now I really know I'm home,' Cannon said as he walked back with Hoskins to where he'd left his bike, wheeled it to the jeep and loaded it.

'Glad I helped,' Hoskins said, but listened attentively as Cannon told him of his earlier visit to Mavis Moyle's cottage. 'Told Maddern I'd look in again on the way back.'

When they reached the cottage, the light was on in the parlour. At the second knock the curtain nearest the door was pulled aside and Mavis stood there.

'You all right?' he shouted. 'I've got Hoskins waiting in the jeep—just called to see you're OK.'

'John, just go home to Liz,' she shouted back, then after a pause added, 'Alan must be desperate for his first pint.'

She lifted a hand in response to Cannon's and let the

curtain drop…and it felt like saying goodbye to hope. She turned slowly but found Bliss's gun-stick levelled this time not at her, as it had been when she arrived home, but towards the window.

'John Cannon?' he said. 'John Cannon?'

'I didn't—' She began a denial of trying to convey any message or meaning to Cannon, but Bliss was not listening and the gun barrel was again focused on her.

'He should be dead, by now he should be dead.' He suddenly turned on her and poked her violently in the chest with the stick. She reeled back as he demanded, 'And Higham, did he die? Tell me! Did Alexander Higham die?'

Hand clutching her breast where the stick had caught her, she stepped back again, tripped on a chair leg, saved herself by grabbing the table, then landed half on and half off a chair.

'Mavis Moyle, useful little Mavis.' He loomed over her, shaking his head, then it turned to a nod as he added, 'But do you know, I have thought of a way you can still help.' He went to her kitchen phone and brought her the receiver.

'You will please ring your friend Peggy Spier and ask her if she has heard whether the great and good Mr Alexander Higham still breathes. You and she like a gossip,' he said matter-of-factly, 'but don't make it too long.'

'But Sergeant Maddern said her husband's in custody. I…' Mavis began. 'I can't—'

Bliss laughed scornfully, pointed at the phone and poked the gun towards her again.

Peggy Spier answered almost immediately. 'Oh, Mavis, *thank you* for ringing, it's times like these that you know who your real friends are.'

'So is it true about Maurice?' she asked.

'Yes, he's really done it this time,' Peggy said. 'He'll be going down for at least two years. How did I come to ever—' She broke off, tears thickening her voice as she questioned, 'And what on earth was he doing in Norway? I didn't even know he had a passport.'

Bliss touched Mavis's other breast with the gun barrel.

'I heard there was some trouble out there with that wealthy Mr Higham from the big house,' she said hastily.

'I know!' Peggy agreed. 'But he must be all right because I've heard he's coming home with his family any day now, so what was that all about?'

'I must go, Peggy,' she said. Bliss now held the gunstick in one hand and was making slashing movements across his throat with the other. 'Look after yourself, I'll be over to see you as soon as I can.'

'Put you in a funny position with that professor bloke and his antique shop,' her friend said, obviously anxious to go on talking.

'Yes,' she said, 'but I'll have to go.'

'So Higham survived,' Bliss said aloud, but certainly to himself. 'It seems even my plans…' His gaze came back to her.

'You have my shop keys,' he said. 'I need to go round there now. I have some spare clothes in the office and my phone is in the drawer.'

'Your keys are there.' She gestured to a row of hooks above the work surface. 'But the police took everything away.'

'Everything?' he snapped. 'My clothes? My phone… yes, of course…but…' He looked at her now as if she was responsible, or at least she was going to be made to pay. 'Let's see,' he said, 'you have a very good old-style pantry, long stone walls, no window, a brick thrall, and an old-fashioned lock and high bolt on the outside to keep children out. Just the place.'

He seized her shoulder and as she resisted he struck her hard, a downward chop across her face and neck. She hit her head on the table as she fell.

She came to in darkness on the cold thrall in her own pantry with her hands and arms secured behind her. She pushed her feet round and sat up carefully, kept still until the spinning sensation lessened, then she put her feet to the ground, stood, went to the door.

It sounded as if Bliss was ransacking her home, and suddenly she did not care; the caution the good Sergeant Maddern had urged on her should Bliss turn up was forgotten. The useful little Mavis Moyle was in revolt. She began to kick at the door and shout as loudly as she could, laying her tongue to obscenities even she hardly realized she knew.

THIRTY-ONE

'NOT THAT LATE,' Hoskins mused as they drove away.

'For?' Cannon asked.

'Never known Mavis Moyle not come gushing out, or invite anybody in.'

'She would have been warned to be careful,' Cannon said, 'though she could see it was me, and I told her you were in the jeep.'

'Was on my way to join you when you turned back,' Hoskins commented. 'Did she say anything?'

'Told me to go home to Liz,' he said, 'and that Alan would be dying for his first pint.'

'She used my moniker, did she?'

'And mine,' he said, 'John, Alan and Liz.'

They both fell silent as Cannon drew the jeep into The Trap car park, switched off the engine, but still sat there. 'We're neither of us quite satisfied, are we?' he asked.

'No,' Hoskins said immediately. 'What you going to do?'

'Think worse scenario and work from that,' Cannon said, pulling out his phone.

Betterson, as he had promised he would be, was on the other end in seconds. Cannon ended his report with 'it's just a feeling'.

'On my way to you,' Betterson said. 'Back door?'

In fifteen minutes his car drew in alongside the jeep.

In another fifteen minutes the pub kitchen had become an isolated incident room, with the door firmly closed between that and the bar. Alamat and Bozena were left in charge with instructions that no further food could be served that evening.

'This feeling,' Betterson asked.

Again the few facts were told.

'And you had no hint that anyone else was there with her?'

Cannon shook his head. 'It was just unsatisfactory.'

'Could I help?' Liz asked. 'Say ring her?'

'The trouble is,' Cannon said, 'if Bliss is there and he's aggravated, he could be pushed into another…'

'Killing,' Betterson provided. 'So presuming he is there with Mavis Moyle…'

'Reckon there's one way we might find out,' Hoskins offered.

All turned to him expectantly.

'Go on,' Betterson said.

'You know I took on Ford's dog?'

'Bounder?' Cannon said. 'No, I didn't know.'

'While you were away.'

'But where is he? I knocked front and back at your place, he didn't bark.'

'No,' Hoskins said, 'done my best but he's one sad dog—grieving still for his master. I reckon if we take him to Mavis's cottage he'd scent the man who murdered his master if he's there.'

Betterson was silently regarding the old man. 'I could just go in anyway, but it would give me more reason if the dog—' He broke off as another idea came to him. 'What if I got something that belonged to Bliss for the dog to smell before we got there?'

'Better still,' Hoskins said, 'much better. Remind him. Might break the dog's grief.'

'It's going to take time,' Liz said.

'It's got to be done right,' Cannon said. 'This man is in a corner—you'll only get one chance if it is Bliss.'

'You think the weapon he'll have is the gun-stick?' Betterson asked.

'I believe so, single cartridge, and that will definitely take a little longer than a modern gun to reload,' Cannon said.

'But he'd have that one shot,' Liz reminded them.

'We're not going to be able to sweet talk this man out,' Betterson said grimly, 'he's too far gone. We have to make surprise and speed our weapons,'

Phone calls were made; Betterson strode up and down and around the kitchen as he motivated men and whole departments of the constabulary. It was however still past midnight when Cannon finally took Hoskins to fetch Ford's dog.

They were to reassemble at the pub, Liz would be in charge there. Alamat and Bozena were now safely in their apartment in the stable block with instructions to take no action about the comings and goings unless directly called upon

'Bounder won't have had his meal,' Hoskins said as he let them in through his front door and groped for the light, 'but I left him with biscuits so…'

'We can't really stop to feed him,' Cannon said.

'No,' Hoskins agreed 'and he'll be the sharper without his stomach full.'

Switching on the kitchen light, Cannon appreciated all Hoskins had said about the dog, for although it certainly looked at them both, that was all it did. The bowl of dog biscuits nearby looked untouched.

'Come on, old boy,' Hoskins said, taking the dog's lead from his dresser and sitting down next to Bounder. 'Time to get your own back.'

The dog rose and put its head on Hoskins' knee, looking up at him with such sad eyes. 'Breaks your heart, don't it,' Hoskins murmured.

The dog came obediently enough, no dragging, no pulling, making no fuss about travelling back to the pub and being walked in through the kitchen to the bar. Here with only a wall light or two still on below the dark beams, Cannon's new clientele looked like aliens out of a sci-fi movie. The armed response group were in full gear, helmets, guns, just waiting to go.

'The only thing we were waiting for is the material from the forensic locker,' Betterson said, 'but the station officer is on his way.' He turned to the officer in charge of the armed unit. 'You could deploy your men now, keep low and observe, and we'll follow with the dog.'

The officer merely nodded first to Betterson, then lifted a hand to his men who all immediately and silently left the bar. Those left listened to the vehicles moving away; in minutes silence settled over The Fens once more.

'We might as well all sit down,' the DI said. 'Does the dog need a drink?'

Liz fetched the bowl they kept for customers' dogs and filled it, but Bounder seemed neither interested nor thirsty.

'You're sure this dog is up to it?' Betterson asked. 'He doesn't look...'

'The dog's grieving,' Hoskins said.

'Grieving?' Betterson shook his head. 'How long is that going to last?'

'Have you never heard of Greyfriars Bobby?' Cannon asked.

Betterson frowned, shook his head.

'He was a Skye terrier who belonged to a man named Gray who was a night-watchman for the police in the 1800s. He was said to have guarded his master's grave for fourteen years. He has a monument in Greyfriars Churchyard in Edinburgh.'

'Well, good way to pass the time, improving my education,' Betterson said. 'I just hope I'm not going to be a laughing stock for going along with this.'

Bounder was the focus of all their attention while they waited. They talked to and tried to fuss the golden retriever but it was totally unresponsive. Cannon began to feel Betterson was regretting committing himself to this operation.

'He really has lost heart,' Liz said, moving the water bowl nearer, but the dog ignored it.

'Let's hope he finds it again fairly quickly,' Betterson said fervently as the lights of a car swung across the bar windows. Moments later a young constable walked in with a large evidence bag.

'This is for you, sir,' he said to Betterson. 'One black academic gown.'

'I wouldn't open that until we're near Mavis Moyle's place,' Hoskins advised when the young officer had gone. 'Let the dog get its scent fresh when he's there.'

'You're the expert,' Betterson replied, 'but once we're at the cottage there's to be no more talking, no noise.'

There was *still* a light on in Mavis's parlour as they grouped themselves just within sight of the property.

Betterson crouched down and in the light of a shaded torch he opened the neck of the bag and advanced it a little towards the dog's nose. Bounder backed off for a moment but as he caught Bliss's scent it was as if he had been touched with an electric probe. First his nose, then his head were in the bag; his heckles rose all along his back and he began to growl.

Betterson moved the bag away a little and as the dog brought its head sharply out it looked a different animal. The DI found himself face to face with a lips-curled, tooth-bared, snarling beast.

'Find,' Hoskins, who was holding the lead, ordered hastily, fearing for Betterson's safety. 'Find!' he repeated. The dog immediately began to pull towards the front path to the cottage, growling savagely in between the high excited yaps of a dog on a hot scent. Betterson said swiftly, if shakily, into his radio, 'We have a positive reaction, be ready.'

When they were nearly to the front gate, Bounder suddenly took off, leaping over the wall, bringing Hoskins hard up against the stones and forcing him to let go of the lead. The dog was now in full cry and, in a repetition of the action Hoskins and Cannon had seen when the dog wanted to get into his dead master, it now pursued the scent of the killer.

The dog scrabbled at the front door in a savage frenzy, snarling, growling, leaping at the windows.

'Go in, go in,' Betterson ordered.

Men seemed to rise up from all points of the compass. One man was at the door with a battering ram and in seconds he was inside—but the dog was in first—then there was a shot, a yelp. Cannon was just in front of Betterson and Hoskins as they burst into the lounge.

Bliss stood at bay trying to reload the gun-stick. Cannon and Betterson were on him before the cartridge was in place. Cannon had thought the two of them would easily overpower this former academic of smallish build, in his sixties, but he had not reckoned on the strength of a madman practised in heaving heavy antique furniture about. Bliss managed to land blows on both of them before Cannon grabbed one of his arms and pulled him to the floor. Betterson joined him and with both of them sitting on the man, Cannon had his arms piniOned and Betterson finally clipped on handcuffs. The struggle had been silent but for the grunts and groans of effort, but now Bliss screamed, raved at them, a meaningless jumble of threats.

Cannon and Betterson stood up and left him to it.

On the carpet near the door Bounder lay in his final death throes. Hoskins bent down to him. 'Good boy, Bounder,' he said. The dog looked up at him and wagged his tail just once.

'Right,' Betterson said, swallowing hard, 'so where's Mavis Moyle?'

There was a shout from the back of the property. 'Phone for an ambulance, someone!' another voice cried.

All three went to where Mavis had been found lying on the floor of the locked pantry.

'Given her a good going over,' the officer kneeling next to her said, 'but she is alive. I can feel a faint pulse.'

Cannon moved nearer. Mavis Moyle had well and truly been beaten and with her hands and arms tied behind her back she had been quite unable to protect her head. He was sure that if the stick had been as heavy as that used on Niall Riley she would definitely be dead.

THIRTY-TWO

THE NEXT DAY Cannon watched Liz preparing their late breakfast. He still felt mistrustful of such normality. Could they just sit and eat, listening to the sounds of their pub being cleaned and ordered, before the day's business?

'Open as usual,' he muttered.

'It's best, I think,' Liz said. 'Routine structures time.'

'Very erudite,' he commented, wondering how structured such as Hoskins' day would seem, once more in a house without another living thing to focus on. He would do his rounds, no doubt, still fulfil his role as temporary gamekeeper. Then he thought sympathetically of Betterson; he would probably be already up to his knees in paperwork. Life went on. People like Mrs Riley and Timmy coping, pulling their lives back into some kind of shape. They were the real heroes and heroines.

There was a tap at the door which startled both of them. Liz dropped her spoon into her cereal bowl with a clatter.

'What now?' Cannon asked, as if some new catastrophe was about to happen.

Alamat put his head around the door. 'You have visitors,' he said.

'Police?' Liz queried, but he shook his head.

'Visitors,' he repeated and turned to beckon before they had time to reach any other decision.

Liz rose from the table in astonishment as Cathy Higham walked in, closely followed by Toby, then Paul and Helen, in uniform.

Cathy fell on Liz and they clung tightly to each other for some long moments, and questions flew around.

'But…what's this?'

'You're home?'

'I'm on duty really.'

'They called on us on their way here,' Paul explained.

'Your father?' Liz queried.

'Mother's in charge of him, and not leaving his side until he can travel home, but he is going to be OK. So once we heard Bliss was caught, that you had…' Toby looked towards Cannon. 'We left everything to come to thank you.'

'A lot of people involved.' Cannon said.

'And a poor dog,' Liz added.

'I've filled them in as far as I could,' Helen said, 'and now I must go, I'm already late.'

'Where's my boy?' Cannon asked her.

'With Mother-in-law until I get back,' Paul answered.

When Helen had left, Cathy and Liz still stood with their arms around each other. 'I…had to come too…to thank you both…' Cathy said, 'and to show…my father… I am independent.' She went on with pride in her voice, 'Toby and I have…come to see the house… is ready for him.' Then she looked at Cannon and said very seriously, 'This is the first time I have *ever* been in a…public house.'

'But it won't be the last,' Paul interrupted. 'I'm enrolling Cathy and Liz as our first students when we begin our painting classes here. Your stable block accommodation is finished, Alamat tells me, and Bozena will clean and caretake once she moves in with him.'

'Hey,' Cannon said, 'hold on!'

'We've talked about it enough,' Paul said. 'Now's the time—get it all up and running for the start of next holiday season.'

'What was I saying about normal routine life before this lot arrived?' Cannon asked.

'Something about it being the best thing,' Liz said, 'but I think this is better. This is something new we can put our energies into.'

'We're never going to forget,' Toby said, 'never, but…' He paused and shook his head. 'I should tell you one more thing. I've been contacted by the nursing home where I visited Bliss's, or rather Evan's father, because I was the only visitor he ever had at the home. Mr Evan died in his sleep, the same day his son was caught.'

There was a deep silence at the irony.

'I've wondered if he had died years earlier it might have made all the difference to his elder son,' Toby said, 'and if he had died before his younger son, would the elder have cared for his brother?'

'We'll never know, but three men might still have been alive,' Cannon added.

'John, don't…' Liz began, but it was Cathy who went on.

'That,' she said, 'cannot be changed, but you two have given us back our lives, our family. I know we will be happy now, and my father will see I do not have to be always under his eye. We will be happy and content even when not all together.'

Toby looked at her in astonishment. It was the longest unbroken sentence he had ever heard her utter and she knew it for she clamped her hand over her mouth in disbelief.

It broke some kind of tension as all of them felt shakily poised between laughter and tears.

ALEXANDER HIGHAM AND Trude came home ten days later. Toby, who now came regularly to The Trap with Paul, brought a message that his father intended to see them very soon, but whatever else he would do two things. First he would ensure that Mavis Moyle, who was making a slow recovery, would always be financially secure. Secondly he would have Bounder's ashes laid to rest in a special grave, with a suitable headstone, next to his old home at the gamekeeper's cottage.

That evening before opening time, Cannon walked through to his bar and asked Alamat if he was all right in there on his own for a time.

'Fine,' Alamat answered. 'Things settle down now, you see, time cures many things they say.'

'I'll open up,' Cannon said and, going through the swing door to the bar, he unlocked The Trap's double front doors and hooked them back—wide and welcoming.

He stepped out and turned in the direction of Hoskins' cottage. He had not walked far before he saw the very man on his bike coming towards him.

'Routine structures time,' he murmured.

* * * * *

Get 2 Free Books,

Plus 2 Free Gifts—

just for trying the
Reader Service!

YES! Please send me 2 FREE Harlequin® Romantic Suspense novels and my 2 FREE gifts (gifts are worth about $10 retail). After receiving them, if I don't wish to receive any more books, I can return the shipping statement marked "cancel." If I don't cancel, I will receive 4 brand-new novels every month and be billed just $4.99 per book in the U.S. or $5.74 per book in Canada. That's a savings of at least 12% off the cover price! It's quite a bargain! Shipping and handling is just 50¢ per book in the U.S. and 75¢ per book in Canada.* I understand that accepting the 2 free books and gifts places me under no obligation to buy anything. I can always return a shipment and cancel at any time. Even if I never buy another book, the 2 free books and gifts are mine to keep forever.

240/340 HDN GLP9

Name   (PLEASE PRINT)

Address   Apt. #

City   State/Prov.   Zip/Postal Code

Signature (if under 18, a parent or guardian must sign)

Mail to the **Reader Service:**
IN U.S.A.: P.O. Box 1867, Buffalo, NY 14240-1867
IN CANADA: P.O. Box 611, Fort Erie, Ontario L2A 9Z9

Want to try two free books from another line?
Call 1-800-873-8635 or visit www.ReaderService.com.

*Terms and prices subject to change without notice. Prices do not include applicable taxes. Sales tax applicable in N.Y. Canadian residents will be charged applicable taxes. Offer not valid in Quebec. This offer is limited to one order per household. Books received may not be as shown. Not valid for current subscribers to Harlequin Romantic Suspense books. All orders subject to credit approval. Credit or debit balances in a customer's account(s) may be offset by any other outstanding balance owed by or to the customer. Please allow 4 to 6 weeks for delivery. Offer available while quantities last.

Your Privacy—The Reader Service is committed to protecting your privacy. Our Privacy Policy is available online at www.ReaderService.com or upon request from the Reader Service.

We make a portion of our mailing list available to reputable third parties that offer products we believe may interest you. If you prefer that we not exchange your name with third parties, or if you wish to clarify or modify your communication preferences, please visit us at www. ReaderService.com/consumerchoice or write to us at Reader Service Preference Service, P.O. Box 9062, Buffalo, NY 14240-9062. Include your complete name and address.

HRS17R

READERSERVICE.COM

Manage your account online!

- Review your order history
- Manage your payments
- Update your address

> ### We've designed the Reader Service website just for you.

Enjoy all the features!

- Discover new series available to you, and read excerpts from any series.
- Respond to mailings and special monthly offers.
- Connect with favorite authors at the blog.
- Browse the Bonus Bucks catalog and online-only exculsives.
- Share your feedback.

Visit us at:

ReaderService.com

RS15

Get 2 Free Books,

Plus 2 Free Gifts—

just for trying the _Reader Service!_